TANGLES

Sharleen Scott

OUT WEST PRESS

YAKIMA, WASHINGTON

Sharleen Scott/Out West Press
PO BOX 185
Naches, WA 98937
www.sharleenscott.com

Publisher's Note: This is a work of fiction. Names, characters, places, and incidents are a product of the author's imagination. Locales and public names are sometimes used for atmospheric purposes. Any resemblance to actual people, living or dead, or to businesses, companies, events, institutions, or locales is completely coincidental.

Editing by Dori Harrell at doriharrell.wix.com/breakoutediting
Cover by The Cover Collection at www.thecovercollection.com

Tangles/ Sharleen Scott. -- 1st ed.
ISBN 978-0-9915890-4-3

To Judy, who is at peace.
To Brett, for meeting the challenge.

Memory is the treasury and guardian of all things.

—MARCUS TULLIUS CICERO

Logan—Now

When the call came, I reacted as a son should. Her heart was failing, and she was fading fast. Without hesitation, I gave the word. Medics were called, and the process of saving a life began. An infection was found and antibiotics were given. A life continued.

Imagine my shock when I was told the situation was handled wrong. Rules were broken, directives not followed. According to her doctors, my moment had come, and I'd failed.

I began to question, just what am I saving her for?

From the moment of diagnosis, her condition was terminal. She lives minute to minute.

She is aggravating and difficult at times. Would my life be easier without her? You bet it would. She only lives minute to minute anyway.

She can't remember my name, but I'm familiar. She may think her son is a daughter she never had, her caregiver an aunt, long gone. Her grandchildren are in the room even when they are miles away. There may be cats in her hospital room, chickens in the nurses' station, and her daughter-in-law is her sister. She can't remember her husband of fifty-four years has died.

Yes, life would be easier without her. She only lives minute to minute anyway.

Does she have an acceptable quality of life? No. There is no quality there. She only lives minute to minute.

But in the peaceful environment created for her, she smiles, laughs, and makes paper flowers and Valentine hearts. When I walk in the door, she smiles and says, "There he is." Maybe she can't remember who I am, but in that minute, I'm familiar.

She can't remember the beach trips, the campouts with friends and family, or her own wedding. She has a taste for sweets that never existed before, but now, a dish of ice cream brings joy.

Yes, my life would be easier without her. She only lives minute to minute.

But in that minute, she looks at me with tears in her eyes and says, "I'm so glad you're here. I missed you so much." She takes my hand and says she loves me. In that minute, I may be her brother, her aunt, her son, or her grandmother. It doesn't matter. In that minute, I'm whoever she needs me to be. Her momentary unconditional love puts our history in the past where it belongs. In that minute, we can love.

Someday, she'll sit in a chair and stare into space. She'll find no joy in ice cream, a pretty flower, or a brightly colored car. Then I may think she is better off gone. I will wish her much-deserved peace.

Her condition is terminal. The plaques and tangles in her brain will win. There is no hope for her.

She lives minute to minute for now.

But those minutes are hers, and in those minutes, she lives.

—Logan

Chapter 1

LOGAN—Then

Logan McKinnon was thirty-six years old when summoned to his parents' home like a delinquent kid in need of a hack from the principal. And what frosted him most was his automatic jump into action when his mother phoned. It must be the shock she'd called at all that had him driving I-5 North, dodging rush-hour traffic and oily splashes in a downpour. He didn't know what she needed to discuss with such urgency. Conversations with his mother ended in arguments, so he avoided the exercise as much as possible. He talked to her when required, nothing more.

When a Suburban darted between his bumper and the Greyhound bus he followed, Logan slammed on the brakes and muttered a curse under his breath. If the windows were down, the offending driver would know exactly where Logan thought the Suburban should be parked and how far up it should go. Luckily, his window remained rolled up tight. Getting the bird for his foul road-rage language was the topper he needed for this unpleasant day.

Road rage. Calm, always in charge Logan McKinnon reduced to road rage.

"Take a breath," he said. "Don't let her do this to you." He inhaled and attempted mental redirection from his mother's demand he hotfoot it to the coast—three long hours from Vancouver to the Washington coast hamlet of King's Bay—as if he had nothing better to do. He only had a wife and son, a company to run, and plans for the evening, which were canceled. Not theater or concert tickets, but romantic plans with his wife that as far as he was concerned were much more important than any concert tickets. Logan sighed. Just recently, three-month-old Joey had begun sleeping through the night. Melissa's hormones were calming down, and they'd made an actual date for some much-needed grown-up time—no babies allowed. When she'd casually mentioned her body would soon be available for recreational use, he'd jotted the estimated date in his planner.

It was that important.

An evening with his mother was an unsuitable alternative for a guy who'd recently begun chewing his nails and feared he was developing a nervous tick. It had been three and a half months, if he counted the two weeks prior to Joey's birth when Melissa felt fat and miserable. Three and a half months. Visiting his mother was not his first choice of evening activities.

He drummed his fingers on the steering wheel as he inched along the clogged interstate, the traffic so thick the state troopers gave up and parked their cruisers on the shoulder. Unable to concentrate on the news, he searched the radio and found a classic-rock station where the Doobie Brothers harmonized "Black Water." He was too busy stewing to listen.

Not only was he peeved about the missed date with his wife but also that he made the trip alone. Melissa and Joey were excluded from the invitation. His mother wouldn't explain why, just said they were expecting him, just him, that evening, as if he lived across town. When he'd asked to speak with his dad, she'd brushed him off and said good-bye. He'd tried calling back to discuss the situation with his father, but the line was busy, and the elder McKinnons didn't believe in cell phones. No need for them, they said. The landline was sufficient for their needs. They sure needed a cell phone now. He'd tried to call throughout the afternoon but continually met frustration in the form of an endless busy signal. At the close of his business day, he gave up, called Melissa about the change in plans, and took off for the coast. He had no choice. The nerve under his eyelid shimmied, and he glanced in the mirror for confirmation. Sure enough, he was twitching.

Two hours into the drive, worry replaced his anger. Something was wrong with this. Rehashing the phone conversation, he realized his mother's voice hadn't held her usual briskness. She'd been anxious, and he'd missed it. Maybe his dad was hurt and unable to come to the phone. Logan grabbed his cell phone and connected with the hospital nearest King's Bay. After a short conversation, he was told neither McKinnon had been admitted. He blew out a relieved breath.

At dusk, he pulled into his parents' drive and sat for a moment. Where was his dad? If they expected him, he'd be at the door to greet his only son. Joe always watched from the window like a kid awaiting Santa's arrival on Christmas Eve, meeting Logan in the driveway with a bear hug. Had Lois been too upset to tell Logan his father was ill? He delayed the moment he'd discover something was wrong.

No, Dad was fine. He was sure of it. She would have said something, given him a hint on the phone. Maybe Mom was trying to reach out to Logan, to make some sort of emotional connection. He snorted with amusement. This was his mother he was dealing with. Warmth wasn't her thing.

With a huff, Logan decided he'd delayed long enough and unfolded his legs from the car and walked to the door. A moderate-sized house, it fit perfectly into the neighborhood of beach cottages. Since his last visit, his parents had repainted the house a pale blue that would appear out of place anywhere else, but on Pacific Drive in King's Bay, it was suitable and charming. A newly planted pink rhododendron flourished near the door, and the monkey puzzle tree sported new growth. Nothing appeared out of place.

He rapped on the door and walked inside, not waiting for an answer. The earlier storm had passed, and the living room glowed with natural light as an iridescent sunset filled the horizon, filtering into the room through a sliding glass door. His parents leaned against the deck rail, their usual cohesive unit. Joe's arm was wrapped around Lois' shoulders, and he bent to kiss her temple. At seventy-seven, Joe stood tall, his shoulders still broad. His nearly black hair had turned gray years before but was neatly trimmed. Lois too appeared healthy and strong. At sixty-eight, she didn't give in to nature's insistent demands and dyed her gray hair to maintain her natural honey blonde. She was trim and well dressed. So what was the emergency?

Logan tapped the glass before sliding the door. They turned to him as a unit, eyes wide with surprise.

"Logan," his father said, turning to embrace his son with the expected hug. "What a surprise. You didn't tell us you were coming." He glanced beyond Logan. "Where are Melissa and Joey? I want to hold that baby boy. What a wonderful surprise this is."

"What do you mean by surprise?"

Joe laughed. "You didn't call first. Of course we're surprised to see you."

"Mom didn't tell you I was coming?" Logan looked at his mother, who appeared bewildered. "Mom? What's up?"

"Did you talk to Logan today, honey?" Joe asked Lois. "You forgot to mention it. No matter. Let's go in and have a cup of coffee. Does Melissa need help with the baby?"

"Melissa isn't here, Dad."

"Why not? You two aren't fighting or something, are you?" Joe said with concern.

"We don't fight." Logan frowned. "What's going on?"

"Nothing is going on," Joe said. "Why would something

be going on? That sounds ominous." He opened the glass door and waited while Lois and Logan walked through.

"Something is weird here. Mom called this afternoon and demanded I drive out here tonight. Alone." He looked at his mother. "Tell him, Mom."

She shrugged, and worry lines formed between her eyes. "I didn't call you, Logan. You must be mistaken."

"Yes. You did. You called my cell phone and insisted I come here to see you."

"Why would I do that? For Pete's sake."

Logan blew out his breath and paced across the room. "I don't know why you called. All you said was, 'I need you home, right now.' When I said something about Melissa and Joey, you said, 'Just get home now.' I thought one of you was sick or something. I tried calling all afternoon and got a busy signal." A quick glance at the phone explained why. It lay on the table, not in the cradle.

"This is crazy," Lois said. "I didn't call you."

Logan pulled the cell phone from his pocket and pushed buttons to display incoming calls. "Then how do you explain your phone number on my cell phone today?"

"I don't know," she said with a scowl. "Apparently, I must be losing my mind."

Chapter 2

Seven years later

From his leather chair, Logan stared out his office window, feet propped on the sill, too keyed up to work. His staff, he knew, sat at their desks, trying to look busy, but they were on pins and needles too. Most likely, they were involved with their social media of choice. It was okay with him, at least for today. By outward appearances they were a rough-looking crew, dressed in faded jeans and T-shirts including logos of classic-rock bands like the Stones or The Grateful Dead. There were T-shirts from the latest vacation destinations and beer companies. One guy had a dirty joke on his back. There wasn't a dress loafer or pump but a lot of tennis shoes and a few pairs of flip-flops. Half the time, Craig didn't comb his hair. If Logan hired people strictly for their fashion sense, this bunch wouldn't make the cut. They were hired for their brilliance. He didn't care if they came to work in boxer shorts and bunny slippers. Creativity, work ethic, and results were what he cared about, and that's what he received by not squishing his employees into a restrictive box. If they received long looks and disgusted glares from the suits in the building, he didn't care. They brought him the results he required.

He shifted in his chair and crossed his feet. Everything Logan had worked for was on the line, all his hopes rolled up in the phone call he willed to come. If it worked out, it was the beginning of a new era at McKinnon Software. No more penny ante small stuff. They'd be in the big leagues. His nerves tingled as he sat at his desk, staring out the window. His lunch sat uneaten on the organized desktop where his fingers tapped a nervous beat. Tension rolled through his broad shoulders.

He tried not to think about the pending deal. He'd done everything possible to ensure success. The programming was brilliant and flawless; his salesmanship had been top of the line. At the ring of the phone, he jumped but didn't answer. He remained cool as his assistant opened his office door.

"Logan, Greg Toliver on line one." She gave her boss a grin and thumbs-up when he turned his chair.

"Thanks, Wendy," he said with false calmness. "Logan McKinnon," he said after she'd closed the door.

Outside the door, they waited for the news. Logan knew they'd huddle close, waiting to hear. He didn't mind, as they'd all been in on the deal and had done their part to make it happen. During the conversation, he retained his cool facade, not letting Greg Toliver know the importance of his call. The exchange completed, he returned the phone to its cradle and took a shuddering breath. Unable to contain it any longer, he punched his fists in the air in victory and spun his chair in a circle.

"Yes! We did it." The moment was sweet, and his first thought was to call his wife and give her the news. Melissa was the senior programmer on the project and was waiting as well. Instead, the phone remained in its place as he jumped from his chair and nearly toppled his scruffy staff as he bounded through the door. Logan, dressed in a suit and tie from the morning's meeting, appeared out of place.

"Well?" Wendy asked, wide eyed.

Logan swallowed and took a breath. "We got it."

"We did?" Wendy asked. "How much?"

"The whole damned thing. McKinnon Software is the new contractor to AmStarInc. We have arrived." He found himself caught in a crush of hugs and screams.

"Have you called Melissa?" Craig asked. True to form, his hair remained uncombed, and he had a spot of ketchup on his vintage Led Zeppelin T-shirt.

"I'm going home to tell her. It's five already. Go and celebrate." He dug the wallet from his back pocket, took out a hundred-dollar bill, and handed it to Wendy. "Take these guys out for a drink on me. I need to go home." He slapped his hand on Craig's shoulder and laughed. "See you tomorrow." He pulled himself from the tangle and headed for the door, smiling as he heard his employees' comments.

"He did it," Craig said with awe. "He really did it. The whole freaking thing."

"Of course he did it," Wendy said. "Logan never fails at anything."

Logan danced his way to the car, his feet barely touching the ground. The news had been better than expected. On a scale of one to ten, he'd rate it a whopping fifteen, maybe twenty. It was so good, he had to control the persistent urge to pull the cell phone from his pocket and spill the news. But he didn't. It was the kind of news deserving face-to-face delivery, and he wanted to see her expression when he told her. A grin spread across his face as he drove his Lexus down the tree-lined suburban street leading home. August heat blew in the window, tousling his light-brown hair. The smoke from a neighbor's barbeque drifted in, causing his stomach to growl and reminding him of the uneaten lunch on his desk. From the audio system, Bob Seger growled out "Katmandu," and Logan thumb-drummed the beat on the steering wheel while he sang along—matching the singer growl for growl. At an intersection, a woman stared his way, shaking her head and laughing as he sang with enthusiasm. He grinned and continued, not allowing anything to spoil his mood. He slowed the car as he maneuvered the drive, pushed the button on the garage door opener, and came to a smooth stop next to his wife's SUV. He sat for a moment, savoring the victory until the adrenalin that carried him home threatened to bounce him from the car.

He hummed as he opened the kitchen door. On the stove, pots of spaghetti and sauce bubbled; their spicy scent filled the air. In denim shorts and a tank top, Melissa moved between them and the refrigerator, collecting salad ingredients while he observed unnoticed. In the living room, young voices whooped and hollered as his two sons played army with G.I. Joes and Tonka trucks. In a basinet to the side of the kitchen, his infant daughter slept in pink sleepers, her heart-shaped mouth making sucking motions. He stepped behind his wife and wrapped his arms around her, snuggling his face into her soft, dark hair.

"Hi," he whispered.

"Hi," Melissa said in return. "You're subdued, Logan. Does that mean—"

"It means we have a baby sleeping in the corner." He chuckled.

"Well? You had the meeting this morning, right? What happened?" she asked softly. He hesitated, making her turn in his arms and stare at him. She fisted her hands on his suit lapels. He tried to string her along and let her wonder, but the excitement of the day took hold, and he grinned.

"We got it."

"We did? How much?"

"All of it."

"Oh my gosh! The overseas offices too?"

He nodded.

"I can't believe it. They said they were splitting it over several companies."

"It's all us, and it's worldwide, baby. One of the largest conglomerates in the country, and they want us." He pulled her off her feet and spun her. They laughed together, forgetting the infant in the corner, who yawned and stretched but didn't awaken. "I'm not surprised," he continued as he set Melissa down. He couldn't contain his confident smile. "Greg Toliver called this afternoon and said they were so impressed with the software samples we'd presented they decided to award the entire contract to us."

"Oh, Logan, I'm so happy for you. You've worked so hard for this. Congratulations." She wrapped her arms around his neck and kissed him.

"It wasn't only me. We all worked hard—you, me, the staff. And it's just the beginning. The next few months will be hectic. I'll need to make a few trips to DC and Houston to get the preliminary work started, which means leaving you home alone with the kids."

She smiled and gave him a peck on the lips. "I'll be okay. If it's too much, Mom and Dad could probably help out a little. Don't worry about me. When will you have to go?" When the stove timer rang, she pulled away and removed the sauce from the burner. "Can we still make the trip to your parents' house next week? The boys are looking forward to spending some time with them at the beach before school starts."

"Yeah, it'll work out. I have work to do here first, and I'll fly out right after Labor Day weekend. Dad sounded tired last time I talked to him, so I think we need to check on him." He dodged aside as Melissa grabbed the steaming spaghetti pot from the stove and drained it in the sink.

"He said he was okay, didn't he?"

"He always says he's okay." Logan laughed. "You know Dad. There would have to be a major nuclear disaster in his backyard before he thought he had a problem. He's always so optimistic about everything." Logan grabbed plates from the cupboard and set them around the table, glancing at the sleeping baby with a smile. "I double-checked on the condo reservations. Dad isn't happy we aren't staying with them, but I think Hannah would keep them awake all night."

"He's probably forgotten what it's like to have a baby in the house. If he heard her yelling at two a.m., he'd wish we were in a motel," Melissa said with a laugh. "She's a good baby but does have her moments. Dinner is ready. Would you tell the boys to wash up?"

"Sure." He nodded and turned to the living room door.

"Wait a sec," Melissa stopped him. "Give me the jacket."

He shrugged out of the jacket and draped it across her out-stretched hand.

"And the tie."

He grinned as he removed the tie and laid it across the jacket. He gave her a mock salute before heading to the war zone in his living room. He crept along so as not to alert the enemy, dropped to a crouch behind the chair, and as luck would have it, his favorite weapon was within his grasp. He grabbed it and planned his strategy. The opposition was canny, and he knew from previous experience he'd have to strike fast or face certain annihilation.

Both boys crawled on hands and knees, pushing jeeps and trucks across the floor, growling like engines and making crash sounds. An army of G.I. Joes leaned against the sofa, stiffly at attention, awaiting their orders. Momentarily distracted from his mission, Logan watched his sons, and a wave of pride ran through him. Seven-year-old Joey, with his dark curly hair, looked so much like Melissa it was as if Logan himself had had little to do with his creation. But Joey shared his father's fascination with technology, thereby proving a link. And little Derek wasn't so little anymore. At five, he'd nearly reached his older brother's height, indicating he would be his father's replica in every way. Derek was tall and lanky with a head of straight, light-brown hair, dark-brown eyes, and a fascination with boats equal to Logan's love of computers.

Logan awaited his opportunity, and when both boys turned their backs, he jumped from behind the chair.

"Incoming!"

The boys jumped but overcame their surprise and launched a loud attack, only to be driven back by the spray from Logan's squirt gun. He lunged and dodged as the boys came at him with pillows and light sabers.

"Hey! No fair. Mom won't let us use squirt guns in the house." Joey, the obvious leader of the opposition, yelled and tried to distract with useless propaganda. The dark-haired boy was an able general, always in control of his troops. To prove it, he waved his hand to his younger brother, and the two ran around opposite sides of their enemy, grabbed his legs, and succeeded in wrestling him to the floor. From there, it turned into a ground war with tickling, hysterical laughter, and superstar wrestler posturing.

"I surrender," Logan called out, laughing in defeat. "You got me again. I surrender." He grabbed Joey for one last tickle, causing Derek to pout.

"Tickle me too, Daddy."

Logan grabbed him and tickled mercilessly, sending Derek into a burst of giggles.

Melissa wandered in, laughing. "Dinner is ready, boys," she said, including all three in the comment. Logan lay on the floor with a boy wrapped in each arm and grinned.

With dinner completed and the boys tucked in bed, Logan kicked back in his chair, put his feet on the desk in his dimly lit office, and made a call on his cell phone. The office was his oasis, his quiet place to think. It was a comfortable room with a bay window and bookshelves lining the walls; blank spaces were filled with certificates and accolades. There were sports trophies, blue ribbons, and letters of commendation. When Logan set out to get something, he generally accomplished his goal. He seldom failed.

"Hi, Mom. It's Logan," he said when his mother picked up the phone.

"Who?" Lois McKinnon said.

"It's Logan, Mom," he said again but was met with silence. "Can I talk to Dad?" He tapped his fingers on the desk as he waited.

"Hello."

"Hi, Dad."

"Logan," Joe McKinnon said with delight. "I'm so glad you called."

"What's up with Mom? She acted...funny, like she didn't know me."

"She's fine, just fine. She was on her way to bed when the phone rang. She's tired, that's all. How are all of you? Have those kids grown since we saw them?"

"Probably. They're eating us out of house and home, so they must be growing." He laughed. "Are you sure Mom is okay?"

"She's great, getting older, that's all. It happens, you know."

"I guess it does. I thought I'd check in and make sure it was still okay to visit next week."

Joe laughed. "Son, you can visit tomorrow if you want. We don't see enough of you and that family of yours. How is your little baby girl?"

"Gorgeous, like her mom."

"I can't wait to hold her again—the baby, that is." Joe laughed at his own joke. "Tell the boys to bring their beach gear. I have an urge to build a huge sandcastle this time. Our biggest ever. And the ice cream parlor has a new flavor I want to try, blueberry cheesecake twist."

"Sounds like you have things planned out."

"There's always more to do than we have time for. Are you sure you can't stay longer?" Joe asked, as he always did.

"I wish we could, but the boys will be in school, and I have to fly to DC right after the holiday."

"DC? That sounds important."

"Sort of...we got the contract I've been working on," Logan said.

"The big one?"

"The really big one, Dad. This is the one that will put

McKinnon Software on the map." He grinned to himself. "And we got the whole thing, not just the part we thought we'd get, but the whole enchilada. Home offices, foreign offices, all of it."

"Oh, Logan. That is wonderful. I'm so proud of you," Joe said with sincerity. "I can't wait to tell your mom. She'll be proud too."

"Thanks," Logan said quietly. Praise from his father always melted him, and he had to stop himself from getting emotional. Praise from his mother? It had never happened, and he didn't expect the situation to change now, no matter how large his success. He figured he could be elected president and his mother would give him one of those odd looks of hers.

"You'll be giving Microsoft a run for their money now, won't you?" Joe chuckled to lighten the moment.

Logan laughed. "Hardly, but at least I'm in the game. We'll be able to expand the games division after this. Melissa had some ideas we haven't been able to implement, and this will give us the cash to do it."

"Just a sec, Logan." Joe had obviously put his hand over the receiver, but Logan could still catch part of the conversation between his parents.

"It's Logan on the phone," Joe said.

Logan couldn't hear his mother, but his father came through loud enough. "Yes, on the phone. He's at his house, Lois. In Vancouver. No, he won't be coming here tonight. He doesn't live with us anymore. Why don't you get your nightgown, honey? The blue one is in your dresser. I'll be there in a minute to help." Joe came back on the line. "Sorry. Mom wanted to talk for a second."

"I'd better get to bed myself. I have to be at the office early tomorrow." He thought for a second. "Dad? Why did she think I'd be at your place tonight?"

"She messed up the date of your visit, that's all."

Logan frowned but decided not to pursue it. "We'll see you next week, Dad. Good-night." He disconnected the call and sat for a moment. There was something going on with his mother, but he quickly shoved aside his concerns when Melissa poked her head in the door.

"I'm going to bed."

"Is Hannah asleep?"

She smiled and nodded.

"I'll be there in a minute." He shut off the lights and ran up the stairs.

⟨⟩

"Are we there yet, Daddy?" Derek whined from the backseat. Next to him, Joey silently played his Game Boy. Hannah dozed in her car seat. Derek squirmed. "I gotta go to the bathroom. Bad." He squirmed again and scrunched his face.

"A few more minutes, buddy. Hang in there," Logan said again, but this time, there was a ring of truth to it as he turned onto his parents' street. It was a pleasant neighborhood of mostly retired people like his parents who spent their days walking the beach and puttering in their yards. Joe and Lois had come to King's Bay twenty years earlier after selling their orchards in the eastern part of the state. Over the years, saltwater mists had faded the blue paint to a pale hue. Logan had to admit it looked good. But then, any house with that ocean view would look terrific, no matter the paint color.

Logan pulled the SUV to a stop and smiled when his father burst from the door, grinning. He didn't appear as tired as he'd sounded on the phone, and Logan relaxed. He stepped from the vehicle and grabbed his dad into a big hug that was returned with enthusiastic back slapping.

"I didn't think you'd ever get here," Joe said. He released Logan and grabbed Derek as he climbed from his seat.

"Let me go," Derek cried as he squirmed. "I gotta pee, Grandpa."

Joe laughed as the skinny boy pulled away and ran for the house, pushing past Lois, who stood in the doorway. Logan waved and wondered why she appeared nervous. She'd allowed her hair to go gray since the last visit, no longer dying it to honey blonde.

"Hi, Mom," he called out. She frowned and gave a tentative wave back. "What's up with her?" he asked Joe, who had moved on to hug Melissa and ogle the baby. Joey said a quick hello and followed his brother's path into the house. Lois frowned as he ran past.

"Mom?" Joe shrugged. "Nothing. She's fine. Tired, maybe. She didn't sleep well last night. Probably the excitement of having visitors today. Come in. We'll get lunch on the table and run down to the beach. It's a beautiful day."

Logan grabbed the diaper bag from the backseat and followed his dad into the house. It looked the same as always, neat and homey. They trooped through the house, past the living room with its comfortable furniture and carefully dusted knickknacks, and into the kitchen, where Joe pulled sandwich ingredients from the refrigerator. He waved for them to sit while he retrieved bread and fixings. Logan watched and wondered why his mother wasn't helping, but stayed silent.

"Logan, there is a bag of chips in the cupboard in the pantry. Could you grab them for me? The jug of juice too," Joe added as he spread mayonnaise on bread and piled lunch meat.

"Sure." Logan got up from the table and returned a moment later with the requested items, setting them on the table. "How are you, Mom?" he asked as he took his seat. She gave him a long look and shrugged.

"Fine, I guess," she said without adding more.

Logan resigned himself to a normal visit with his mom. She'd never been particularly talkative with him, but this behavior was odd, even for Lois. She appeared uneasy.

"Get washed up, everybody. I'll have these sandwiches ready in a minute," Joe said as he set plates on the table.

Logan observed Lois throughout lunch. She ate slowly and methodically, concentrating on her sandwich as if the task was difficult. Conversation swirled around her, but she added nothing. Joe sat next to her, anticipating her needs. If she required a napkin, he handed it to her. If her juice glass was empty, he refilled it. When she finished eating, she wrapped the last bit of sandwich in her napkin and stuffed it in her pocket.

After lunch, they piled into their cars and drove to the public beach a mile from the house. The afternoon was spent building sandcastles and hunting seashells. The day was indeed beautiful. The sun glistened on the breaking waves, and seagulls added their cacophony to the ocean's roar. The group carried their gear down the beach to a driftwood log partially embedded in the sand. Joe sat in the middle with Lois to one side, and on the other side Logan leaned comfortably against the log with his bare feet buried in the sand. Later, he'd let the boys bury him. It was tradition.

Again, Logan observed Lois' behavior and found it odd. She was quiet and edgy. When the boys went into the surf to play, she became agitated, wringing her hands. Logan was distracted by his father's conversation and didn't notice Lois had left her seat on the nearby driftwood log until he heard the commotion at the water's edge. When he looked up, she was yelling at the boys.

"Get out of the water this minute!"

Joey and Derek stopped splashing for a moment. "Why?" Joey asked.

"Because I said so. Get out of that water right now. It isn't safe."

"Daddy said we could play here," Derek said. When she grabbed his arm and yanked him from the water, Derek cried out. He didn't weigh much, and she pulled him with ease.

"Logan, I said get out of that water, and I mean it." She pulled him to the shore, holding his arm tightly.

"Grandma! Ow! You're hurting me!" Derek tried to twist away and began to cry when he couldn't wrench free. "Daddy!"

Logan was on his feet and running. "What's wrong?" He took in the scene, his distressed mother and his squirming son with tears streaming down his face. "Mom, what's going on?" Lois looked from Logan to Derek, confusion in her eyes, and released Derek's arm. Logan took Derek in his arms and held him. The boy sobbed into his shoulder. Joey stood behind Logan, peering at his grandmother. "What's the problem, Mom? I was watching them. They were fine."

Lois blinked a few times and strode back up the beach to Joe. Melissa walked to his side with baby Hannah sleeping soundly in her Snugli. She rubbed her finger across Derek's arm.

"She made a mark, Logan. What's wrong with her?" Melissa said as Lois walked away.

"I don't know," Logan said. "But I intend to find out."

After dinner at Polly's Beachside Restaurant, Logan dropped his tired family at the rented condo and returned to his parents' home alone. Joe answered the door with a smile, but Logan didn't match it.

"I need to talk to you," Logan said as he walked into the dimly lit living room. "Where's Mom?"

"She went to bed early. What's troubling you, Logan?" Joe said as he followed.

"I want to know what's going on with Mom."

"There isn't anything going on. She's fine."

"No. She isn't. There's something wrong with her, and I want to know what it is. She bruised Derek's arm and scared him half to death today." He paced across the room. "If you don't know what's going on with her, then we'd better get her into the doctor and find out. She's not right."

"Keep your voice down. You'll wake her." Joe motioned for Logan to follow into his den. He dropped into his desk chair and indicated for Logan to sit on the love seat along the wall.

"What makes you think something is wrong?"

"What makes you think she's okay?" Logan countered. "She's not acting right, Dad. You have to see it."

"She's fine. She has occasional memory problems. It's hardly a crime."

"Why didn't she help with lunch today? Why did she sit there and not say anything?"

"I like to fix lunch. I'm retired and have a lot of free time. I like to do things for her." He frowned. "And who says she has to chatter like a magpie? If she wants to be quiet, it's her right."

"Dad." Logan lowered his voice and tried a new approach. "You're doing everything for her. She seems lost. There's this look in her eyes I don't remember seeing before, like she isn't quite sure what's going on around her. I don't think it's a simple memory problem anymore." He took a breath and stared into his father's eyes. "When she grabbed Derek today, she called him Logan. You heard her. How can you deny she has a problem?" He watched as the emotion played across his father's face. Anger turned to sadness, and Logan was sure he saw a tear form in his father's blue eyes, but he blinked it away.

Joe nodded and sighed. "I know what it is." He closed his eyes and blew out a breath.

Logan waited.

"I've known for some time now."

"What is it, Dad?"

"Alzheimer's disease." He looked at Logan with stricken eyes as if the admission was physically painful.

Logan was stunned. "Alzheimer's? Are you sure?"

"Very sure. She's been through a battery of tests, and by

process of elimination, that's the doctor's diagnosis. They say the only way to know for sure is after death, by autopsy. But she has all the classic symptoms. Her doctor is as positive as he can be."

"What can we do? Is there treatment? What are you doing for her?"

"She takes medication, but the doc says it will only help for a couple of years. She's doing okay with it for now. She gets depressed, so she has medication for that too. Otherwise, there isn't anything else we can do."

Logan felt as if the floor had been pulled from under him. He wasn't sure which upset him more, the horrible diagnosis or the fact his father had kept it from him. Wasn't he a part of this family too?

When he spoke, his voice was a hoarse whisper. "Why didn't you tell me? You've always been honest with me about everything, haven't you? Why didn't you tell me about this?"

Joe hesitated. "I've always tried to be honest with you, but I couldn't bring myself to tell you about this. I couldn't stand the thought of people seeing her as less than perfect."

"Even me?" Logan whispered.

"Especially you." Joe sighed. "Your mom has always worried about what other people thought of her. When she first started having problems, I didn't tell anyone out of fear people would laugh at her failing memory and think less of her."

"How long has she had these problems?"

"Years. She first started noticing it before your wedding, little things we attributed to age. But it kept getting worse. She was so afraid of what people would think of her."

Logan sighed. "What can we do for her?"

"Nothing." He shook his head.

"There must be something. Have you talked to any specialists, or are you relying on these small-town hacks?"

"She has very good doctors."

Logan huffed out a breath and jumped to his feet. "Well,

not good enough, apparently. I think we need to get her into Virginia Mason in Seattle and have a specialist look her over. With all the medical research going on, I can't believe they can't help her." He paced, unable to control his momentum. Though he couldn't say he had a great relationship with his mother, the instinct to protect her took hold.

Joe looked at Logan with tired eyes. "Sit down." Joe motioned to the love seat and waited while Logan settled. "We've been through all that. I've taken her to Seattle. Remember a few years ago when we were spending a lot of time in the city? We weren't going to Mariners games. We were making the rounds and talking to the experts. She's been tested, poked, prodded, and received psychiatric evaluation. She has Alzheimer's disease, and there is absolutely nothing we can do about it."

"There are always solutions, Dad. Maybe you haven't been asking the right questions." He felt so helpless, and that wasn't a feeling he allowed. There were always paths to follow for success. Always.

Joe smiled sadly. "I've asked every question there is to ask." He opened a desk drawer, and removed a pile of books. "I've been studying this for years." He handed Logan the pile of dog-eared medical books. "Take them if you like. I've nearly memorized them all." He leaned back in his chair. "Believe it when I say I've tried everything. I felt like you did when she was first diagnosed. It wasn't fair. Why Lois?" Joe frowned. "You're my son, and I love you with all my heart, but she is my heart, and you can bet I've done everything possible for her." He turned away as tears filled his eyes. "I would do anything to protect her, and I have. I always have."

Logan felt a lump in his throat. "I'm sorry, Dad. I didn't mean to imply you haven't done your best for her. What can I do to help?"

Joe shook his head. "I know your offer is sincere, but there isn't anything right now. We go on, day to day. Some days are better than others, but it isn't anything I can't handle. We're doing okay, like we always have. You have your life to take care of. Your young family needs you. Your company is growing. Let me worry about this."

"But..." Logan began but stopped when Joe leaned forward and took his hand. Despite his advanced age, the grip remained strong.

"We're all right for now, but there may come a time when I'll need your help. I'm a lot older than your mom, and it is conceivable I could...that something could happen." He looked seriously into his son's eyes. "When the time comes I can't handle this anymore, I'll let you know, and I'll trust you to take care of her for me. I don't want you to worry about it until then. Agreed?"

Logan nodded reluctantly. "There must be something, Dad. With all the research going on, isn't there something we can try?" Logan was grasping for anything. The heartbreak in his father's eyes was killing him.

Joe shook his head. "Just love her. It's all we can do."

Chapter 3

Logan sat at his home office desk, staring at the latest e-mail from AmStarInc. In the two months since the contract was finalized, his life had become a whirlwind of meetings, red-eye flights, and restaurant food on the run. He was home for the time being, at least until another situation arose requiring his personal attention. He'd never been happier.

Another e-mail popped up as the phone rang. He absently grabbed it as he continued to read.

"Yeah."

"It's Dad. Am I interrupting something?"

"Just reading e-mail. How are things?" He relaxed in his chair and rubbed his eyes.

"Good."

"Don't give me that 'everything is just fine' crap, Dad. The truth, please," he scolded his father, who laughed.

"We're doing fine. Mom isn't any worse, so I look at it as a good day. She's on what the doc calls a plateau. When things change, I'll tell you. How is business?"

"Hectic. I just got home from Houston last night and may need to go again. But I'm keeping up."

"You must be tired, so I won't keep you long. I saw something in the *AARP Magazine* I thought you should know about. Have you heard of the Elf Virus? It's supposed to hit around Christmastime."

"I guess I missed that one." Logan glanced at his computer screen and saw a new e-mail. He opened it while his dad talked.

"I'll send the article to you. Sounds like a bad one." Joe

paused. "Have you made your vacation plans for next summer yet?"

"No, haven't thought that far ahead. Why?" He perused the document on the screen.

"Just an idea I had. I was thinking we could all make a trip home to Henley next summer. The boys are big enough to do some fishing, and I thought it would be fun to take them to the mountains. You always liked to fish when you were that age."

"Still do," Logan said. He closed one document and opened another. "That would be fun. Hannah will be a year old then, so it'll be easier to take her along. I'll talk to Melissa about it."

"Maybe we could drive by the old house and see if the young pup who bought the place is taking care of the orchards right."

"He isn't such a young pup anymore, Dad. I graduated with him, so he must be forty-three or forty-four."

"I suppose you're right…" He trailed off. "Do you think the old Apple Blossom Café is still there?"

"It's gone," Logan said. "There's a Lowe's Hardware there now."

"Oh, yes, I remember reading about that now you mention it. Old Tony sure made a good apple pie. Left all the apples in big chunks, not those skinny little slices. Maybe we could drive up Lang's Hill for a look-see around the valley. Your mom would enjoy it."

"We could," Logan said, "but you can't see much since a gated community went in. It's prime real estate now."

"Oh well. That's progress, I suppose. A lot of memories sit on that hill," Joe said. "You know I proposed to your mom up there."

"Yeah, I know."

"She was so pretty. When we were dating, we'd sit on Lang's Hill sometimes, listen to romantic music, do a little kissing," he said with a chuckle. "Things were different back then. One thing stayed the same though."

"What's that?"

"Lois is still the prettiest woman I've ever seen. Fifty-four years we've been married, and she's still the prettiest."

They continued to talk about the old times until Melissa stuck her head in the door and said she was heading to bed. Logan checked the clock and decided he needed to get moving as well.

"I need to go, Dad. Talk to you later."

⚜

The next week was as crazy as the previous two months. Logan barely had time to eat. Occasionally, the thought crossed his mind he needed to check on his parents, but another crisis presented itself, and he was off and running again.

He sat at his desk, contemplating the next trip he'd need to take, when his cell phone rang. He answered absently.

"Yeah?"

"Is this Logan McKinnon?" said an unfamiliar voice.

"Yes, it is."

"This is Harry Thomas from King's Bay."

Logan frowned and tried to remember if he'd met a Harry Thomas at his parents' house and couldn't place him. "What can I do for you, Mr. Thomas?"

"I was wondering when you'd be coming to get your mom. She's already been here over an hour and isn't particularly happy about the situation. She wants to go home."

"I don't understand. Why is Mom with you?" Logan's full attention shifted to the conversation now. "Where is my dad?"

"They took him to the hospital."

"The hospital? What's wrong?"

"Didn't they call you?"

"No. No one called me. What's going on?"

"Well, hells bells," Harry muttered. "I'd have called you myself if I'd known they weren't doing it." He sighed. "You'd better get here quick. Your father had a stroke."

Chapter 4

Logan packed a suitcase and was on the road in minutes, making the normal three-hour drive in less than two hours. He collected his mother on the way to the hospital and sat waiting for news. The smell of sickness permeated the air.

"Where is Joe?" Lois asked. "I want to see Joe." She fidgeted in her chair as her fingers made nervous motions on her sweater sleeve.

Tension gripped Logan, and he wished his mother would stop asking the same irritating question over and over. He tried to speak in a calming way, but his voice came out clipped. "The doctors are with him, Mom. We can't see him right now." He leaned forward in his chair, resting his elbows on his knees. He'd been waiting an hour for news. All he knew so far was Joe had collapsed on the living room floor. His mother had managed to walk to the neighbor's house and actually remembered the message she needed to relay. Mr. Thomas called 9-1-1, and Joe was brought into the emergency room. Someone had promised to call Logan from the hospital, but it hadn't happened. Lois stayed with her neighbors, growing progressively more agitated.

Logan stood and paced. He couldn't help but feel guilty for the present situation. His father had brushed off his offer for help, and Logan let him do it. He should have persisted and maybe Joe wouldn't be in this situation.

As he paced, he reflected on the past two months. Had his father given him signals he'd missed? Was he too absorbed in his own life to realize his father was overwhelmed? Probably. The AmStarInc deal had consumed every waking moment for months, and he hadn't hesitated to take the easy way out when his father gave him the opportunity.

"Mr. McKinnon?" said a doctor standing in the doorway, his eyes shifting between Logan and Lois. "May I talk with you out here for a moment?"

Logan's heart drummed in his chest. "Sure." He followed the doctor to the hall.

"I'm sorry, Mr. McKinnon. We did everything we could, but...we've lost him." He looked at Logan with sympathetic eyes.

"You've what?" Logan asked, sure he'd heard him wrong.

"We've lost him. Your father has passed away. I'm sorry." He placed his hand on Logan's shoulder and squeezed.

Logan shook his head. "No, that can't be. He's been fine. There must be something..."

The doctor shook his head. "I'm sorry. If you like, the chaplain is waiting. If it would help, he'll be there when you tell your mother."

Logan swallowed hard and fought the surging emotions. "No, it's okay. I'll talk to her." He tried to control a shake running through his body. "In a second, I'll tell her." The doctor patted him on the shoulder and walked away.

Logan glanced in the waiting room at his mother and wondered how to tell her Joe was gone. What would become of her now? He willed his feet to take him into the waiting room, but he remained rooted. They had been together fifty-four years. How would she survive now? He stepped away from the door and began to shake in earnest. The tremor began in his shoulders and soon encompassed his entire body, and he wrapped his arms around his middle in an unsuccessful attempt to steady himself. He leaned his head on the cool wall and tears cascaded down his face. He was helpless to stop them and squeezed his eyes tight in a vain attempt. It couldn't be true. Joe couldn't be gone.

A hand on his shoulder startled him, and he opened his

eyes to find an elderly man in a clergy collar looking at him with grave concern.

"Come with me, son. We can find a better place than this." He squeezed Logan's shoulder and began to walk. Tempted to follow and let the minister take control, Logan had to stop and remember his new responsibility. He wiped his sleeve across his face, removing tears.

"I can't leave, sir. My mother is in the waiting room. I need to tell her." The elderly man nodded and led the way to Lois. She sat alone, looking so small and vulnerable.

"Where's Joe? Can I see him now?" She stood, but Logan took her small hand and stopped her. He sniffed and wiped at his eyes. He gently pulled Lois back to her seat.

"Mom. We can't see Dad. He, uh…" He swallowed hard. "Mom…Dad didn't make it."

"Didn't make what?" she asked, confused.

"He…" Logan swallowed. "He died, Mom. Dad's gone."

Lois' lip quivered. "He's gone?" Her face contorted. Logan wrapped his arms around her and held her as she leaned into his shoulder. Waves of tears soaked his shirt.

"Yeah, he's gone." They sat that way for a while until her tremors subsided and she pulled away. Lois looked from the minister to Logan, her brow knitted in a frown.

"Who is he?" she asked Logan, pointing to the minister.

"He's the hospital chaplain. He's here because of Dad."

Lois looked thoughtful for a moment and then looked at Logan with wide eyes. "Where is Joe? Can I see him now?"

Chapter 5

Logan was at the end of his rope and wishing someone would hang him with it. The demands upon him were walls closing in, squeezing the breath from his lungs. He'd heard the term sandwich generation for years, but until recently it hadn't applied to him. But now he felt its pressure as he was firmly pressed between two slices of family—young and old—trapped without room to move.

He stood stiffly, braced against the winter wind driven from the ocean below, tossing rain-like icicles against his skin. Wrapped in his thoughts, he was vaguely aware of discomfort but unwilling to leave the solitude of the deck railing yet. For a few minutes he could have peace and the freedom to think uninterrupted, a luxury he'd come to treasure the week he'd been stuck in King's Bay.

He leaned against the cedar rail, his back to the house lit only by a chairside lamp. It was nearly midnight, but it was the first time all day he'd been free to escape the confines of his mother's home and her maddening behavior.

He frowned as he stared into the night, made darker by the falling rain. Had it been two months since he'd visited his parents and they'd built sandcastles on the beach? Two weeks since the last phone call? Logan closed his eyes, took a deep breath, and imagined his dad's voice in his head. Would the memory fade? Would he remember the timbre of his voice or the roll of his laugh five years from now? He thought about their last conversation, the reminiscing, the plans they'd begun to make, and Logan wondered if his father had recognized his time was limited. They always talked about the old times together, but this had been different, and Logan had missed it.

Movement in the living room grabbed his attention. He turned from the solitude of the night, shelved his emotions, and reluctantly returned to the house and his current responsibility. He wiped the remaining rain from his face as he entered the sliding glass door.

"Who is this?" Lois said into the phone, her voice escalated in panic. Worry etched her lined face, and her pink flannel nightgown was partially unbuttoned and slipping from her shoulder. Her hand gripped the phone. "Who is this?"

Long strides brought Logan across the room to stand by his mother. He reached for the phone, but she moved away.

"I don't understand what you're saying." Lois frowned.

"Mom, let me have the phone." Logan held out his hand, but she ignored him.

"Who are you?" Lois said again. "You want who? I don't understand. You want Logan? He's away at school. I haven't seen him in weeks."

Logan put his hand on the receiver. "Mom, let me have the phone." He gave it a slight tug, and she released it. Confusion filled her eyes. "Why don't you go back to bed? I'll take care of this. Hello. This is Logan," he said. His mother stood at his elbow, wringing her hands.

"Hi, honey. I thought she'd be asleep, or I wouldn't have called."

Logan sighed with relief when he recognized his wife's voice. "It's fine. She's up and down all night anyway. Did you make it home okay?" he asked, trying to mask the fatigue in his voice. Melissa had enough on her plate at the moment with the kids and the company. He didn't want to add to her worries.

"Yeah, the boys talked me into stopping for milkshakes. It took longer, but we made it. I wish we could have stayed there with you." Melissa sighed. "This isn't a night for you to be alone. I should be with you."

"I'd love to have you here, but you know how Mom is with the kids. It's easier to handle things if it's just us."

"Are you okay?"

"I'm surviving. Mom slept for a while, so I went out on the deck. I froze my butt off, but the fresh air felt good. I'm still a little soggy from the rain." He ran his hand across the damp dress shirt he'd worn since his father's funeral that day. He'd already tossed the tie and belt he'd worn. He flinched when his mother slapped his arm.

"Watch your mouth, young man. I won't have that language in my home." Lois slapped his arm again, harder. "Are you listening to me? I'll be talking to your father about this when he gets home."

He thought back to what he'd said to Melissa that had been offensive to his mother. Probably the frozen butt comment. "Just a sec, Melissa." He turned to Lois, scowling. "Will you stop hitting me? I'm forty-three years old, and I'll talk however I please." He instantly regretted lashing out at her when her lip quivered. She dropped her head, covered in gray chaotic curls, and began to cry.

"I'll tell your father." She turned away and wandered from the room.

Logan blew out a frustrated breath. "I'll have to call you in the morning. I just set off Mom again, and I need to see where she disappeared to." He glanced in the direction she'd gone. "This is so damned difficult. I swear she's into everything like a five-and-a-half-foot-tall toddler. But at least with toddlers, you can lock them out of things or set hazards up high. She can reach everything. I get one mess cleaned up, and she makes another one. I have to watch every word I say, or she's mad or crying or both. I don't know what I'm doing—but apparently it's all wrong."

"I wish there was something I could do to help you," Melissa said.

"Me too. But the more people around, the worse she is. I hate this." He ran his hand through his damp hair and let out a frustrated groan. "I'll have to call you in the morning. Love you." He hung up the phone and walked through the house, searching each room. He found her in her bedroom, digging through the closet. Clothing, boxes, and shoes were strewn about haphazardly.

"What are you doing?" he asked as he watched her take the shoes from the closet and stuff them into a dresser drawer.

"I need to do this," she said with determination as a pair of sandals went into the drawer.

"Shoes belong in the closet," he said with similar determination. He picked up the sandals and returned them to the closet floor. Lois picked them up again and stuffed them in the drawer.

"Mom," he said with impatience. "Shoes belong there." He pointed to the closet.

"I need to do this." Despite her son's protests, she continued moving shoes.

Logan threw up his hands and walked from the room. He'd let her do what she wanted and clean up the mess later. It was easier than fighting with her when he knew he couldn't win.

He found himself in his father's den staring at pictures on the wall, mostly of Logan at various ages, with his light-brown hair ranging from extreme buzz cut in the sixties to long and shaggy in the seventies when he'd had more control over the frequency of his haircuts. Little League, Boy Scouts, his prize FFA pigs, high school and college graduations were commemorated on his father's wall. An only child, he'd had no one with whom to share the space, so it was dedicated to him and his achievements.

There were pictures of Logan with his smiling father at every occasion and pictures with his mother as well, but there was seldom a smile on her face. He'd often wondered when he was younger if an only child later in his parents' marriage had meant he was an unwanted or accidental child. Questions to his father had netted him a laugh and a hug. Joe had wanted him, he was sure, but he'd often wondered about his mother. Stories were told of Lois being unable to conceive in the early years, so she had made her life what she wanted it to be. She'd worked in a grocery store, belonged to a women's club, and had many friends.

Everything changed when she'd found herself pregnant at thirty-one. While her friends' children were in school, Lois changed diapers and washed bottles. Forty-three years later, Logan still wondered if his existence made her unhappy.

A loud crash from the other room forced Logan back to the present, and he flew through the house to locate his mother.

"What are you doing now?" he asked as he skidded to a stop in the kitchen. She stood surrounded by pots and pans pulled roughly from the bottom cupboard. She fussed with the sleeve of her nightgown. Her eyes held childish innocence.

"I need to fix dinner."

"It's nearly one in the morning. We ate dinner hours ago when everyone was here," Logan said as he surveyed the mess with disgust. Pots and pans covered the floor, sugar from the canister was spilled on the counter, a package of frozen steak sat in a skillet, and a bag of potatoes lay in the sink.

"Someone was here?"

"Yes, everyone. Melissa and the kids, Uncle Larry and Aunt Marian, and about twenty others. We had a huge dinner." He bent to retrieve a pan and set it on the counter.

"Well." She pursed her lips. "And where is Joe? He should be here to help clean this mess. That man is never around." She kicked a pan with her bare foot. It skidded across the floor and banged against a table leg. "I'm going to give him a piece of my mind. Where is he?"

Logan sighed. A tremendous weight pressed on his shoulders. "Mom," he began as he had repeatedly for the past seven days. "Dad is gone. He died last week, and his funeral was this morning."

Tears filled her eyes and her lip trembled. "Why didn't anyone tell me?" She looked at him with anguished eyes. "How dare you keep that from me? He is my husband."

Exhaustion crept through his body. He rubbed his hand on his neck to ease the tension. "I didn't keep anything from you. The funeral was this morning, and you were there. Reverend Miller gave a nice sermon. George Henderson from the VFW gave the eulogy and handed you the flag."

"What flag? I don't understand what you're talking about." Lois stepped over the scattered pans and drifted from the room. He followed her through the living room and guided her back to her room.

"It's time for bed." Logan walked her to the bed and straightened the pale-blue blankets. "Just a second, I need to fix this." He readjusted her nightgown and fastened the buttons. Lois dutifully climbed in the bed and closed her eyes as Logan tucked the blankets around her. "Good-night," he said as he ran his hand over the light switch and shut the door.

༄

Logan woke to the smell of bacon frying and thought how wonderful Melissa was to fix breakfast, when he knew she'd been up with the baby during the night. He stretched and yawned, savoring a contented moment. For the most part, he had a good life. He had a beautiful and intelligent wife, three great kids, and was successfully self-employed in his profession. When the smoke alarm screeched through the calm, his eyes flew open, and he remembered he wasn't home. His mother, not Melissa, was frying the bacon. Jumping from bed, he ran through the house in boxers and bare feet. Smoke filled the air, and he was reminded of the flaw in his perfect life. He arrived in the kitchen to find his mother staring at a grease fire threatening to spread. Menacing flames shot from the skillet, nipping the wall.

"Damn it, Mom!" He searched under the sink for the fire

extinguisher. Unable to find it, he grabbed the baking soda from the cupboard and dumped it on the flames, dousing the fire. "Are you trying to burn the house down?" He turned on the stove fan and fanned the smoke with a towel. Lois stood still with a faraway look in her eyes.

"I can't do anything anymore," she said and walked from the room.

Hours later the stench of burned bacon lingered in the air. And if that wasn't bad enough, while he cleaned the mess in the kitchen, Lois spent her time in Logan's room. He'd searched an hour before finding his razor and toothbrush stuffed in his jacket sleeves. At this rate, he'd be insane in less than a week.

"Mom!" he called as he searched the house again. He was forever searching for her and usually found her tearing something apart or piling junk. Somewhere in the house he knew he'd eventually find a carton of soured milk and a bunch of bananas, but he hadn't located them yet. They'd disappeared a week ago, and he waited for a rotten stench to guide him. It was possible she'd thrown them in the ocean, and that worried him. Having no physical impediments, Lois moved fast, and he worried she would make it to the deck and fall off the cliff to the ocean below.

A thought crossed his mind, making him ashamed. What would it matter if she fell off the cliff? Her mind was gone. She spent her days in fear and confusion. What kind of life was that?

The guilt came. She was his responsibility now. He owed it to his father to care for the woman he'd loved. Even though Logan himself had never understood her, he'd do his best for her now. He'd do it for Joe.

He found her where he feared, standing on the deck gazing expressionless out to sea. The previous night's storm had cleared, but the sky remained sullen and gray. Rough November waves crashed with violent anger on the jagged rocks below. If Lois fell, she'd be gone in a moment. Something needed to be done, and fast.

He guided her back to the house and settled her in front of the TV with a cup of coffee. After a brief search, he located the remote control and ran through the TV stations, landing on The Food Channel. He hoped it would hold her attention while he made a call. He pulled his cell phone from his pocket.

"I need some help," Logan said to Melissa with a shaking voice. He wandered from the room, keeping an eye on Lois from the den door.

"I'll see if Mom and Dad can take the kids for a few days and be there as quick as I can," she offered.

"I don't want to impose on your parents. Your dad hasn't been feeling well, and with Hannah teething, it would be too much." He dropped into his dad's desk chair and ran his fingers through his hair. "She's driving me insane, Mel. I haven't slept in over a week, and I'm getting as loopy as she is. I was so unprepared for this. I thought I knew what to expect after reading those books Dad gave me, but the reality is unimaginable. I'm thinking of calling one of those home nursing services and getting someone in here during the day so I can get some of this stuff done. I need to get to the lawyer's office to see about the will and power of attorney. Bills are piling up, and I'm not sure if I can write checks from their account. I think Dad had me sign something a few years ago."

"I remember him handing you some papers. If not, can Mom still sign her name?" Melissa asked.

"I don't know. We're out of groceries, so I need to take her to the store today. That should be a nightmare." He closed his eyes. "Why didn't Dad tell us it was this bad? How did he do this? I'm half his age, and I can't keep up with her. I wish he'd said something."

"He was like that, Logan, always taking care of things himself. He wanted to take care of us too."

"I know, but I wonder if he would've had the stroke if he'd brought in some help. Were there warning signs he missed because he wasn't taking care of himself? If I hadn't been so busy, would I have noticed it?"

"Don't torture yourself, honey. He chose to handle it his own way, and there isn't any way to change that now." She paused. "What are you planning to do with her? We can't have her here with us," she said with a small amount of panic in her voice. "She scares the kids, and you can't stay there forever."

"I know. First thing I'll do is get a nursing service in to help, and I need you to do something for me. Mom needs to be in a care facility where they can watch her twenty-four seven. This house isn't safe for her. I'm afraid she'll fall off the cliff, and this morning she almost burned the house down cooking bacon."

"Oh, Logan."

"I caught it before it spread, and turned off the breaker for the stove so she can't do it again. But I can't keep this up. We need to find an Alzheimer's care place near us and get her moved."

"All right. I have the yellow pages right here. Just a second."

"I'll need to know cost, if they take her long-term care insurance, and when she can move in. Yesterday, if possible." He laughed but sobered when he saw movement in the living room. Frowning, he moved to the door and watched as his mother moved methodically around the room. First, she went to the front door, stopped short, and opened the hall closet. She stood staring. After a moment, she pulled a jacket from its hanger and put it on. Logan took a step, thinking she was heading out the door, but she turned and walked into the living room. Stopping near her mother's piano, Lois picked up a glass hummingbird figurine and stuffed it in the jacket pocket. That accomplished, she returned to the hall closet and hung the jacket on its hanger.

Logan continued to watch, his curiosity piqued. Lois left the closet, went to the bookshelf, removed a small book, and returned to the closet. The book joined the glass bird in the jacket pocket.

"I see four places fairly close by specializing in Alzheimer's. That's promising," Melissa said, but Logan didn't respond. "Logan? Are you still there?"

"Huh? Oh yeah. Sorry. I was watching Mom." He described what his mother had been doing. "It's wild. She keeps making this circuit around the room. I'm thinking I may find my shampoo in the closet. It disappeared yesterday." He continued watching as she took the jacket from the closet again and slipped it on. Next, she removed her winter coat and put it on over the jacket. She didn't appear interested in the front door, so he relaxed.

"What did you say about the care places?" He kept his eye on his mother as he continued his conversation.

"There are four nearby. That's good."

"It sure is. Find out what you can and call me on my cell phone. Don't use the land line anymore. It confuses her. She can't make the connection between your voice and who you are, so the cell phone is the better way to go."

"I'm already gone from her memory, aren't I?" Melissa sounded hurt at the prospect.

"I think you and the kids are gone to her, honey. In her mind, I'm a kid again, and I don't have a wife and kids. She hit me last night because she didn't like the language I used on the phone." He had to laugh. If he didn't, he'd lose his mind. "When she saw the kids at the funeral, she thought they were cute, but she couldn't connect them to herself at all."

"I suspected that. I don't think the kids will care much, really. Every time she's seen Joey and Derek lately, she's yelled at them. I wish they could have known her before this disease messed her up. They think their grandma is a crazy old lady.

Just a sec." She moved the phone from her mouth. "Joey! Quit fighting with your brother and come say hi to your dad."

Logan heard running feet, and his breathless dark-haired boy came to the phone.

"Daddy! When are you coming home?"

"Soon, Joey. Why are you fighting with Derek?"

"Cause he won't leave my G.I. Joes alone. He got that one of yours and tried to take the clothes off it. It's old and really special," Joey said with his new lisp making "special" sound like "spethal." The night before the funeral, he'd lost his second front tooth and had been stunned when the tooth fairy found him in King's Bay.

"Why don't you play with him and show him how to take care of them?" Logan smiled to himself at the thought of his boys playing with his old toys. The G.I. Joe had been a special gift from his mom's uncle in Seattle, and Logan had stored it away for his kids.

"I don't want him touching it. He breaks everything," Joey said.

"You guys need to help Mom and get along. I'm not sure how long I'll be stuck here with Grandma, and Mom's handling things by herself. You're the man of the house until I get back, so don't be fighting with Derek." He tried to sound stern but had difficulty when all he wanted to do was go home and hug them all. He would love to walk away from this and return to his life, but he was trapped until all the legalities were settled and his mother was safe somewhere with locked doors. "I know I haven't been home much lately, and I'm sorry. I'll fix it as soon as I can. Let me talk to Mom again. I love you, Joey."

"I love you too, Daddy. Here, Mom. He wants to talk to you. Bye."

"Yeah," Melissa said as she took the phone.

"Tell Derek I'll talk to him next time. I need to get Mom ready for the store. Call me later, okay?" He tried to keep the desperation from his voice. Melissa was his lifeline, his sanity, and he didn't want to disconnect the call. "I love you."

"I love you too. I'll call you tonight."

Logan went in search of Lois and the next fight. She was standing in her room, clothing scattered across the floor. The jacket and coat were gone, but she'd replaced them with three pairs of pants, two shirts, a fishing hat, one sandal recently removed from her dresser, and a snow boot. If he believed in reincarnation, he'd have to wonder what sort of evil he'd committed in a former life to deserve this punishment now. Maybe he'd been a serial killer. He took a calming breath.

"You don't need so many layers. You'll cook." He started to slide a shirt from her shoulders, but she stopped him.

"I need this. It's freezing in here."

"It's eighty degrees. I'm sweating," he said. "We need to go to the grocery store, and you can't wear all those pants. They won't zip." Lois looked confused as he helped her remove two pairs and the sandal. "You need both boots." He found the second boot in the closet and slipped it on her foot.

"Okay. You're ready to go. Come on." He led her to the living room. "Sit here and I'll grab my jacket." Logan ran to his room, slipped on his hiking boots and jacket, and retrieved his wallet from its hiding place in the closet. When he returned, his mother was standing in the center of the living room surrounded by her clothes. Only her panties remained.

Logan let out a frustrated sigh. "You were ready to go. What did you do that for?"

"What?"

"Why did you take off your clothes?"

She looked down at her nearly nude body and back at him. "I don't know." She looked at the clothes on the floor. "Why did Joe make this mess and leave it? I'm going to give that man a talking to." Anger flared across her face.

"For the hundredth time, Dad is dead. He didn't make this mess—you did. Stand still so I can get you dressed again."

Logan took a deep breath and tried to calm his temper. He knew she couldn't help it. He knew the plaques and tangles forming in her brain kept her from functioning, but he'd always fought with his mother. It was their relationship history, and he was having difficulty switching gears and dealing with her impaired mental state.

"Joe is dead?" She blinked owlishly. "Why didn't you tell me?"

"I told you. Now put these clothes back on."

"You shouldn't be here when I'm dressing," Lois said with indignation. "Young boys shouldn't see their mothers naked. It's not right."

"I'm not a young boy anymore, and you can't do this alone. Put these pants on." And on it went—pants, bra, shirt, socks, and the boots. He led her to the kitchen and sat her at the table with a cookie. Logan sat as well, watching her as he would a small child.

She concentrated on her treat while Logan grabbed his cell phone and searched for phone numbers. Finding what he needed, he called.

"I need to inquire about nursing services for my mother. She has Alzheimer's disease." He grabbed a pad and began taking notes. "Per hour?" He gulped at the cost, "All right, that sounds...fine. Can you have someone here tomorrow? I need help during the day." He held his breath while the woman checked the schedule and said she was doubtful they could help him that soon. She put him on hold and had good news on returning. Someone would be available. He jotted more notes as she spoke. "Great. Eight is fine. No, as terrific as it would be, I can't afford twenty-four-hour care. I'll have to handle the rest for now." He gave directions to the house. "I'm Logan McKinnon. Her name is Lois McKinnon." He nodded as he listened, jotting down the name Maxwell. "I'll expect him tomorrow. Thanks." He disconnected the call and watched as Lois folded her last bit of cookie into her napkin and stuffed it in her pants pocket.

"Let's go shopping," he said when she'd finished.

Lois perked up immediately at the mention of the store. His father, he knew, had taken Lois somewhere every day to get out of the house. This past week had broken her routine, and he hoped to get her back on track. He locked the front door and held his mother's elbow as they walked to the car. There was a spring to her step as she climbed in.

As he drove, she watched out the window. Leafless trees, damp sidewalks, and walkers wrapped in warm coats hustling by the shops filled the gray winter landscape.

"This is all new. I don't remember this," Lois said as she pointed at a strip mall.

"It's been there at least twenty years, Mom."

"Are we going to see your dad at the hospital?"

Logan sighed. "Dad is gone." And it started all over again.

⁂

Logan pushed the cart through the grocery store aisles, picking up milk, bread, margarine, and other necessities. Lois loaded the cart with everything they didn't need: six boxes of tea, an armload of Lucky Charms cereal, and two jars of sweet pickles. She didn't like sweet pickles but insisted she needed them. Logan argued with her at every turn, trying to explain those items weren't necessary. Saying no made her cry, which earned him a few glares from other elderly ladies.

"Hold this." He handed her a can of coffee, hoping to keep her hands busy, and noticed an immediate change. Holding the coffee can, Lois walked happily through the store telling other shoppers she was helping. It was the darnedest thing he'd ever seen. After that, he made sure she held something.

After the groceries, he decided to take a chance at the hardware store. Lois was tiring, but he only needed two things. He parked in front of Dailey's Hardware and led her inside. The store was familiar with its piles of shovels, countertop racks of Swiss army knives, and row upon row of hardware. Joe always had a project in the works when Logan visited, so the two men spent many hours combing the bins together. He stood in front of the lock display when Josh Dailey, a burly man in overalls, stopped to speak with them.

"Lois," he said. "I'm so sorry to hear about Joe." He took her hand and squeezed.

She looked at him with confusion as she pulled her hand back. "What about Joe? Is he here?"

Josh looked to Logan for help. Logan held out his hand to him. "I'm Logan McKinnon, Joe and Lois' son."

Josh shook the offered hand. "Oh yes. I've seen you here with him. I'm sorry about your loss." He looked at Lois again.

"Mom has Alzheimer's disease, Mr. Dailey. She can't remember Dad died. Heck, in two minutes she won't remember seeing you."

"I'm sorry to hear that." Josh took Lois' hand in his again. "Take care, Lois." He released her and walked away.

"Who is that man?" she asked. "He's fat, isn't he?"

Logan frowned at her inappropriate comment. Luckily, the storeowner was out of earshot. "He owns the store and was friends with Dad. Stand right here while I get what I need, okay?" He turned from her and selected a locking doorknob for the guest room and a lock for the deck door. He was tired of searching for his razor and afraid to leave the deck door unsecured. When he turned back from the display, Lois was gone.

"Mom!" Logan sprinted down the aisle, looking in all directions, unable to locate her. He'd turned away for a moment, and she'd gotten away from him.

"Mr. Dailey," he called as he neared the cash register. "My mother disappeared. Have you seen her?" He continued to glance around as he set the locks on the counter.

"No, but I'll help you look."

They located Lois in the parking lot. A light drizzle fell, and her wet hair stuck to her head.

"I can't find Joe," she said as she continued to scan the parking lot.

"He isn't here, Mom. Come back in before you get soaked. Thanks, Mr. Dailey," he said to the store owner as he guided her back to the store. He was tempted to yell at her for wandering off but stopped himself. What purpose would it serve? She wouldn't remember what he said and would cry. And Logan figured he'd had enough disgusted glares from little old ladies for one day.

Chapter 6

Logan woke the following morning more tired than when he'd gone to bed. Lois jumped out of bed every few hours, and at 4:00 a.m., she was up for the day. He was thankful the nursing service cavalry would arrive soon to save the day. Somehow, he'd managed to pull on a pair of jeans and a T-shirt between Lois' outbursts, but he had yet to brush his teeth, comb his hair, or shave. He was sure his wife would wrinkle her nose at the sight and smell of him.

When the doorbell rang, he nearly danced a victory dance rivaling any major leaguer's performance. If he'd had the energy, he'd have done a jig too. He frowned when he opened the door and faced a six-foot-four-inch, dark-haired giant who couldn't possibly be a nurse.

"Yeah?" he said as he took in the size of the man. Logan was lanky and at just over six feet tall had never felt small. Next to this guy, he felt scrawny.

"Mr. McKinnon?"

"Right. I'm Logan McKinnon," he said, yawning.

The man looked at his watch. "I'm Maxwell Roth from Home Health Care. I thought you'd be expecting me."

"You're the nurse?" He looked the man over again. "Thank God," Logan muttered, and then laughed. "Sorry. I'm completely exhausted and am so glad to see you. Come in." Logan motioned him in and waved at a living room chair. "In fact, I'm so happy to see you I'd give you a kiss if you weren't so big and hairy." Logan laughed as he looked at the man who would be more at home on a football field than in his mother's moderate-sized house.

Maxwell sat in the offered chair and laughed. "It's the thought that counts. You've been having a rough time of it?"

"Oh man. Rough doesn't begin to describe the nightmare. Living hell comes closer." He blew out a breath as he sat on the sofa. "I don't know how my dad did this, and I keep wondering if the stroke that killed him could have been avoided if he'd called in help."

"It's possible. Unfortunately, many caregivers will die before the patient. The stress of living with this disease is staggering. That's one of the reasons I do this."

Logan nodded. "I understand completely. I've only been here for ten days, and I'm not doing well. I hope Mom is receptive to this, or I may have to be committed right along with her."

"We'll have to approach her right," Maxwell said with a confident nod.

"You've dealt with Alzheimer's before?"

"It's become my specialty," he said with an easy smile and a gentle voice Logan liked immediately. For such a large man, he exuded a sense of calm, putting Logan at ease, and he hoped Maxwell's lack of nursing attire would help Lois accept him in her home. He dressed as Logan had in jeans and T-shirt. The only indication of his occupation was the ID hung by a lanyard around his neck. He could easily be mistaken for a friend who had come to visit. In Lois' presence, that's exactly how Logan planned to treat him.

"Good, because I don't have a clue what I'm doing." As if on cue, Lois wandered in the room wearing her swimming suit and snow boots. Logan cringed, but Maxwell didn't acknowledge Lois' wardrobe irregularity He stood, walked to her with a smile, and took her hand.

"Lois, aren't you looking pretty today? Purple is a good color for you. It brings out the color in your cheeks."

She appeared confused for a moment, not knowing the large man, but his calm manner put her at ease. "Yes. Purple is my color, isn't it?" She beamed at Maxwell, who patted her hand.

"My name is Max. How about if you and I take a tour around the house? You can show me your room, and we'll find a sweater to match your pretty swimming suit."

"Okay," Lois agreed with a nod.

"Mr. McKinnon?"

"Logan, please."

"Logan. I think Lois and I will get along fine. Maybe you'd like to get a little sleep this morning. You could pack your whole wardrobe in those bags under your eyes." He laughed. "That's something my wife always says. Get some rest. I'll take care of her. You and I can talk later. Come along, sweetheart."

Logan watched in awe as the big man led his mother from the room. Following suit, Logan left as well, dragging his feet, but there was too much to accomplish to waste time on a nap. There were locks to install, lawyer appointments to schedule, bank accounts, and insurance policies to investigate. He sat on the bed with his new doorknob in hand and couldn't keep his eyes open. "Okay, a short nap," he mumbled before crashing on his bed.

Logan woke with a start hours later. Long afternoon shadows filled the room. The house was quiet, and worry crawled through him, knotting his gut into a now familiar ball. He rolled from the bed, bumping the uninstalled doorknob, and set out on another search for his mother.

"This is a pretty color for you, Lois. Here, have a sip of your tea." Logan heard a low male voice from the kitchen. He walked in and was stunned to see Max applying pink polish to Lois' nails.

"Logan," he said. "You look a lot better. There's water for tea on the stove, if you'd like some."

"Thanks." Logan grabbed a cup from the shelf and frowned at the tea box on the counter. "Green tea?" He wrinkled his nose.

"Some research shows indications green tea may help Alzheimer's patients." Max pushed Lois' cup to her. "Drink up, sweetheart."

Logan shrugged. "If it helps, I guess it's worth a try. Too bad it tastes like grass." He sniffed the bag before placing it in his cup. He leaned on the counter to watch Lois' manicure.

"We've been busy," Max said. "Haven't we, Lois? She's had her lunch and bath. Then we decided a manicure was in order." Lois smiled and nodded her head, enjoying the attention.

"You got her to take a bath?" Logan was awestruck again. "I haven't been able to do that all week."

"I have some experience with it. There is soup in the refrigerator, if you're hungry. I also put a roast in your slow cooker. I hope you don't mind." Max dabbed more polish.

"I have a slow cooker?" Logan looked around and smiled when his gaze landed on an appliance perking on the counter. "Wow. How did you do all this?"

"Getting a full eight hours helps," Max said with a smile.

"I should've called you last week. Sure could've used the help." Logan dipped the tea bag a few times and tossed it in the trash. A quick sip had him digging out the sugar canister.

"I'm here now and will be until five, so go do what you need to do. Lois and I will hang out."

"Great." Logan sipped his tea, made a face, and set the cup in the sink. "I need to make a few calls and install some locks." He dug his cell phone from his pocket and dialed home on the way to his room.

"Logan," Melissa said. "You sound better today."

"The nursing service sent a great guy over who kept Mom busy so I could get some sleep. She likes him too. Any news on the care facilities?"

Melissa was silent a moment. "Yes, but it's not great news."

"Oh?"

"Well, cost-wise, these places are expensive. Anywhere from $3,800 a month and up, depending on what she needs."

"Okay. I think we can handle it with the insurance and her income. I was expecting it."

"But that's not the bad part."

"Oh?"

"Every care facility in town is full. There is one called Eagle Crest expecting a vacancy, and Mom would be first on the list."

"Did you put her name on it?"

"Yes, as it's the best hope."

"How long do they expect the wait to be?"

"That's the bad part. One of their residents is on life support." She took a breath. "This person has to die before your mother can move in."

"That's gruesome, isn't it?" He let out a frustrated breath. "I'm going to ask a tacky question. What condition is this person in? Do they have any idea?"

"They have no way of knowing for sure, but maybe a month. The family won't disconnect life support yet."

"I'm stuck with her for a month?" Panic welled up. "I don't know if I can handle it. She's driving me crazy."

"Can you afford to keep the nursing service that long?"

"I haven't been to the bank yet, but I'll have to figure out a way to do it. I can't do this alone. How Dad did amazes me. I'll talk to Max and see if he's available." He sighed. "A month."

His call home concluded, Logan checked on Lois, saw she was content with Max, and spent the remainder of the afternoon making appointments and visiting the bank. He was more optimistic after the conference with his father's banker. Joe had planned well. The money from the orchard sale had been wisely and safely invested and produced a healthy income. The papers his father had had him sign several years earlier were indeed signature authorizations, and Logan was on all the accounts. He was thankful his father had planned ahead. By late afternoon, he'd done what he could and headed home to relieve Max.

The house was quiet as he walked in the front door, with only the kitchen radio breaking the silence. He walked in the kitchen to find Max loading the dishwasher. Classical music played softly.

Max glanced up from his task. "Hey, Logan. I hope you don't mind—I changed the radio. Beethoven is much more soothing for Lois than talk radio."

"Sure, that's fine." He looked around. "Where's Mom?"

"Bed."

"Already?"

"She's a sundowner," Max said, his tone matter of fact.

"A what?"

Max wiped his hands on a towel as he spoke. "Some Alzheimer's patients go to sleep with the sun. It doesn't mean she won't be up later, but at four thirty, she said it was bedtime."

"She never said anything like that to me." Logan frowned, wondering if he'd missed something.

"With all the turmoil around her this past week, I'm not surprised. Today I kept her in a peaceful atmosphere and busy. She may sleep well for a while tonight." He glanced at the clock: 5:00 p.m.

Logan noticed. "I appreciate you being here today. You'll be back tomorrow, I hope?"

"I'm not going yet. Since Lois is asleep, we'll have a chance to talk. Fix a plate, and I'll stay for a bit." He grabbed a plate from the cupboard and handed it to Logan. "Don't worry. I'm off the clock at five."

"You don't have to do that. I can pay you."

"Not necessary." He grabbed a cup, filled it with coffee, and sat at the table.

Logan brought his filled plate and sat in the chair across

from Max. "Your wife must be a happy woman." Logan sampled the beef and potatoes and hummed with satisfaction. "You cook, clean, do manicures. If my wife ever gets wind of it, I'm sunk. I'm a Neanderthal in comparison."

"It all comes in handy in this line of work. Anything I can do to make your life easier is a plus."

"I'll say. I don't know how you stand it though. One week and I'm going crazy." He took another bite.

"I don't have to live it. I go home at night, see my family, and get a good-night sleep." He sipped his coffee. "And I like it better than what I did before. I spent fifteen years at the hospital before going into home care." He smiled. "And go ahead and ask the question sitting on the tip of your tongue. Why is a guy like me doing this?"

Logan shrugged. "So far, I'm just thankful you're here. But now you mention it, shouldn't you be playing linebacker for the Seahawks or something?"

Max laughed. "My father thought so. He was horrified when I wanted to go to nursing school. I'm probably the only guy to get a nursing degree on a football scholarship." He laughed again. "He was convinced I was gay, until I married Linda and had a few kids."

"He's okay with it now?"

"After a while he was. Mom was on my side though. She's always said compassionate hearts come in all sizes of bodies." He leaned back in his chair. "My size comes in handy in this occupation. You'd be amazed at how strong some Alzheimer's patients are. I've seen skinny elderly ladies lift up mattresses and carry them across the room. I guess they don't have the mental restraints to tell them they can't do it, so they do. Anyway, what is our situation here? The office told me you didn't know yesterday how long I'd be needed."

"I have a better idea now." Logan explained the care facility situation. "Can you stay on the job for the month? I don't think I could handle it alone."

"You don't need to. My schedule is open, so I'll be here as long as I'm needed. And you know the old song, 'If you got the money, honey, I got the time.'" He stood and put his empty cup in the sink. "Crass, but true." His laugh was deep and hearty. "I'll get out of your way and head home. Lois may sleep through the evening or all night. It's hard to say. Try to get some sleep, and I'll be back in the morning."

"I can't sleep yet," Logan said. "I have locks to put on the doors. The deck worries me, and Mom won't stay out of my room."

Max looked thoughtful. "Okay. Finish your dinner, and I'll give you a hand."

The locks were installed an hour later, and Max had offered suggestions on kid-proofing the house for Lois. Max left for home, and Logan was able to start his next task of searching his father's files.

He'd exhausted the file cabinets by 9:00 p.m. and still hadn't located the insurance policies. Thinking there could be more files in the closets, he poked around until he found a locked box marked Personal in the top of the guest room closet. It was heavy and locked. He didn't find a key, but rather than give up, he jimmied it open with a screwdriver. Hoping to find file folders, he was disappointed when the contents were books and notebooks, all numbered and dated.

He sat on the floor and selected a white book marked Number One. He opened it to the first page and was stunned by what he found. The first entry, with its childish scrawl and misspelled words, made him smile.

April 1936
Dear Jurnal, My name is Lois and I am six. Mama says girls like to rite stuff so she gave you to me. I hope we can be frends and I can tell you my secrets. Love, Lois

July 1936
Dear Jurnal, Larry called me a bad name today. I
dumped mud on his head. Daddy spanked me. It hurt.
Big brothers are icky, and I hate him. Don't tell any-
one. Love, Lois

Logan doubled over with laughter as he read his mother's
diary. He knew it was wrong, but he couldn't stop. The entries
were short but telling of Lois' early life, and he found himself
engrossed. Hours passed as he read the entries detailing her
fights with her older brother, Larry, stories of her cat named
Puffpuff, a dog named Hunter though he was gun shy to the
point of terror, and he sniffled when he read about the day she
stopped hating Larry.

April 1939
Dear friend, my grandpa died today and I'm sad. When
Mama told me, I ran to the barn and cried until my
stomach hurt. Puffpuff tried to make me feel better but
it didn't help. Larry found me and I yelled at him to
leave me alone. He said he was sad, too, and wanted to
cry with me where no one would see him. Boys aren't
supposed to cry. He held my hand and we cried togeth-
er. I promised I wouldn't tell anyone he cried. I think
Larry is an okay brother after all, but don't tell anyone
I said that. Love, Lois

Logan placed the journal in the box and closed the lid. He
stared at it, debating if he should return it to the closet where
it belonged and leave it alone. His curiosity won, and he
shoved the box in a corner and covered it with a blanket. The
late hour caught up with him, and he stripped off his clothes
and climbed into bed. Blissful sleep came quickly.

He woke with a start when a finger jabbed his shoulder.
Moonlight through the window highlighted his mother standing over his bed. Saying she was severely agitated would have
been an understatement.

"What are you doing here?" she whispered as she poked him again. "You have to leave. Now." She shook his shoulder. "What?" Logan said, groggy with sleep. He tried to pull the blankets over his head. "I'm sleeping. Go away."

She became more persistent and shook his shoulder again. "Nate. Wake up. You shouldn't be here."

"Mom? What are you talking about?"

"Nate," she said again. "You have to go before Joe gets home."

Logan sat up and turned on the bedside lamp. He blinked several times. "Mom? What are you doing?" Lois gave Logan a long, confused look. "Why are you up?"

Lois shook her head and frowned.

"What time is it?" He rubbed his eyes and glanced at the clock—5:00 a.m.—and resigned himself to getting up. "Are you hungry?"

She looked at him with owlish eyes and shrugged. "I don't know."

"I suppose you don't. Well, we're awake. How about if we make some pancakes and some of the yummy green tea Max left us? Does that sound good?" He climbed from bed and pulled on a pair of sweatpants and a T-shirt he'd left lying in the chair. Once he shook off the grogginess, he was amazed at how good he felt from one decent night of sleep. He walked from the room with Lois on his heels. "Mom, who's Nate?" he asked as they wandered to the kitchen.

Lois frowned. "I don't know."

⌖

Max arrived promptly at 8:00 a.m., relieving Logan for the day. He showered and was off by nine to meet with the lawyer, who informed him his father had planned exceedingly well for Lois' care. All the proper papers had been signed for community property transfer, and paperwork would be started to have Lois declared mentally incompetent.

"Is it necessary?" Logan asked. "It sounds so harsh."

"Unfortunately, it is a necessity to invoke your power of attorney and declare guardianship. She isn't able to make decisions any longer, is she?"

"No. She can't do much of anything for herself anymore. I'm taking care of everything."

"Then this is necessary. We'll get the forms for her doctor, and we can proceed." With that, the attorney concluded the meeting with Logan and sent him on to his next duty: life insurance policies. He left the lawyer's office relieved to have accomplished something, but also sad about having Lois declared incompetent. She'd always been an extremely competent woman. She was always brisk and efficient, whether he had fallen from a tree and broken his arm or flunked geometry and needed a butt chewing. She was always on top of things. And now, she was mentally incompetent, and that stank. He may not have agreed with Lois often, but he would never have wished this on her.

He returned home in a drizzling rain to find Max and Lois laughing in the living room. If he hadn't seen it, he wouldn't have believed it. He stood in the doorway, biting his lip to keep from laughing as Lois and Max did aerobics with a skinny woman on TV.

"Hey, Logan!" Max called when he noticed him. "Throw off your coat and join us." He did a spin and kicked a large foot.

"As much as I would love that," Logan said with a laugh, "I'd better get some work done." He watched a moment longer as his mother followed along, and again was struck by the injustice of her disease. Physically, Lois was in terrific health, but mentally, she was slipping away fast. He thought of his father's comment and had to agree. Lois was still a pretty woman, and if not for the disease, she'd have all the men at the senior center looking her way. He thought of the precocious girl who'd written about dumping mud on her brother's head, and he wished he could have known the girl or even the woman his father had loved. As Logan's mother, she'd always been reserved, even cold at times, and he'd spent his childhood trying to make her love him. He'd become an ambitious overachiever because of it, always trying to get her attention and maybe a smile. She smiled at Max, a stranger, more than she'd ever smiled at him, and it hurt.

"You okay, Logan?" Max called to him.

Logan shook free from his thoughts. "Just thinking. Have fun. I need to find insurance policies." He left the room and hung his wet coat in the bathroom to dry. In his father's den, he dug into the file cabinets again and located the files that had eluded him earlier when he'd been exhausted. A handful of calls later, Logan had begun the claims process, and forms were being sent.

Tucking the files back in their proper places, he smelled something wonderful wafting from the kitchen and went in search of its source. As he entered the kitchen, Max was removing an apple pie from the oven, and Lois beamed with pride.

"That smells heavenly," Logan said with a deep breath. "I may take you home with me when I leave here. My wife would love you."

"I can't take all the credit. Lois did most of the work." He smiled at Logan's stunned expression. "She can do a lot with assistance."

"Wow, Mom. You did a beautiful job. I can't wait to eat it." He smiled and was stunned when she smiled back.

"After dinner," Lois scolded in a voice he remembered well from his childhood, but she smiled when she said it.

"If you'll help Lois set the table, I'll finish up over here, and you can eat." Max stirred a pot on the stove.

They set a place for Max, and he stayed for dinner and dessert. At 5:00 p.m., Lois announced she was tired, and Logan assisted with her bedtime routine. When he returned, Max had done the dishes and was wiping the counters.

"You know, Max, you don't have to do everything. I don't remember all this cooking being in the job description."

"You know what they say about idle hands," he said as he hung the dish towel on the stove.

"Can I ask you something before you go?" Logan asked as he fixed a cup of coffee. "Want a cup?"

"Sure."

Max took a seat at the table as Logan poured a second cup. He set it on the table near Max and sat in the opposite chair.

"I'm not sure how to ask you this. It's kind of personal." Logan frowned. "I'll start by telling you my mother and I have never gotten along well. I don't know why, but she's always been cold to me. And because of that we've always fought. I guess it was my way of getting her attention. She couldn't be cold if she was yelling at me." He chuckled and shrugged, embarrassed by the admission of his childhood behavior.

"I know what you mean. I fought with my old man every day," Max said. "And it heated up when I went into nursing. The tough construction worker couldn't handle my choice of professions. But we made our peace."

"I envy you. With Mom's condition, we'll never be able to make our peace." He sipped his coffee and continued. "I found something last night, and I'm wrestling with some guilt today. I opened a box in the closet. Clarification, I jimmied the lock on a box in the closet, and I found something very personal of Mom's." He sighed. "It appears she has been keeping a diary since she was six, and from the number of books in the box, she kept it up most of her life. I read one of them last night."

"And you're wondering if it's okay?"

"I wanted to know if you' do the same in this situation. Before you answer, I want to tell you more. She wrote to her journal as if she were writing to her best friend. All of her little girl secrets are in there." He laughed softly. "She's always telling her diary not to tell anyone. It's cute." He smiled. "I sat there reading last night, completely fascinated, and I couldn't put it down. I know it's wrong to read a personal journal without her permission, but I feel like I'm getting to know my mom. She writes so openly of all her thoughts and fears. There's stuff in there about my grandparents I never knew. I feel like I have a chance to know her by reading this. It's like looking through a window." He laughed. "Does that make me a Peeping Tom?"

Max shrugged. "You have to justify this with your own conscience, but knowing your history with Lois and her present condition, I have a hard time condemning you for reading it. If I was in your situation and had a chance to get to know my parent better, I think I'd read it too." He leaned on his elbows and looked at Logan seriously. "But you may want to consider something first."

"What?"

"You may find out something you don't want to know."

Logan laughed. "My mother may be a cold fish, but I don't think we have any skeletons in the family closet. My family is as boring and average as white bread."

"You never know. There could be a couple of slices of pumpernickel mixed in your loaf." Max shrugged. "If it were me, I'd read it with caution. And on that bit of advice, I best be off. My wife will worry if I'm late. Petite thing that I am, she sees danger for me around every corner." He laughed. "See you tomorrow." He left Logan sitting at the table in the graying evening light, contemplating what he'd said.

After his last gulp of coffee, Logan cleared the cups and checked on his mother before retiring to his room for the evening. He'd given up watching TV in the living room, as the noise woke Lois. After changing into sweats and a T-shirt, he pulled the unlocked box from the corner and debated reading her private journal, finally deciding to continue, as it was the best chance he had of understanding her.

He opened the book where he'd left off the night before and prepared to meet his mother.

Chapter 7

Lois

September 1942
My friend, we had a picnic at our house after church
today. Everybody talked about the war. Mr. Ford tried
to beat up Mr. Yamada when he came to talk to Daddy.
He says it's just prejudice brought on by grief and I
shouldn't listen to him. Mr. Yamada is Daddy's friend,
even if he is Japanese. Terry Morris tried to kiss me.
Okay, he did more than try...

"Lois Mae Delaney!" Fern Delaney yelled from the kitch-
en door. "I need help in the kitchen...Lois!"

"Coming, Mama!" Lois huffed her breath at having her
game of tag interrupted. "I gotta go, Terry. Mama's calling."
She spun, nearly snagging her head on a low-hanging apple
tree limb. Harvest would begin in a few short weeks, and the
branches hung heavy with bright-red apples. She grumbled
under her breath as she wound her way through the orchard,
tall grass whipping against her legs. She was sure Mama
would be mad when she saw the stains on her good church
stockings. Terry had been impatient to start the game, and
she'd not changed to her overalls as Mama had instructed.
Now she'd pay the price. The slap of the porch screen an-

nounced Lois' arrival, and Fern scowled at her twelve-year-old daughter.

"What have you done to those stockings, young lady? You know how hard it is to get new ones right now."

Lois shuffled her feet, ready for the blast and the grounding she was sure to get.

"Fern!" Harriet Sedge called in from the living room. "Mike and the boys have the tables up and the tablecloths on. We're ready for the food."

"All right, Harriet, we'll start carting it out." Fern glared at Lois. "We'll talk about this later. You can help me now and then go change into your play clothes before eating."

"Yes, Mama," Lois said meekly. A clothing change before eating would put her at the end of the line, which meant she'd miss out on the best pieces of chicken. Grounding was a better punishment than losing out on the chicken legs.

Fern handed Lois a platter of rolls and shooed her from the hot kitchen. The September day was warm, and Lois was happy to escape the stifling indoor heat. She skipped through the house and out the front door to where Daddy had set up the picnic tables and folding chairs in the shade of the giant willow tree. Sawhorses and plywood formed the buffet table. She deposited her platter on the makeshift table, but she delayed her return for the next dinner item, hanging back as the men gathered for a smoke before dinner. Leaning against the backside of the tree, she overheard them, mostly older men, discussing the war and its effects on the town. At thirty-five, Mike Delaney was the youngest in the group, as most other men were off fighting. Mike attempted enlistment after Pearl Harbor but was denied due to a foot injury. He was committed to doing his part at home for the war effort and volunteered every chance he had.

"We've got a scrap-metal drive coming up. You have anything over to your place, Herman?" Mike asked as he leaned against the old tree. "I'll toss it in the truck when I go into town. No point in using our gas if we don't need to."

"Yeah," Herman Ford said. "There's some stuff behind the barn. I'll take a look."

"I'll give you a hand," Mike said to the older man. Herman Ford was in his early sixties and tougher than an angered mountain lion, but he had his slow days when his gout flared up. He was a crabby character since his wife passed on. Mike always included the sassy neighbor in the get-togethers though they never knew what the old man would do or say. Today was a mellow day.

"Appreciate it. Apple harvest coming up. Not sure how I'm getting mine off the tree." Herman puffed his cigarette and blew smoke from the side of his mouth.

"They're letting the kids out of school to help, and I hear some stores are closing in the afternoons so the town folks can lend a hand," Mike said. "Lois, honey, didn't your mama tell you to help her in the kitchen?" he asked with a smile when Lois poked her nose from behind the tree. Lois glared and meandered back to the house.

"That girl of yours is sure going to be a pretty one," she heard Mr. Ford say. "You'll be fighting those boys back with a stick soon."

"Sooner than I'm wanting—that's for sure," Mike said. "I noticed Terry's eye wandered her way a while ago. He's about thirteen now. Just the right age to be keeping an eye on, I'd say."

"Best be keeping that stick handy," Herman said with a chuckle.

Lois snuck back into the kitchen without catching her mother's eye, grabbed another platter, and was gone before Mama could reprimand her for dawdling. She deposited her platter on the table and ran to her second-story bedroom. Her overalls lay across her bed where she'd left them that morning. She stripped off her dress and dressed in play clothes. As she started for the door, she reconsidered leaving her church dress lying in a pile and hung it across her desk chair. Mama might reconsider the grounding if Lois showed her sense of responsibility and hung up the dress.

She ran down the stairs and was in line for dinner within moments, her stomach growling. Plate in hand, Lois waited, shifting from one foot to the other, watching fretfully as Terry Morris grabbed the last chicken leg. Her heart sank when she reached the platter to find nothing but a scrawny wing. Mama sure knew how to deliver punishment. She sighed with resignation and forked the last piece of chicken. Her plate heaping with potato salad, rolls, carrots, and the puny wing, Lois made her way to the kids' table and sat next to Terry, looking at him with a pronounced glare.

"What's your problem, sourpuss?" Terry asked.

"Nothing."

"I have something for you," he said with a smile.

"I don't want anything from you, Terry Morris." She continued to glare at the owner of the last chicken leg, glancing at his plate with envy.

Terry smiled. "Not even this?" He picked up the chicken leg and offered it to her. "I'll trade you for that wing." Lois gave him a smile and readily agreed to the switch. As she ate the chicken, she glanced at him from the corner of her eye and thought Terry was looking kind of cute with his blond curly hair. He winked and smiled, causing Lois to blush.

"Let's play hide-and-seek after we eat," announced Terry's younger sister, Sue. "I'll be it first." The kids at the table agreed, and after they cleaned their plates, the group ran into the orchard.

Lois ran fast and found a hiding spot beneath the heavily laden branches of an apple tree. The fruit bore enough weight to pull the branch nearly to the ground. She waited patiently, trying to hold her breath so as not to alert Sue to her spot. A few minutes went by, and she heard footsteps. She was sure she was caught when the branch lifted and Terry crawled into her hiding spot with her.

"Shhh."

"Shhh, yourself. Find your own hiding spot," Lois whispered in return.

"It's more fun hiding with you." He sat for a moment before poking his head out of the tree. "Sue's way over by the barn. She'll never find us." He looked at Lois and swallowed hard. Lois looked back with big eyes as she realized she was alone with a boy in a good hiding place. No one would ever find them.

"Have you ever been kissed, Lois?"

Lois' heart pounded like a herd of tap-dancing elephants. "No," she whispered. "Have you?"

He nodded his head. "Yes." He swallowed and licked his lip.

Lois felt perspiration form on her skin. "Is it…is it…" She swallowed as she looked at his lips. "Is it nice?"

"I thought so. Want to try it?" He swallowed again.

She took a nervous breath. "Okay." She continued to look at him with wide eyes as he leaned closer.

"Close your eyes, silly." His lips were a breath from hers.

"Oh, sorry." She closed her eyes, and he touched his lips to hers. When she made no attempt to push him away, he leaned in closer, putting his fingers in her honey-blonde hair. Lois wasn't sure if she was doing it right, but it did indeed feel pleasant. Terry had been practicing, she was sure. Their breath intensified as he pressed his lips tighter to hers. He moved his hand from her neck to her breast. Yelling from the house startled them, and Lois pulled away.

"We should see what's going on." She crawled through the branches with Terry on her heels. They ran to the house and found several men restraining Herman Ford as he screamed at a small Japanese man.

"Goddamn Jap. Get him out of here before I kill him!" He struggled against the men who held him. Tao Yamada looked at Herman with sadness and a healthy amount of fear. His wife sat in their dilapidated pickup, her eyes filled with panic.

"Now, Herman," Mike said in an attempt to calm the man. "Mr. Yamada isn't our enemy. He's been in this country for a long time. He's our neighbor, just like you."

"There ain't nothing about that scum that's anything like me. Murdering bastard!" He spat at Mr. Yamada, who stepped aside quickly.

"Herman! Mr. Yamada hasn't murdered anyone. Calm down, or get out of my yard."

"I won't calm down!" Herman shrieked. "He killed my boy. Slant-eyed bastards. They killed my boy!" He fought harder against the men holding him.

"Mr. Yamada didn't kill your boy, Herman," Mike said.

Mr. Yamada held his hand up to Mike and spoke for the first time. "I offer my condolences for your loss, Mr. Ford. I know your son was in Pearl Harbor, but I personally was not involved." He spoke softly, rolling his hat in his hands. "My son also serves this country somewhere in Europe. He is an American citizen. As Mr. Delaney has said, I am not your enemy. America is my home."

"Goddamned spy is what you are. I ought to report you to the government for spying." Herman spat again.

"That's enough." Mike said. "George? Could you and Harvey take Herman home? I think he just wore out his welcome here today."

"Sure thing, Mike. Come on, Herman." Neither man loosened their grip on Herman as they walked him to his truck. After Herman departed with his escort, Mike turned to Tao Yamada.

"I'm sure sorry about that, Mr. Yamada. Grief can do terrible things to an otherwise sane man."

"Thank you, Mr. Delaney. It is not your fault. I happen to be in the wrong skin at the wrong time. Mr. Ford is not unique in his opinions. You, sir, are the exception. "

Mike smiled. "Would you and your wife care for some pie and coffee, Mr. Yamada? We've plenty."

Mr. Yamada looked cautiously at the remaining group. "My thanks for the hospitality, but I must decline. I have come today to speak with you in private about a most important matter. My apologies for intruding on your guests, but my time grows short."

Mike nodded. In February, President Roosevelt had called for the internment of citizens of Japanese descent living on the coastal areas. In August they began transferring those in Eastern Washington to relocation centers in Wyoming. It was the Yamada family's time to go.

"Let's go for a walk." Mike excused himself from his remaining guests and walked with Mr. Yamada to the orchard, stopping to lean on an apple bin setting in the tree rows where Lois was hidden.

"I have known you and your father before you many years, Mr. Delaney, and have always found you to be fair-minded people. I come to you now hoping your character is as I have always suspected," Mr. Yamada said solemnly.

Mike waved his hand. "Let's cut to the chase, Mr. Yamada. I know what's happening with all the Japanese folks in our area, and if I can help you, I will. What do you need?"

Mr. Yamada sighed with relief. "We have been unable to withdraw our money from the bank. People will not buy our crops, and we will lose our land lease in a few days. The owner, of course, will not extend our lease, and another farmer will take over our land soon."

Mike nodded.

"We are to go to Portland in less than a week and then to Wyoming, and we have nowhere to keep our belongings. Everything we own is in the house we will lose soon."

"I've got a loft in my barn I haven't been using much," Mike said. "It's secure and weathertight. If you'd like, pack your stuff and bring it over. There's room for your truck too.

I'll keep it safe for you."

Tears filled Mr. Yamada's eyes.

"If you need a place to stay, I've got those cabins out back. We won't use them until harvest when the pickers arrive. It's nothing fancy, but you're welcome to it if it helps you out."

"Oh, yes, that would be wonderful." Mr. Yamada said as he wiped his sleeve across his damp eyes. "Thank you."

"There are six of them if you know of anyone else with a need of a place to stay," Mike offered. "But keep it quiet, okay? You know how people are right now."

"Of course. I don't know how to thank you."

"Just come home safe. You've always been a good neighbor, and we'd like to have you back when all this craziness is over." He stood and clapped Tao on the shoulder. "Now, how about we cut a few pieces of pie?"

Lois ran through the trees and met them as they walked from the orchard.

"Is Anne with you, Mr. Yamada?" she inquired.

"My daughter has stayed at home today," he said to the young girl who walked by his side.

"Oh well. Maybe we can play next weekend," she said as she skipped off to find the other kids.

After the Yamadas and the other guests departed, Lois approached her father while he cleared the tables and chairs from the yard.

"Daddy, what was Mr. Ford so angry about? What did Mr. Yamada do?"

He sighed and thought for a moment. "Let's sit down, honey, and I'll try to explain it." He took her hand and led her to the porch step.

"It's the war. Mr. Yamada was born in Japan, and right now a lot of people hate him for it though he's been in this country for thirty years. Mr. Ford's son John was an officer on one of the ships bombed in Pearl Harbor, and Mr. Ford wants to blame someone for his son's death. The Japanese killed his son. Mr. Yamada is Japanese, and he's close enough to blame. Grief does strange things to people."

"But you don't hate Mr. Yamada, do you?"

"No, honey, I don't hate Mr. Yamada. He's as loyal to this country as I am. He has a son who is an American citizen and is serving in the army in Europe. It's wrong his family is being sent to a camp while his son fights for his country."

"Does Anne have to live in a camp too?" Lois asked in horror when she thought of losing one of her best friends. She hadn't understood her father's earlier conversation, but it became clear to her now.

Mike sighed. "Yeah, honey, she does. Her whole family has to leave in a few days."

"Oh, Daddy." Tears welled in her eyes, and Mike put his arm around her.

"She'll be staying in one of the cabins for a couple days, so you can see her before she goes," he whispered.

"Why are you helping them, Daddy? Won't people hate you for that?"

"Maybe, but it's the right thing to do."

"Why?" she said with a sniffle.

"See, a long time ago, my grandpa came here from Ireland, and people weren't nice to him."

"Why?" she asked.

"Because he was Irish. People back east were awful to him, so he worked his way out west and settled here. This land we have was his homestead." He hugged Lois tight. "And because of the hatred my grandpa experienced, I'll help Mr. Yamada. It's the right thing to do." He rubbed his hand across Lois' hair. "Can you give me a hand with these chairs, and then we can both go in and listen to the radio before bedtime." He glanced back at the house. "Looks like your mama is already pulling the blackout curtains. We better get a move on, sweetie, or we'll both be in hot water."

...Daddy and I said good-bye to Anne and her family today. I gave Anne a silver locket with my picture so she wouldn't forget me. I cried as the train pulled away. It's so unfair my friend has to go away. I'll pray for her until she comes home. Love, Lois

Chapter 8

Logan

Logan closed his mother's journal and felt a tug at his heart. He'd never heard any stories about his grandfather's part in helping his Japanese neighbors during WWII. He knew about the foot injury from a farming accident and that his grandfather was instrumental in the local war effort, but the rest was news to him. Apparently, the secret had been kept. He tucked the journal in the box and peeked in on his mother. She slept soundly, so he returned to his room and dialed his cell phone.

"Hey, baby," he said softly when Melissa answered.

"What time is it?" she said with a yawn.

Logan looked at the clock: 11:00 p.m. "Sorry. I didn't realize it was so late. How is everything?"

"Fine. We miss you. The boys keep asking when you'll be home. How are you?"

"Much better. Max is a lifesaver. He cooks. He cleans. He got Mom to take a bath, which is nothing short of a miracle." He chuckled.

"You certainly sound better. I was getting worried about you."

"So was I." He lay back on the bed and kicked up his feet. "I'm much better tonight. With Max handling Mom during the day, I may survive this. I know you aren't getting enough sleep either, and I should let you go to bed, but I found the most amazing thing, and I couldn't wait to tell you about it."

"What is it?" she asked.

"My mother's diary."

"Logan! You didn't read it, did you?"

"I started it." He frowned at her reaction. "Hear me out before you go ballistic on me. She started writing when she was six, and for the first time, I feel like I'm getting to know my mother. She never talked about herself or her family much, and now that her mind is going, I can't ask her. Tonight, I read about what my grandfather did during WWII."

"Oh? What did he do?"

"Maybe I shouldn't tell you. It's private stuff," he said with a laugh.

"Logan! I guess it doesn't hurt anything for you to read about your grandfather."

"Thank you for your approval. Grandpa was either a hero or a traitor, depending on who you asked at the time. When his Japanese neighbors where being shipped off to the camps, he stored their belongings for them until the end of the war. It was a fairly brave thing to do, I think, what with the attitudes toward the Japanese at the time. I wish I could've known him longer. He died when I was kid. She also wrote about things like gas rationing and her first kiss."

"How old was she?"

"Twelve, and he was thirteen. An experienced older man with wandering hands, and from the sound of it, she enjoyed the whole experience a great deal." He laughed softly. "Do you still want to blast me for reading her diary?"

"I guess not. It is an unusual situation since you can't ask her about things."

"Max said I should read with caution. He thinks I might find a family skeleton. I doubt that."

"You never know." She yawned loudly. "Sorry. Hannah

kept me up late last night. I sure miss you, but I need to get some sleep."

"Just a few minutes longer." He lowered his voice and smiled as he spoke. "What are you wearing?" He imagined she was wearing her pink flannel pajamas she'd worn since Hannah was born. Because she had to be up in the night with the baby, sexy lingerie was stuffed in the back of the drawer.

She lowered her voice like he had. "Absolutely nothing."

At dawn, Logan was again awakened by prodding to his shoulder. He was becoming accustomed to the early morning wakeup call and his temper remained under control. But he would love to know why she continued to call him Nate.

He dressed and led her to the kitchen for their breakfast ritual. This morning, he fixed French toast, and at Max's urging, decaf coffee. Caffeine caused agitation. She sipped coffee while Logan prepared the meal. After cutting her toast into bite-sized pieces, Logan sat across the table and looked at her thoughtfully.

"Mom? You had a friend named Anne, right?"

She looked confused for a moment and then smiled. "Yes," she said. "Anne Yamada. She was…" Lois struggled for the words. "She…was Japanese."

"That's the one. What happened to her dad? I don't remember him." He took a bite of toast and waited to see if Lois could continue the conversation. She frowned as she tried to grasp some long-forgotten memory. Sometimes if he prompted her, she could remember small bits.

"Camps. Her family was sent to the camps." She smiled, obviously pleased to have remembered. Logan persisted. Apparently, Anne was an old memory that hadn't disappeared.

"Did her family come back for their stuff?"

Lois nodded. "After the war. She and her mother came back to live. Her father died of…" She frowned, unable to remember the word. She patted her chest.

"Pneumonia?" Logan filled in.

"Yes. In the camp. Very sad. He was a nice man." She smiled at Logan and ate a bite of toast.

"Was Nate a friend of yours back then?"

She gave him a long look. "I don't know."

After breakfast, Lois assisted Logan with the laundry and dishes. At eight, Max arrived, and Logan left for the grocery store.

On his return, he found Max and Lois making paper flower bouquets at the kitchen table. She grinned as she handed one to Logan.

"Pretty for you." She smiled.

"It is. Thanks, Mom." He surprised them both by giving her a hug. She looked at him, startled. "Well," he cleared his throat and stepped away. "I need to pay some bills. Have fun."

He spent the large part of the day in his dad's den with the checkbook until he felt the pull of his mother's journal. Despite his guilt, he decided to continue. After a quick trip to the refrigerator for a pop, he lay on his bed and picked up the next volume.

Chapter 9

Lois

1950
My dear friend, I had a date tonight with Lana's friend
Henry. It was a disaster, but I met another man, not an
immature boy like Henry, an older man. He's tall and
handsome with dark hair and the prettiest blue eyes
I've ever seen...

"Lois!. Your young man is here to pick you up."
"Thank you, Mrs. Smithwick. Tell him I'll be right down!"
Lois yelled down the stairs from her apartment door. "He's
not my young man," she grumbled under her breath. Henry
was merely a friend of a friend, a casual date she'd accepted
because no one else had asked her out. She ran back in the
shared bathroom for a quick once-over. Her short blonde hair
was sprayed in place, and her rhinestone earrings looked fine.
She turned back and forth in the full-length mirror, please
with the pale-blue dress she wore. The style was flattering
with its full skirt and fitted bodice with buttons down the
front. The belt narrowed her waist, and the straps showed off
just enough shoulder. If it was cold, not likely in August, she
carried a short, fitted jacket as well. She blew out her breath,
grabbed her clutch purse, and walked down the stairs to the

front door. Of course, her landlady, the pudgy Mrs. Smithwick, waited right alongside Lois' date, a short, thin young man who leered when he smiled. She thought he looked like he was leering anyway. He was probably a pleasant fellow, if she gave him a chance.

"Hello, Henry," Lois said with a polite smile. "I have my key, Mrs. Smithwick, so don't wait up." Mrs. Smithwick was the consummate busybody, and Lois knew she'd stay up to see if she could catch one of the girls who rented her apartments kissing boys on the steps. She hadn't caught Lois yet, as there hadn't been anyone she wanted to kiss, but the woman appeared forever hopeful.

"Good-night, Mrs. Smithwick," she called as Henry opened the door and followed her down the steps.

"You sure look pretty tonight, Lois." Henry opened the passenger door of his Ford sedan for Lois to slide in.

"Thank you," she said politely as he closed the door. Henry climbed in behind the wheel and cast an expectant gaze toward Lois. "You can sit by me, honey. I won't bite. Much." He winked and patted the seat next to him. Lois cringed, already regretting her hasty acceptance of his invitation. Resigned, she moved closer but not right next to him. He grinned as he pulled away from the curb.

As he drove, Henry turned on the radio, dropped his hand on her knee, and tapped in tune with Hank Williams singing "Honky Tonkin'." Lois moved Henry's hand. He tried again. She removed the offending hand again. He sighed and placed both hands on the wheel.

"I thought we'd see that Lloyd Bridges movie *Rocketship X-M* at the Bijou. That sound all right to you, honey?"

"It's a space movie, isn't it?" she said as she looked out the window at the passing houses. She disliked science fiction and didn't want Henry to see her frown.

"You betcha. I love that stuff. All those Martians and spaceships are really neat." He drove his car into the theater lot and parked. As he turned the key, he looked at her and smiled. "The only other movie playing is *Harvey*, and I don't think I could stand watching a six-foot-tall invisible rabbit. Sheesh." He opened his door, slammed it shut, and went around, opening Lois' side.

"I've heard Jimmy Stewart is good in *Harvey*," she said as she stepped out.

"Honey, I'm not watching any bunnies," Henry said with disgust. He grabbed her hand and led her to the theater. The line for the show was short. In minutes they were buying popcorn and finding seats. Henry walked toward the back row, and Lois stopped him.

"I prefer the middle," she said, knowing full well why people sat in the back row, and she had no desire to snuggle with a boy she barely knew.

Henry grinned. "I like the back row, honey."

Lois cringed and decided to kick him the next time he called her honey. Sheesh.

They settled in the back row, nearly alone at the early showing. They munched popcorn and sipped pop during the previews, and Lois thought she could make it through the evening. Unfortunately, the movie proved as bad as anticipated, and Henry couldn't keep his hands to himself. She tried to pull away, but he held her hand tight. When she managed to reclaim her hand, his arm slipped around her shoulders. As Lloyd Bridges' ship winged its way to Mars, Henry pulled her to him and kissed her. Her first thought was, Terry Morris had been a better kisser at thirteen than Henry was at twenty. When he plunged his tongue into her mouth, she nearly gagged. Her next thought was of escape. Henry had somehow been misinformed and thought she was fast. She wasn't and planned to leave before Henry got any ideas about playing backseat bingo with her.

When Henry released her, she smiled as best she could and whispered she needed to find the ladies' room. He nodded, stuffed a handful of popcorn in his mouth, and continued to watch the movie. Lois made her way through the dark theater and ran as fast as she could out the front door, the concession stand workers snickering behind her.

Once on the street, she leaned against the building and wiped her mouth. She paused in the dwindling daylight and debated her next move. It was at least ten blocks to her apartment, but her other choice was calling her parents. She could be home before they arrived.

She'd walked two blocks through downtown when she heard footsteps behind her, and her nerves jumped. Henley was a quiet town and crime was minimal, but the newspaper had stories of robberies now and then. Lois continued on, holding her purse and jacket tighter to her middle, not daring to look around. As she passed the Apple Blossom Diner, she saw several teenage boys reflected in the windows, following close behind her. She contemplated entering the diner but decided that was silly. The boys appeared harmless enough. The night grew darker as dusk settled. She stepped beyond the edge of the last streetlight and immediately wished she'd followed her instincts and gone into the diner.

"Hey, pretty lady," a voice said from behind.

Lois continued walking. In moments, the boys, dressed in scruffy jeans and T-shirts, surrounded her, making her stop. "I'm talking to you," a tall boy said as he stepped in front of her.

"Let me pass," she said with false bravado. Her heart skidded in several directions at once.

"I don't think so." He rubbed his finger across her cheek. "Very pretty. What's in your purse?"

Lois clutched her bag tighter. "Nothing. Just a lipstick and some tissues."

"The way you're holding it, there must be some money in there." The boy grabbed for the purse, but Lois dodged.

"There isn't, or I would've called a taxi." Lois swallowed

as the other boys closed in on her.

The tall boy grabbed her arm and pulled her to him. "If you don't have any money, maybe you have something else I want."

"I doubt that very much," a low male voice said from behind the group.

"This isn't your business, mister. We're talking to the lady."

The kid continued to hold Lois. She winced as his fingers dug into her arm.

"Maybe I'll ask the lady myself." The man stepped out of the shadows, and Lois could see him. He was tall, dark haired, and wearing a jacket and slacks. He certainly looked safer than the hoodlums accosting her.

"Do you want to talk with these boys, ma'am?" he asked as he stepped closer.

It was four to one, and she didn't feel confident he could help her on his own. "No. I don't know them."

"All right then. I'll ask you boys to let her go and be on your way."

"This ain't your business, mister," the tall boy said again.

The man took an impatient breath. "I'll ask you nice the first time. Let her go." He stared into the eyes of the obvious group leader. "If I have to ask twice, there is a real good possibility you may find out what I learned in the war. There's a whole load of Germans who found out. Do you want to be next?" His eyes narrowed, and the boys appeared to reconsider their evening entertainment and stepped away.

"It's okay, mister. Don't have a cow. We were joking with the lady." They stepped back. "Let's split," the leader said before disappearing into the dark.

The man rushed to Lois. "Are you okay?" he asked as he reached her side. She nodded and took a breath.

"I'm fine, thanks to you. I think they wanted to steal my purse."

"I think they were planning a lot more than that. You're shaking. Are you sure you're okay?" He looked at her with concerned eyes.

"Just tense. Thank you for your help." Lois turned and continued down the street.

"Wait a minute. Are you walking somewhere in the dark?" he said as he caught up and matched her steps. "They may come back,"

"I dumped my date at the Bijou, and I need to walk home." She continued walking.

"You can't do that. It isn't safe. My car is back at the Apple Blossom Diner. I can give you a lift."

"Thanks, but no. I don't know you, and I don't get into cars with strange men."

He stopped and held out his hand to her. "I'm Joe McKinnon. It's nice to meet you. Now you know me. Will you let me take you home?"

She smiled and shook her head. "I still don't know you, Joe McKinnon."

"Well," he said with exasperation. "You can't walk home alone in the dark. Walk back to the diner with me. It isn't far. They know me there and will vouch for me."

She hesitated.

"I'll buy you a cup of coffee."

Lois smiled at his persistence. He was sharply dressed and well mannered, so maybe he would be safer than the dark street.

"You win." She held out her hand to him. "I'm Lois Delaney. It's nice to meet you too." He shook her hand and smiled. A short walk back, they entered the brightly lit Apple Blossom Diner. The tension between her shoulders lessened, and she was glad her rescuer had made the suggestion.

"What are you doing back, Joe? I thought you'd gone home," a heavyset, older man called from behind the lunch counter. He wiped his wet hands on his apron.

"Saving a damsel in distress," he said with a wink to Lois. "Some boys were roughing her up outside, and I offered to drive her home. But she doesn't know me and won't ride with strange men." He grinned at Lois' discomfort.

The man behind the counter laughed. "You're safe enough with this guy, ma'am. Ol' Joe McKinnon is a real good guy. He won't hurt you. He's a war hero."

"Oh, well, if he's a war hero." She laughed at Joe's obvious discomfort.

The man continued. "Joe went to high school with my kid. He's steady as they come."

"Thanks, Tony." He looked at Lois. "Can I buy you that coffee now?"

"All right. I guess I'm not in a hurry." She looked at him in the light of the diner and thought he was the sort of guy she'd like to have coffee with. His short hair was dark, nearly black, and his eyes a vivid blue. His smile came easy and his laugh was genuine, and Lois had to consciously stop staring. Joe McKinnon was wonderful to look at.

"Tony, can you get us a couple of cups of coffee? Cream for mine. How about you?" he asked Lois.

"Please."

"Two with cream."

They sat in a booth near the window, and after a few minutes, Tony brought cups and a pot of coffee. When he departed, Joe looked at her across the table.

"So there is an unhappy guy sitting in the Bijou tonight?" he asked with a smile.

"I did say that, didn't I?" She laughed. "I doubt he's noticed yet. He was truly enjoying that Martian movie." She wrinkled her nose.

"Not your choice of shows?"

"I'm not fond of sci-fi. I'd have preferred *Harvey*, but my eloquent date said he wouldn't watch a movie with invisible bunnies."

"I haven't seen it, but I hear Jimmy Stewart is good in it."

Lois smiled. "I heard that too. So, you're a war hero." She noticed Joe cringed.

"I guess."

"Germany?"

"Yeah. I, uh, dragged some guys from a burning truck." He shrugged. "Anybody would have done the same. I just happened to be there. They made a big fuss over it at the time."

"But you don't?"

"No. I didn't get them all." Joe looked down at his coffee cup, frowning.

"I'm sorry," Lois said.

"Me too." He paused for a moment before looking up at her. "Delaney? Are you related to Mike Delaney?" He changed the subject smoothly back to her.

"My dad. You know him?"

"Not well. I bought the Hanson place down the road from his. Met him a while back at Jenny's Café. He was having pie and coffee with a bunch of gabby know-it-alls." He laughed.

"You stumbled onto my dad's vice in life. Two or three times a week he gets together with some of his orchardist buddies. Apple pie is his favorite."

"I have to admit a weakness for it myself."

"So, you bought the Hanson place. I'd heard they sold and moved to town, but I hadn't heard about the new owner. I moved into town last year, so I miss some of the neighborhood gossip."

"The Hansons let the place go some before I bought it, so there's been a load of work to do to get it productive again. I've been tearing out old orchard and replanting some apples into pears and peaches. It's a job." He sipped his coffee. "But I'm catching up now, so I may get off the ranch once in a while. This is the first evening I've been in town for months."

"Tony said you were here earlier. Do you eat here often?"

"When I can, I stop in to see Tony. His son was a friend of mine. High school, and then we enlisted together."

"Was a friend?"

"He didn't make it back. So I stop in to see Tony now and then, talk about old times. It helps us both." He fiddled with his napkin, appearing unhappy with the maudlin course the conversation had taken. "You moved into town last year?"

"Mm hmm. Mrs. Smithwick's house. Her kids are all grown and gone, so she converted her upstairs into apartments during the war. It's cozy, and my father thought it was safe. Mrs. Smithwick acts more like a chaperone than a landlady." She sipped her steaming coffee, looking at Joe over the brim. "I work during the day, sometimes in the evenings, so I'm not there much."

"Where do you work?"

"Milton's Variety. It's busy, and I like the people."

They talked for an hour and stopped only when Tony announced he was shutting off the lights. As they walked into the balmy August night, Lois was thinking she didn't want the evening to end. Joe was different from anyone she'd met. She'd like to spend more time with him but couldn't imagine him wanting to spend more time with her. She was sure he was much older than her twenty years. When he walked to a red Chevy ragtop and opened the door, her eyes lit up and she smiled.

"I like your car," she said as she climbed in.

"Me too. I just bought it a few months ago. Not very practical, but that's what my truck is for. This is for fun." He looked at her perfectly arranged hair and frowned. "Should I put the top up?"

"Don't you dare," she said with a laugh. "I've never been in a convertible with the top down."

"Well then, I'll take you for a ride." The engine roared to life, and he pulled away from the curb. On the radio, Nat King Cole sang "Mona Lisa," and Lois was in heaven.

An hour later, he pulled in front of Mrs. Smithwick's house. They were both silent. Finally, Joe stepped out and around the car to open her door. They walked to the front porch as if trying to drag out the inevitable end to the evening. "That was certainly a different evening than I'd planned to have. Thank you for the coffee and the ride." She looked at Joe, wishing she didn't have to go in.

"You're welcome. I'm glad I came into town tonight. Right place at the right time." He shuffled his feet. "I guess I'd better be going. Good-night, Lois."

"Good-night, Joe," she said as he turned away. "Joe?"

"What?" He turned back.

"Wait." She walked up to him and placed a kiss on his cheek. "Thank you for saving me this evening. I shudder to think what those hooligans may have done if you hadn't come along."

"I'm glad I was there." He smiled. "Um, do you think, I mean..." He took a nervous breath. "Can I see you again?"

Lois smiled. "Yes."

"Tomorrow night? I hear there's a great flick about invisible bunnies playing at the Diamond Cinema. Would you like to go with me?"

"I'd love to."

He grinned. "I'll pick you up at seven, and we'll have a bite to eat first."

"I'll see you tomorrow."

He turned and walked away as Lois climbed the steps to the door. She wasn't surprised to find Mrs. Smithwick waiting in the foyer.

"That isn't the young man who picked you up tonight," she said as she stared at Lois' wind-tussled hair.

Lois smiled. "Oh, didn't you hear? Instead of dish night, the theater had a trade-in night."

"Trade-in?" Mrs. Smithwick looked puzzled.

"Yes. I traded in a heel for a hero. Good-night, Mrs.

Smithwick," she said with a giddy laugh as she skipped up the stairs.

...I can't believe I kissed him but I'm glad I did. He smelled of aftershave, and I didn't want to step away. I may never go to sleep and will spend the night thinking of Joe. He is so dishy. Love, Lois

Logan smiled as he set the journal on his nightstand to finish later. It was nearly 5:00 p.m. and Max would leave soon. He entered the kitchen, inhaling. Lois sat at the table, spooning soup into her mouth.

"How goes the reading?" Max asked. "Have some soup."

"I will. Thanks." He grabbed a bowl, ladled soup into it, and sat with Lois at the table. "The current chapter," he said vaguely, "is the beginning of a love story. She just met him. It's sweet." He looked at Lois. "Do you remember how you met Dad?"

She looked confused for a moment.

"He took you to the movies, right?" Logan prompted.

"Yes." She grinned. "Invisible bunnies." She laughed.

Max looked confused this time. "Invisible bunnies?"

"*Harvey.* Jimmy Stewart. It was their first date. But the night you met him, you were on a date with someone else."

Lois blew out a disgusted breath. "He was awful. I left him in the theater."

"You did what?" Max sat at the table. "I want to hear this, Lois."

She laughed, and her blue eyes danced. "He was...yucky."

Logan helped her with the details. "He couldn't keep his hands to himself, so Mom said she needed to use the bathroom and left him sitting there. No backseat bingo for that guy, right Mom?" He laughed.

"Good for you, Lois. You had spunk." Max patted her hand. "So how did you meet Joe then?"

"My hero." She stopped, so Logan again helped out.

"After she left the theater, she had to walk home. It was getting dark, and some rough boys tried to steal her purse. Dad scared them off, bought her a cup of coffee, and drove her home. Her hero." He smiled at Lois and felt a tender tug at his heart. He'd never known any of this. He knew their first date had been the movies, but his dad hadn't told him the story about the boys. It probably would've embarrassed him to be considered a hero.

Lois took another bite of her soup and became distracted.

"Everyone needs a hero," Max sad as he stood and began clearing the cooking pots. When her bowl was empty, Lois announced it was time for bed. Logan helped her get ready, tucked her in, and returned to talk with Max.

"Is it my imagination, or is she getting better?" Logan asked as he sat at the table.

Max frowned. "I hate to say this, but she won't get better. It's the nature of the disease. The deterioration may level off for a while, but there will only be decline."

"But she seems better to me. Last week she flew into uncontrollable rages and argued with me constantly. Now we're having conversations. She couldn't do that last week."

"Compared to last week, she is better in some respects." Max sat at the table and folded his large hands in front of him. "She had just lost her husband, best friend, and lover, and in her impaired mental state, she can't process the information, so she becomes angry. It doesn't soak in that the man she loved and depended on most of her life is gone."

"I don't know how many times I told her Dad died. And every time I tell her, it's like it's the first time. She grieves over and over at the same intensity."

Max nodded. "Lois has lost most of her short-term memory. She'll continue to decline, but she'll have good days and bad. Someday, she'll stop asking about him completely." He paused and smiled. "Since I've been here, the biggest change I've noticed has been in you."

"Me?"

"The way you're interacting with her. I know most of the problem was lack of sleep, and I'm not criticizing, just making an observation. Your attitude toward her has softened. You told me your history with her was mostly arguing, and I'm seeing something different happening here. You, my friend, are mellowing. She hasn't changed—you have."

"Sleeping does help. This is difficult to deal with when I'm feeling good." Logan looked thoughtful. "I think it's that and the journals. I feel like I understand her better."

"You may be right," Max agreed. "I wasn't sure about it when you told me you were reading her personal journals, but I like what I'm seeing now. You're able to jog her long-term memory and have conversations with her, and that's terrific. I doubt she'll figure out where you're getting the information, and she seems happy to talk about these things with you. It's great. Just be careful not to mention her journals. She might get angry." Max stood and headed for the door. "Gotta go. Have a nice evening, and I'll see you tomorrow."

"Night, Max." Logan cleared the dinner dishes, finished loading the dishwasher, and returned to his room. After changing into sweats, he picked up the journal and continued to read.

Chapter 10

June 1951
My dear friend, he asked me to marry him and I said
yes. It won't be long and I'll be Mrs. Joseph McKinnon.
I'm so happy I might cry...

"Ouch!" Lois cried out. "Be careful, Anne. I don't want blood on my wedding dress." She balanced on a footstool.

"Sorry," Anne Yamada apologized from her perch at hem level. "If you'd hold still, I could be done by now. I'm beginning to wish you'd bought a wedding dress."

"Oh, Anne. No. You've done such a beautiful job. I could never have bought a dress this lovely."

"Stand up straight." Anne laughed. "Your wedding is a week away, and at the rate we're going, I'll never have this hem finished. I have work to do on my dress too."

"I still can't believe I'm getting married. It won't be long, and I'll be living with him in his house, cooking his meals, and having lots of babies." She flushed. "I'm kind of nervous about that part, Anne. What if I don't like it? What if he thinks I'm fat? I have to take my clothes off in front of him. Oh my. I hadn't thought of that."

Anne laughed again. "You're asking the wrong person. Teddy and I won't be married until after you and Joe. I'll be asking you for advice soon." She stood and took Lois' hands in hers. "But I can say with certainty you don't have an ounce of fat on you, and Joe is a lucky man." She leaned in and whispered, "And from what I hear, you'll like it." She giggled at Lois' shocked eyes. "I hear it's lots of fun."

Lois giggled with Anne. "I'll stop worrying."

"You probably won't." Anne sighed. "I'm envious, Lois, that you are getting married first. I want to start my family too. But Teddy says we have to wait until next year when the store is better established. He says we can't afford babies yet."

"You can help take care of mine," Lois said. "We plan to have a houseful. Joe loves children."

"And they will be beautiful, well-behaved children like you were," Anne said with a sly smile.

"Oh dear. I hadn't thought about them being like me. I gave my mother all sorts of fits." She frowned. "What a thing to wish on a person, Anne. Maybe they'll all be like Joe. I can hope, can't I?"

"Take this dress off so I can finish it and then get going. If Joe is taking you out tonight, you'll be late."

Lois glanced at the clock. "Oh, I am." She jumped from the stool, and Anne helped remove the gown. She dressed quickly, gave Anne a hug, and ran out the door.

They sat quietly, looking out over the valley from their perch high atop Lang's Hill, named for the family who had originally homesteaded the base of the hill. At Lois' request, the top was down on Joe's red convertible. The crisp, early summer air provided an excuse to cuddle with the man she loved. Joe lounged against the driver's door with Lois' back snuggled against his chest. She rested her head on his shoulder. He took her hand in his, caressing her fingers.

They watched the last sputter of sunlight sink below the horizon. Bing Crosby crooned on the radio. In a week, they wouldn't need Lang's Hill anymore. After they wed, the need to find a private place would be gone. He'd take her home, and she'd be his. Joe laid gentle kisses in her hair.

"Tell me again, Joe."

"Again? How many times a night do you need to hear it?" He chuckled.

"As many times as you have breath for," she sighed. "I'll never hear it enough."

"I love you." He kissed her cheek. "I love you. I love you." He started to laugh. "Do you have anything to say?"

"Like what?" she teased. "Oh, you mean like, I love you too?" She giggled as he wrapped his arms around her and squeezed her tight.

"You got it. I think I need to hear it over and over too. It has a nice ring to it."

"It will always be this perfect, won't it, Joe?"

"It will only get better, sweetheart. We'll always have each other. I promise you. And we'll have a few children too."

"How many?" she asked. They'd discussed it often, but she liked to hear him say it.

"A houseful, if you like. Little girls who look like you," he added wistfully.

"And little boys with dark hair, blue eyes, and their daddy's sweet nature." She reached her hand back and tangled her fingers in his dark hair. "At least four, okay? It's what I've always wanted."

"How about five, and we'll have a basketball team? Or nine for baseball?" He laughed.

"I'll have to think about that." She sighed. "Okay, a baseball team is good. We'll have to build on to your house." She turned in his arms and placed her lips to his. Joe pulled her to him tighter, needing more than a few kisses.

"Oh, Lois." He sighed into her hair. "I do love you so much." He rubbed his hand gently across her cheek and kissed her again.

"Joe," she said between kisses.

"Hmm?" He broke the kiss, trailing his lips down her neck and nibbled his way back up. She was nearly breathless.

"Let's go to your house."

"Why?"

"So we can...start working on that baseball team." There,

she'd said it. "We'll be married in a week. What's the point in waiting?"

"I can wait a week."

"I know…sex is important to a man. Why wait?"

"It is, and I'm hoping it will be important to you too." He kissed her nose. "We'll wait because it's right. Our first child will be conceived in marriage, not before." He took her in his arms and kissed her again. "But that doesn't mean we can't have fun now."

⌘

June 1952
My friend, today marks our first wedding anniversary. I love Joe more today than I did a year ago. He is everything I thought he'd be: gentle, kind, loving, and passionate. My only sorrow is we have yet to conceive a child. Joe says not to worry. Sometimes it takes longer. But every month that goes by weighs heavy on my heart. I want nothing more than to hold a baby in my arms.

June 1953
My friend, again we celebrate an anniversary without the sound of little feet in our home. Joe says we must relax and it will happen.

June 1956
My friend, Joe marked our fifth wedding anniversary with a candlelight dinner, dancing, and a beautiful necklace. I tried to be joyful but the day only drives home my failure to conceive. At this rate we'll never have that baseball team and may have to reduce our plans to basketball. To fill my time, I've been helping Joe in the orchards and handling the books, but it isn't enough. Anne invited me to attend her women's club today. Listening to other women talk about their families didn't do much to ease my mind…

"Oh! Look who's here. Lois McKinnon. We're so glad

you're here today," Ellen Trent called out from the kitchen. Lois cringed at the older woman's enthusiasm—she certainly didn't share it. Ellen wrapped her heavy arms around Lois and gave her an affectionate hug.

"Hello, Mrs. Trent," Lois said, trying to muster warmth.

"We'll have none of that Mrs. Trent formalness. I may be a friend of your mother, but at the Friendship Club, it's first names only. Come in, dear. Everyone is in the front room having coffee. We're sewing a quilt today and will have coffee cake later." Lois followed in Ellen's wake, finding herself in the middle of a large group of chatting women sitting at the edges of a large wooden quilting frame. Needles in hand, they stitched the intricate quilt stretched across it. Lois inwardly groaned. She'd agreed to attend at her mother's insistence and already wished she was home.

"Lois," Anne Yamada, now Taki, called to her. "Come sit by me." She smiled and patted the sofa next to her. "Would you like to hold Jimmy?" she said as Lois sat down.

"I'd love to," Lois said, hoping to sound convincing. Anne handed her the sleeping baby, and Lois' heart sank. She should be holding a child of her own, not Anne's. She watched his little chest rise and fall as he slept.

"He's so beautiful. How old is he now?" She lifted his little fingers with her own and felt a catch in her throat.

"Nine months. He'll be walking soon."

"Yes, he will," Lois agreed. "Oh, thank you," she said as Ellen handed her a cup of coffee.

The women made her welcome, included her in their gossip, and handed her a needle to assist with the quilting. She forgot her troubles for a short time and began to think her mother correct. She needed out of the house more, needed to stop obsessing about things she didn't have, and find activities to occupy her mind.

"So, Lois," Irma Thorp, a solid woman in her fifties wearing blue paisley, said as she stitched her quilt square. "When

94 · SHARLEEN SCOTT

will you and Joe end the honeymoon and have a few children?"

Lois was stunned by the question. "It will happen when it happens, I suppose."

Irma laughed. "I wish I could've had a five-year honeymoon. My Earl got me pregnant right after the wedding and kept at it for the next ten years. Had a baby every year until little Don came along. Thank heavens he was the last of them."

"Our first child came nine months to the day after our wedding," Sally Tillman volunteered, nodding her head of blonde curls. "Luckily, he was born on time, or people would have looked at us funny." She giggled.

"We just made it through the chicken pox," Janice Harrington chimed in, her fingers pushing and pulling her needle quickly. "All six kids at once, but we're done with it now."

"Oh, I remember that." Irma chuckled. "I wish all mine had had it at the same time. But no, we went through it about five times. Miserable, it was."

"Speaking of miserable," Sally Melbourne said, "my fingers are aching. Can we cut the cake soon and take a break? I'll give you a hand, Ellen." She rose from her chair, brushed the skirt of her cotton dress, and followed Ellen to the kitchen.

"You know," Irma said to Lois, her voice a loud whisper everyone could hear, "if you and Joe are have troubles in the, you know, bedroom, there are things you can do." She nodded her head. "I heard if you don't do the deed for a while, you'll get pregnant for sure. You may want to try it. Let things build up, you know." She patted Lois' hand and gave her a knowing look.

Lois was certain her face revealed the horror she felt. "We're fine. Thank you for your concern, Irma."

"I heard," elderly Mavis Campbell said, also in a loud whisper, "if you do it standing up, you'll be sure to be pregnant."

Lois swallowed hard and wondered how she could escape this room before dying of embarrassment. Her cheeks felt crimson hot. Luckily, Ellen returned with the cake and began cutting slices. Lois ate hers with determination, hoping to make her excuses and leave.

"Now that everyone has cake, Anne has an announcement she'd like to make." Ellen indicated Anne should stand. Anne looked at Lois and shook her head. "Not right now, Ellen." "Come on, dear. Don't be shy. Everyone, Anne and Teddy are expecting another baby this winter." Ellen beamed as the ladies offered a chorus of congratulations.

"Anne, maybe you should be offering some advice to Lois. She and Joe are having troubles that way, you know," Irma said with authority.

For Lois, it was the last straw. She set her cake plate down with a thud and ran, red faced, from the room and out the door. Anne caught up with her as she flung open her car door. Lois stopped and sobbed into her hands.

"Nosey old busybodies," Lois cried. "It's none of their business."

"No, it isn't," Anne said with sympathy. "And I wasn't going to say anything about the baby. It wasn't the time."

Lois looked at Anne, red eyed. "No, Anne. It's wonderful. Celebrate your blessing. It's not your fault I'm a total failure." She began to sob again.

"You aren't a failure, Lois. It'll happen—you'll see."

"No, it won't. I'm a complete failure. What other women can do at the drop of a hat, I can't." She sniffled. "Poor Joe. He wants children so badly. Sometimes I think he should divorce me and marry a woman who can give him what he wants."

"Now that's foolishness, Lois. Joe loves you. He'd never do such a thing." She put her arms around Lois. "Go home. I'll give those old biddies a piece of my mind."

"You do that," Lois laughed, wiping tears from her face.

She climbed in her car and drove home.

As she scaled the steps, she saw Joe sitting on the porch, wearing a worried frown.

"Anne called."

Lois' shoulders shook, and she began to cry. He held his arms out to her, and she crawled into his lap.

"Lois, sweetheart, I would never divorce you. How could you say such a thing?" He held her tight. "I love you."

"Because I'm a failure. I can't give you the children you want. I'm useless." She looked at him, her face tearstained.

"No, you're not. If we never have children, it's fine. We'll be okay, just you and me. We have a good life together."

"But that isn't the way it's supposed to be. We should have several babies by now." She began to cry again. Joe ran his hand across her hair to comfort.

"Hush now. We're okay. If we have kids, that's good. If we don't, it's okay."

"Did Anne tell you what those old biddies said to me?" Her voice caught.

"No. She said they gave you a rough time and you thought I should divorce you and find a woman who can give me children." He took her face in his hands and looked at her with intensity. "I'll never divorce you, no matter what. I married you for better or worse, and so far, it's been the best thing I've ever done."

"Oh, Joe. You're so wonderful." She kissed him. "I'm sorry to be so emotional, but if you'd heard those women, you'd be mad too."

"What did they say?"

"Irma announced to everyone we are having problems in the bedroom."

Joe grimaced.

"And she thought Anne should give us some advice since she's pregnant again. Then they started telling me things we could do to increase the chances I'd get pregnant. Irma said we shouldn't have sex for a while, let things build up." She blushed as Joe's eyes widened. "And Mavis Campbell said we should do it standing up. I was horrified." She buried her face in Joe's shoulder.

"I can see why you're upset. That is kind of personal." He was quiet a moment. "Standing up, she said?"

Lois sniffed and looked at Joe. "Yes. Standing up—can you imagine suggesting such a thing?"

"Oh yeah," he said, distracted. "It's awful."

"Joe? What's wrong?"

"Just thinking. You know, Mavis has eight kids. Maybe she knows something." He looked at Lois with a smile. "Maybe we should take her advice. Standing up could be...interesting."

Lois looked at him and smiled. "You want to try it standing up?"

"Would you?"

Lois giggled. "I'll think about it."

"You'd better think fast." He dropped her to her feet and pulled her through the door.

"Now?"

"Why not?" He pulled her toward the bedroom with a laugh.

...I may need to thank Mavis for the advice at the next Friendship Club meeting. Love, Lois

⟨≈⟩

October 1960
My friend, I write today with a heavy heart and I can confide in no one but you. My period came again today and I don't want to tell Joe again. He says it doesn't matter, but the look in his eyes says otherwise, and I fear we are running out of time for his basketball team and will be lucky to have a tennis double or even a single long-distance runner. I'm thirty and Joe will be forty soon, an age when most men have sons to take

*fishing and hunting. I have given him nothing and I
despair...*

"Lois?" Joe called as he knocked on the bathroom door.
"Are you okay in there?"

Lois sniffled and splashed cool water on her cheeks. "Fine.
Why?" She patted her face dry and opened the door.

"I thought I heard you crying. Are you all right?" He
looked at her with concern.

"Perfectly fine. I was washing my face."

Joe looked at her expectantly, but she didn't confide in
him.

"I'm fine," She smiled. "How is your picking crew getting
along? Have you finished the Reds yet?" She took his arm and
guided him to the kitchen.

"They're doing fine. We should be finished in a few days."
He looked at her seriously, waiting.

Lois turned away. "Are you in for coffee? I'll put on a
pot." She grabbed the pot and filled it with water.

"That would be nice. Will you have a cup with me?" he
asked with stiff formality.

It was her fault and she knew it. Joe was wonderful, always loving and supportive each month when she failed him.
She considered telling him she'd been unsuccessful again but
decided she'd done that for the last time. From now on, she
would bear her failure in silence and not burden Joe each
month. He was bound to figure it out for himself anyway. She
turned and smiled.

"Certainly I'll sit with you."

He sat at the table, afternoon sunlight streaming through
the windows, and watched Lois putter around the kitchen. She
felt his gaze and wanted him to look away.

"Come here, honey." He held out his arms.

"Why?"

"Just do, please." He waved her to him. She sat on his lap,
and he took her in his arms. She stiffened as he kissed her, his

lips tentative at first, then demanding. "I'm sorry I've been neglecting you, Lois. If I've upset you, I apologize."

"I'm not upset. You've been busy with the harvest. I understand."

"You've been acting as if something was bothering you. I thought I'd done something, or not done something. You've barely talked to me lately. What's wrong?"

"Nothing." She gave him a strained smile and tried to stand. He held her in place.

"We can make up for lost time now. The crew won't miss me." He attempted to kiss her again.

She stiffened. "Not now, Joe."

"Why not?"

She swallowed, debating what to say. She didn't want to tell him she'd failed again. "Well, it's the middle of the afternoon, and you've been working. I don't think you have time for a bath first." She slid from his lap and walked to the cupboard.

"I see." He stood and walked to the door. "Forget the coffee. I'll get a pop from the cooler." The screen slapped as he walked out.

Lois stood still, listening to the perk of the coffee. They'd been doing that a lot lately, talking but not talking. She found herself unable to confide in Joe. There had been a time not too long past he had been her best friend, but now she couldn't talk to him about what bothered her most. When she did try to discuss things with him, he would hug her and say it was okay. It wasn't okay. Lois McKinnon was a failure as a woman, and it wasn't okay. She wanted to scream and cry. She wanted him to be upset right along with her, maybe shed a few tears. She needed him to acknowledge with her there was something wrong, but he remained eternally calm, patient, and quiet. If he experienced any emotion, he kept it locked inside, and she resented it.

She pushed him away for a week, long enough for her time

of the month to pass. They began to drift apart further. At night, Joe reached for her, but their lovemaking was mechanical. Joe retreated into his orchards more and more.

...We have lost our passion and I have myself to blame.
Lois

⁂

Logan wondered if he was invading an area of his parents' marriage where he shouldn't intrude. He contemplated what he'd read, and while it explained a lot, it also muddied the waters in other areas. Lois had been unable to conceive, causing her to withdraw from Joe. Her lack of childbearing ability affected her greatly. Each month she was unable to conceive made her sink further and further into depression and self-doubt. Then why, he wondered, had she treated Logan, the long-desired child, with such apathy?

A noise in the living room forced him to put his thoughts on hold. He tucked the journal in the box and went in search of the sound. He turned on the living room light and was surprised to find Lois standing in the center of the room, crying. Large tears rolled down her creased cheeks.

"Mom?" He walked to her, and she continued to sob. "What's wrong?"

"I don't know." She sobbed louder.

"Are you hurt?" He looked at her face, her arms, walking around her to see if something obvious was bothering her. He didn't find anything. "Are you feeling sick?" He knew she probably couldn't tell him, but he asked anyway.

She nodded. "Yes. Sick. On the floor."

"Can you show me where you were sick?" he asked as Lois sobbed harder. "Never mind. I'll look." He retraced her steps as best as he could guess but couldn't find where she had been sick on the floor. When he reached her bed, he realized immediately she hadn't been sick. She'd wet the bed and the floor where he stood in bare feet. With a sigh, he stripped the bedding and tossed it in the wash. He grabbed a can of carpet cleaner and scrubbed the floor. Last, he cleaned the mattress, laid a towel on the wet spot, and remade the bed.

He remembered he'd left his mother standing in the living room in wet bedclothes and ran back to find her in the same place, sobbing quietly. "Come on, Mom," he said. "We'll take care of you now. You aren't sick." With his arm around her, he led her to her bedroom. She leaned into him, and her crying quieted. "Let's find you a fresh nightgown and underclothes," he said softly, afraid she'd begin crying again. He helped her remove the wet gown and underclothes and wrapped her in a robe. "Stay here for a second," he said and ran to the bathroom, returning with a warm washcloth, hoping she would understand what she needed to do. "Here, Mom. You need to clean yourself. Do you understand?" He motioned with the washcloth, and she seemed to get it. Logan was thankful. There were some things he didn't want to do for her. After she'd finished, he helped her into the fresh gown and back into bed. She settled down, the incident already forgotten.

Logan thought about his dirty feet with a scowl and took a shower before turning in for the night. Before drifting off to sleep, he wondered again how his father had handled this situation without losing his sanity.

Another day began with a prodding finger, this time in his stomach.

"Get up, Logan. You'll be late for school."

"Go back to bed," Logan mumbled, his mind mired in much-needed sleep.

"Logan, you'll miss the bus. Get out of bed." She gave him another poke to the stomach, this one harder.

"Ouch!" He leaned up on his elbow and looked at Lois in the dark. "Quit poking me, Mom."

"You'll miss your bus."

"What bus?" he said, momentarily confused. He sighed when his brain cleared enough to remind him of where and when he was. He was forty-three. Mother has Alzheimer's and thinks he's ten again. Actually, being ten again might be okay—he wouldn't be dealing with this. He glanced at the clock: 5:00 a.m. He groaned and rolled from bed. His late nights were catching up. Last night he'd read until midnight, unable to put down Lois' journal.

"Might as well fix breakfast." He grabbed his robe and led Lois to the kitchen. He rubbed his eyes as he filled the coffeemaker, popped bread in the toaster, and dug through the refrigerator for jam, finding marmalade. He set the jar on the table.

Lois picked up the marmalade and smiled.

"Your favorite," she said with a smile.

Logan turned. "Marmalade? Not mine. I've always preferred grape."

"He loved it." She ran her finger over the label.

"Dad? He loved apricot or blackberry, but he bought marmalade for you." He busied himself with butter and toast, turning from her. "But what I remember most was the apple butter you used to make. That stuff was great. Melissa has bought every brand in the store, and we haven't found one as good as yours." He glanced over his shoulder.

"Nate," she whispered as tears filled her eyes, "liked marmalade."

He frowned. There was that name again. Nate. "Maybe while I'm here," he said, "we can dig through your cookbooks for your apple butter recipe. Melissa would like to make some." He turned to the table with toast in hand, noticing the tears on Lois' face.

"Or not, if it bothers you." He watched Lois stare at the marmalade jar. As far as he knew, there wasn't anything about the jam that should make his mother cry. But then, in this condition, anything could make her cry. She hadn't any control over her emotions anymore. He set the toast down and attempted to distract her. "Maybe we should have some grape jam?" He took the jar from her and traded it for the other flavor. Lois sniffed but made no comment.

Max arrived to relieve Logan, carrying a large cardboard box. Lois brightened when she saw him.

"There he is." She grinned at the huge man in flannel and jeans.

"Morning, cupcake," he said, returning the grin. "Morning, Logan."

"What's in the box?" Logan asked as Max set his load on the sofa.

"Hats," he said.

Logan gave him a funny look. "We have a lot of them, but thanks."

Max laughed. "It's something for Lois to do if she wants. The last woman I cared for loved hats and fancy clothes, so we dressed her up and had tea parties like when she was a girl." He pulled out a purple hat with a feather and placed it on Lois' head. "When the woman passed, her daughter gave me the hats. She thought other women would have the same fun with them her mother did." He laughed as Lois adjusted the hat. "That looks stunning on you."

"If you two have plans, I'll take care of some things I need to do today. I'll stop at the store for some groceries. Oh," Logan frowned. "Could I talk to you for a second?" He tilted his head in the direction of the kitchen.

"Sure. Lois, dig through there and see what else there is." Max followed him to the kitchen. "What's up?"

Logan frowned. "Mom wet the bed last night, and it was traumatic for her, so I thought I'd warn you."

"It happens eventually. They wake up in the dark, confused, and may not remember how to find the bathroom. Does she have a nightlight in her room?"

"Not that I know of. I'll pick one up today if it'll help."

"Get several. One in the bathroom would be good too. And you may want to try some adult diapers at night. It may save her some anxiety."

"So far, having you here is the best anxiety reducer. She's doing a lot better."

"A quiet atmosphere is the best thing for her. Soft music, soft lights, and a little attention are all it takes sometimes. At least at this stage anyway." He clapped Logan on the shoulder. "Go do your thing, and I'll take care of things here." He walked from the kitchen. "Oh, Lois, the pink one is nice on you. I think there may be some beads in the box too."

Chapter 11

Lois

July 1961
My dear friend, I've given up the notion of motherhood.
There, I've said it bluntly. After ten years, I must relin-
quish hope and find other things to occupy my time. I
haven't confided my decision to Joe for I fear he'll be
upset with me. I confide to you, dear friend, as no one
else will understand my desolation. Anne can't as she
has four little ones of her own. My mother is sympathet-
ic but is still of the mind it isn't too late to conceive. It's
not unusual for women to become pregnant in their
thirties, and I'm now thirty-one. I have to give up or go
crazy. I've helped Joe in the orchards for ten years but
lack the desire for another harvest sitting in a tractor
seat. The bookkeeping occupies little of my day. Mr.
Sloan posted a sign in his window this morning and
I've applied for the job...

They sat in silence, the meal completed. She'd prepared
his favorite: spaghetti with meatballs, salad, and ice cream for
dessert. Lois twisted her wedding ring, crossed and uncrossed
her legs, waiting for the right moment. She wore a sundress he
liked.

Joe complimented her meal, and they fell into customary

silence. It had been so long since they'd had easy conversation, and Lois was pensive as to how to raise the subject she wanted to discuss.

"There was a sign in Mr. Sloan's window the other day," she said.

"What kind of sign?" Joe asked.

"Help wanted. He needs a store clerk, someone to run the register and restock shelves." She again looked at him.

"That isn't unusual. He hires new people occasionally. I heard Fred was quitting there and going to work at the feed store. Maybe he needs to fill his spot." He sipped his coffee and shrugged.

"Yes. Exactly. Fred is leaving." She swallowed. "I applied for the job." She knotted her hands together in her lap.

"Why would you do that? We don't need the money." He leaned on his elbows and looked at her.

"I know we don't need the money." She frowned and worried he wouldn't understand her reasons.

"You have plenty to do around here. Peach harvest starts soon, and you always help with it."

"I know," she said.

"He'll probably hire a man for the job anyway. I'd think it would take a lot of lifting to stock shelves." Joe returned to his ice cream.

"He didn't hire a man for the job."

"How do you know?"

"Because"—she paused and gave him a level stare—"he hired me, a skinny, scrawny woman who probably can't lift a thing." She pushed back her chair, tossed her napkin to her plate, and stomped from the room, leaving Joe to stare after her.

She was in the bedroom, folding laundry—or abusing it, depending on a person's perspective. A pillowcase snapped crisply, pants folded roughly, and Joe's favorite plaid shirt was wadded into an unattractive ball.

"I didn't mean—"

"To point out I'm weak and useless? That I can't do anything right? That I can't do anything other women do?" she snapped at him as she scrunched up his socks.

"I didn't say that."

"You didn't have to say it. I know it's what you think." She wadded his shorts and tossed them in a pile.

"Don't put words in my mouth, Lois. I said no such thing, and I've never thought of you as useless. I've always depended on you to help run the picking crew. You've done a great job of collecting the tickets from the pickers and making sure they're paid properly at the end of the day." He frowned when she continued folding the laundry with merciless vigor. "I wasn't thinking. That's all. I've always thought you extremely capable at anything you did, and if I haven't said that, I apologize for the oversight. Sometimes I think they'll have a man on the moon before I figure out how to talk to you."

She gripped a bath towel in her hands. "You really feel that way?"

"Yes, I do. I know you'll do a wonderful job for Mr. Sloan at the grocery store."

"You don't mind if I take the job?" She dropped the towel and walked to him. "But who will handle the harvest? I wasn't thinking that far ahead. If I'm not here, who will take care of it?"

Joe smiled. "I'll find someone. Maybe you could still help a little? Maybe teach someone to take your place?"

She nodded. "Okay. I'll do that, and I won't be working every day anyway. He needs me three days a week, and I could be here helping you the rest of the time."

"You'll be awfully tired if you work that much."

"We'll see how it goes. Are you sure you don't mind if I take this job?"

"I've had a moment to think on it now. If it makes you happy, do it. I want you to be happy. I'll figure out a way to survive here a few days a week."

Lois smiled and stepped into his arms. "I can fix sand-wiches and things for your lunch before I leave in the morning."

"No, you won't." He laughed. "I lived alone for years be-fore I met you, and I think I can still fix a sandwich."

"Thank you, Joe." She looked up at him. "I need to do something to fill my time. The harvest is short, and I need to do something the rest of the time."

"Don't thank me, honey. If you want to work, do it. I've never told you what to do with your time, have I?"

"No, you haven't."

"That settles it then. My wife is a workingwoman now." He turned to the door, his arm around her shoulders. "How about if we celebrate with another dish of ice cream? I think the first one is melted by now. To prove I'm capable in the kitchen, I'll scoop it."

⁓

The job at Sloan's Grocery was the necessary tonic to lift Lois from her doldrums. Three days a week she rose early to stock shelves before opening, worked the cash register, and swept the wooden floor. Each morning, she walked in with a lighter heart, surveying her new domain with enthusiasm. There were rows of turquoise-painted shelves filled with canned goods, boxes, and jars; the meat counter where Mr. Sloan did the meat cutting and sausage making; and the freez-er case full of ice cream and frozen foods. At break time, she pulled a bottle of Coke from the water-filled cooler in front of the store and found a shady spot to rest.

There were customers to assist and visit. Mr. Jones refused to wear glasses and required Lois' eyes to find the Ivory Soap. Harvey Thompson asked for assistance with rice and oatmeal. Since his wife died, he had new things to learn. The candy aisle was always full of children debating whether to spend their nickels on candy cigarettes, Chick-O-Sticks, Bazooka

Gum, Sugar Daddy Pops, or a handful of penny candies.

Elderly Mrs. Cooper had yet to adjust to the self-service idea and insisted Lois walk with her along the aisles, carrying her basket, all the while discussing the virtues of Jell-O versus Royal Gelatin. A considerable amount of time was spent in the soap aisle while Mrs. Cooper informed Lois that not only could Fels-Naptha Soap remove any stain but could also be a very effective poison ivy treatment.

"And for that pretty skin of yours, Lois, you do know Lux soap would work well."

"Yes, Mrs. Cooper. I've heard that." Lois tried not to laugh as the aged woman talked, apparently thinking Lois was much younger than her thirty-one years and in need of beauty instruction. Considering Mrs. Cooper's hair had a strange blue tinge, Lois reserved judgment on any advice she received from her. "Is there anything else I can help you with?"

"I need a sack of cat food," she said, and Lois led her to a shelf on the far wall. Mrs. Cooper purchased cat food with the same determination as soap. Every bag was studied in minute detail until Lois felt the urge to pull out her hair. Luckily, Mr. Sloan was at the register, or his other customers would have been severely neglected. As she waited for Mrs. Cooper to decide, she heard Mr. Sloan direct a customer in the direction of the cat food, and out of the corner of her eye saw a man walk around the toilet paper display at the end of the row and patiently wait his turn.

"I'm not sure if Bubbles will like beef better than chicken flavor. Do you have cats, Lois?" Mrs. Cooper asked with seriousness the subject did not deserve, looking at Lois over the top of her glasses.

"Yes, I do, and they are particularly fond of fish-flavored food," Lois said with earnest.

"Hmm. Fish gives Bubbles gas. Which smells better?" Mrs. Cooper leaned in for a whiff of the bags, and Lois heard a snicker from her left. She turned to see a tall, lanky man trying to maintain a serious demeanor, but he failed miserably. He was young, maybe twenty-five, had light-brown hair in need of a cut, and brown eyes, and Lois thought him quite handsome. Unable to control his humor, he winked and smiled. Lois shrugged her shoulders and returned his smile.

"I think the chicken smells better than beef, and I think Bubbles will agree. Here, Lois, smell this and give me your opinion." She held the bag to Lois' face, forcing her to sniff.

"Uh, yes. I agree. Bubbles should like that one fine. Your basket is full. Is there anything else you need?" she asked as the cat food bag was shoved her way. She hoped to conclude the sale and not offer the tall man further entertainment. When she glanced his way, he was trying hard to contain his laugter.

"No, dear. That will do for now." She walked away with Lois on her heels, the shopping basket in one hand and the cat food sack precariously balanced under her other arm.

"Miss?" the man called after her.

Lois stopped and turned, nearly dropping the cat food sack. "Yes?"

"When you have a moment, could I have some assistance?"

"Certainly." She nodded. "I'll take Mrs. Cooper up front and be right back." She juggled her load to the front of the store, nearly dropping the sack as she hoisted it to the counter.

"Did you find everything you needed, Mrs. Cooper?" Mr. Sloan inquired from behind his horn-rimmed glasses. He was a pleasant man, prone to small, tight-lipped smiles.

"Oh, dear me, yes. Lois was wonderful as usual." She gave Lois a gracious smile.

"Thank you, Mrs. Cooper. If you'll excuse me, I have another customer who needs my assistance." She stepped away before she could be drawn into another of Mrs. Cooper's lengthy stories. She'd learned as much as she needed about soap and flatulent cats to last her until the elderly lady's next shopping visit.

Lois returned to the young man who solemnly studied the cat food, looking perplexed.

She wiped her hands on her apron, removing bits of pet food that had shaken from the sack. "How can I help you?" He looked at her seriously. "I need cat food, and imagine my surprise to find Mr. Sloan employs the area's foremost cat food expert. I'm awed by your knowledge of flavor and bouquet. It must be a learned skill, like tasting fine wine." His face remained serious while Lois digested his comments. She stared at him with a lifted brow, trying to think of something to say, when he burst out laughing. "Don't take me so seriously. I'm joking with you. I've never seen anyone sniff a bag of cat food before. It must be disgusting."

Lois smiled at his teasing. "If the truth be told, it's revolting, but I'd never tell Mrs. Cooper. She'd be here the rest of day trying to decide."

"Probably so." His serious look returned. "Now in your expert opinion, which cat food is most likely to please the discriminating palette of a calico barn cat?" He picked up a bag. "Sniff this one and tell me what you think." He held it up and laughed. Lois couldn't help herself and joined his laughter. He was obviously flirting with her, and she shouldn't have been laughing with him, but it had been so long since a man had flirted. She decided to enjoy the innocent moment. As soon as he realized she was much older than he, the fun would end.

"Calico?" she said. "They are particularly finicky eaters and like only fish. But only the sniff test will tell." She picked up a small bag and held it to his nose, laughing.

He turned away while making a face. "You're right—it is disgusting. How can a cat eat this stuff?"

"Most cats will eat just about anything. Is this your first experience with cats?"

"Yeah. I'd rather have a dog, but the cat adopted me. I haven't been able to catch the stupid thing yet. It's either wild or it hates me. Not sure which." He took the bag from her.

"I doubt it hates you. Are you trying to tame it?"

"Not really, but it's there, so I thought I should feed it. So far, I haven't been able to get close to it. Any suggestions?"

She shrugged. "Just put the food out. I'm sure it'll eat it." An uncomfortable silence filled the space between them as he looked at her seriously. She flushed.

"I guess that about covers my cat food problem. Maybe you could direct me to the meat counter, and I'll get some sliced meat for sandwiches."

Lois relaxed. "This way." She led him to the glass meat case and walked behind, feeling more secure with the refrigerated counter between them. When he stopped his teasing, he had an unsettling way of looking at her. "What can I get for you?"

He studied the meats, pointing at the ham and roast beef. She filled his order and handed it to him.

"That should do it," he said.

"Mr. Sloan can take care of that up front. Thank you for shopping Sloan's."

"You're welcome." He smiled, apparently amused at her sudden formality.

She watched as he left, then turned and walked into the restroom in the storage room. She closed the door and leaned against it, wondering what had come over her. A man flirted with her, and she had blatantly flirted back. Lois McKinnon, married ten years, behaved shamelessly with a younger man. She moaned into her hands. Heat radiated from her cheeks. What would Joe think of her behavior?

"Oh my gosh." Her fingertips rubbed across her ringless finger, and she wondered if that had brought his attention to her. Her wedding ring sat at the jeweler's for repair. She vowed to get it back immediately, if she could.

"Lois? Are you all right?" Mr. Sloan called through the door, tapping with his knuckles.

"Yes. Fine. Thank you." She turned on the faucet and

splashed her face with cool water.

"Sorry to bother you. You've been gone for a while. I thought I should check on you."

"I'll be right out." She took a deep breath, waited for Mr. Sloan's retreating footsteps, and emerged from the restroom. The canned green bean display needed restocking, so she grabbed a case and began filling the shelf, hoping the activity would occupy her mind.

It didn't. She couldn't stop thinking about her brazen behavior. Joe would be hurt and angry if he knew she'd flirted with another man. Every time she thought of it, her cheeks flushed pink.

"Lois," Mr. Sloan called. "Can you take care of some gift wrapping?"

"Certainly," she said as she stood, brushing the wrinkles from her skirt. "I'm on my way." She rushed to the counter, thankful for the distraction.

The tall, lanky young man returned to Sloan's Grocery the following week, which in itself was not unusual. Sloan's wasn't the largest grocery in the area, but it was convenient for a lot of the rural folks to drop in for a quick shopping trip and a visit. Mr. Sloan was a friendly man with a large number of children and knew everyone in the area personally.

Lois was on her hands and knees, stocking the lower cereal shelf with oatmeal, when she heard footsteps. She glanced up to say hello and nearly bit her tongue when she found the handsome young man grinning at her.

"Hello," he said.

"Hello." She paused, thinking she needed to say something more. After all, he was a customer, and it was her job to be friendly. "How is your calico getting along?"

"Fine, I suppose. I put food out and it disappears." He shrugged. "I still think the thing hates me."

Lois finished stacking cereal cans and began to stand. He extended his hand to help her up. She hesitated and took his hand reluctantly. It was strong and calloused from work. She released it fast once on her feet. He smiled, obviously amused by her.

"Why would it adopt you if it hates you?"

"Not sure. I think someone dumped it off on my road, and mine was the first barn it came to. It's a fat thing, so someone was taking care of it."

"That could be. Can I help you with anything?"

"Not really. I wanted to stop in and say hello. And now I've done that." He hesitated. "It's three o'clock. Do you get a break?"

Lois swallowed. "I do." The voice in the back of her mind nudged her to speak up and tell him she was married, but she remained silent.

"Could I buy you a pop?" He smiled, and his eyes were hopeful.

Lois' inner voice stopped nudging and began to scream. *Be honest. Tell him you're married.* "Oh, you don't need to buy one for me. Mr. Sloan lets me have one for free in the afternoon." She dodged and swallowed hard.

"Okay. I'll buy one for me, and I'll sit with you while you drink yours."

"I don't think that would be…"

"Lois," Mr. Sloan called from the end of the aisle.

She turned, grateful for the interruption. "Yes?"

"I need to make a phone call. Could you handle the register?"

"Oh, yes, certainly." She looked at the young man. "Excuse me," she said and walked away.

⸎

He returned two days later. Lois hated to admit it, but she'd watched for him. She'd decided her imagination was running wild, and the attractive younger man wasn't flirting with her. He was one of those friendly sorts who laughed and smiled easily, and she enjoyed talking to him. And the more she thought about it, the more she convinced herself she hadn't been flirting with him either. It had been innocent conversation with a customer, that's all.

The day was hot. Heat rose in waves from the pavement, and the store's swamp cooler did little to ease the uncomfortable temperature indoors. Mr. Sloan suggested she grab a pop and find a cool spot for a few minutes, and she eagerly accepted the offer.

She dipped into the cooler for a Coke dripping with ice-cold water, popped the bottle cap with the church key hanging from a string on the side of the cooler, and wandered to the picnic table in the shade of a maple tree near a corner of the parking lot. Lois watched passersby, admiring Joann Carlson's new dress, and waved hello to Mr. Zirkle, the pharmacist. She closed her eyes a moment, setting the pop bottle against her forehead, and was surprised when a shadow fell across her. She opened her eyes to find the friendly young man wearing a blue plaid shirt, baseball cap, and a big grin.

"Hello," he said, continuing to smile.

"Hello."

"This is a nice shady spot. Mind if I sit with you?" He indicated his own dripping bottle of Nesbitt's Orange Soda fresh from the cooler.

"Help yourself." She smiled and waved at the opposite picnic bench. "It's certainly warm today," she said as he sat.

"Too hot for work, so I decided to come to town. Are you on your break?"

"Mr. Sloan suggested I cool off. I didn't see any point in arguing," she said, wondering why they were having this silly conversation. She sat primly, back straight and hands in her lap, causing him to smile.

"What's your name?"

"Lois. And yours?"

"Nate."

"Nice to meet you, Nate." She smiled.

"Nice to meet you, Lois. Pretty name for a pretty girl."

Lois laughed. "That's a line if I ever heard one."

Nate laughed with her. "Sorry. Guess I'm not very original. Have you worked at Sloan's long?"

"About three weeks."

"Like it?"

"Yes, very much." She smiled at the inane conversation.

"Seen any good movies lately?" he asked with an amused smile.

"No."

"I guess that covers all the bases."

"What bases would those be?"

"The bases needing to be covered before I tell you that you are the prettiest woman I've ever seen." He gave her an admiring look.

"Oh." She flushed and looked away. "Nate, I'm..."

"I'm sorry. I didn't mean to embarrass you. It's just...I can't stop looking at you." His brown eyes studied her. "I tend to blurt things out. I'm sorry if I made you uncomfortable. I've been told I'm fairly impulsive. My parents thought I might grow out of it, but I guess I haven't. At least not where pretty women are concerned."

"It's okay. It's just that..."

"I made you uncomfortable." He blew out a breath. "Well, damn, it's the truth. You are the prettiest woman I've ever seen."

Lois couldn't help but be amused at his intensity. "Prettier than Marilyn Monroe?" She laughed, teasing him.

"Much. She's nice for a movie star, but you're in another league entirely."

"I'm thinking you don't get out much, Nate."

"That's true for the past couple of months, but before that, I got around quite a lot. I spent a lot of time around Seattle and Portland before coming here."

"I see. So you are an expert on pretty women then?" She

couldn't stop herself from flirting with him. It kept popping out.

"I know what I like." He reached across the table and ran a calloused finger across her hand, causing her to tense. "I came here today intending to ask you out. Could I take you to the movies or out for a bite to eat? Maybe both?"

"Oh, well, I can't—" Mr. Sloan stepped out the door, looking for her.

"Lois! Your break is over. I need to get some things done in the back room."

"I'll be right there." She looked at Nate, relieved to have an excuse to leave. "I'm sorry—I need to go." She hurried back to the store, berating herself for not being honest with him.

As she worked through the afternoon, her thoughts continually wandered to Nate. She should have revealed her marital status before he entertained ideas about taking her on a date. She was flattered and couldn't possibly be interested in the younger man. She loved her husband. Joe was a wonderful man, and she had no business flirting with Nate. None at all.

But as the day wore on, Lois thought about him and the way he looked at her. It was the way Joe had looked at her when they'd first met. Passion lit his eyes back then, back before they'd grown apart. She still loved Joe so much, but they didn't have that spark anymore.

At the end of her workday, she picked up a few groceries and planned to fix a romantic dinner for her husband and see if she could muster a little spark. If she could, maybe she'd stop thinking inappropriately about Nate.

Lois rushed home and tossed potatoes in the oven before heading into the bathroom. She emerged an hour later smelling of bath salts, her hair combed back and flipped softly, and wearing her prettiest floral dress that reached just above her knees. She felt pretty and feminine and thought Joe would get the idea.

The steaks were broiled, potatoes baked, a cake sat on the counter, and by 8:00 p.m., she hadn't seen anything of Joe. She paced the front room windows, waiting and wondering. Unless involved in the fruit harvest, he was never this late. She turned on the TV set and watched *Gunsmoke* without paying attention to the story, all the while keeping her eyes riveted to the door. At some point, she drifted off to sleep on the sofa and didn't awaken until 10:00 p.m. when she heard his boots shuffle in the back door. She walked quickly to the kitchen.

"Joe. You're awfully late tonight."

He sighed. "We spent the day propping trees, and about halfway through, the truck broke down. Bert and I have been out there with flashlights tearing the thing apart." He kicked off his muddy boots at the door and washed his greasy hands in the kitchen sink.

"It couldn't wait until morning?" She stood, waiting for him to notice her dress. He didn't.

"Could have, I guess, but neither of us had any plans, so we decided to work late and get it done. I'm starved." He sat in his chair with a thud and waited for Lois to bring dinner.

"And you didn't bother to ask me if I had anything planned this evening?" she said sharply.

"We never have plans," he said absently as she filled his plate with a shriveled potato, dry steak, and shrunken peas.

"It looked better at six." She sat across the table from him, folding her hands tightly together.

Joe shrugged tiredly and ate his meal in silence. When he finished, Lois cut a piece of cake that he ate in silence. He stood and left the table. She heard the bathwater running and thought maybe there was still a chance to get his attention after he cleaned up. She straightened the dinner mess, stored the leftovers in the refrigerator, and made her way to the bedroom, where she was greeted by her husband's snores. Lois stood in the bedroom door, the hall light streaming in from behind, highlighting the sleeping man. A lump formed in her throat when she thought of the effort she'd put into this evening and he hadn't noticed any of it. Not the pretty dress she'd worn for him, not the nice dinner or the fresh sheets she'd placed on the bed.

She turned from the room, lay on the sofa, and sobbed.

Chapter 12

With the beginning of the peach harvest, business at Sloan's Grocery increased enough for Mr. Sloan to request that Lois work an extra day a week. Lois gladly accepted and rose early to begin her workday with the rising sun. Migrant workers filed into the area to pick the ripe fruit, pitching their tents near the river and in any open space near the orchards. The schools filled temporarily with their children, and Henley enjoyed a brief population surge.

Business in the little store was brisk, so much so that a week went by before Lois realized Nate hadn't been in for groceries. She thought it silly, but for some reason, she kept expecting him to pop in and say hello.

He didn't, and even though it was inappropriate, she missed him.

She worked the cash register. First, ringing up bananas Mr. Sloan had carefully checked for tarantulas and other creepy crawlies that made their way in the shipping boxes from South America, a box of crackers, and a bottle of milk. After she'd counted back the customer's change, Mr. Sloan interrupted.

"Lois, would you mind making a delivery?"

She looked at the short line of customers and back to Mr. Sloan. "I didn't know you delivered."

"We don't get many requests. I usually have Billy do it when he comes in the afternoon, but he has plans today. I'll take care of the register if you'll do it."

"Certainly. I'll go right after I finish here."

"I'll get the order together. Let me know when you're ready."

When the last customer departed, she found Mr. Sloan loading bags into her car. "Where am I going?"

"The old Ford place. You know where Herman Ford lived, don't you?"

"Sure. It's a few miles from my parents' place." She slid in behind the wheel of her white Chevy Corvair and closed the door.

"It's nearly lunchtime. Take your break while you're out, if you like," he said through the open window.

"Fine. I will." She started the engine and pulled away from the parking lot and headed out of town. The Ford place had been vacant since old Herman passed away, and she didn't know who lived there now. The thought came too late that she should have asked.

She followed the gravel lane past her parents' house, tooting her horn at her father as he rode his tractor through his pear orchard. She hummed along with the Platters as they sang "Harbor Lights" on the radio. The day was beautiful; the late morning air blowing in her window was soft and warm, not yet hot. She was still humming as she pulled into the orchard road leading to the Ford house. It was located a fair distance from the road and surrounded by fruit trees. The Corvair bumped along as she twisted to avoid potholes and a few rocks. From the condition of the orchards, whoever had purchased Herman Ford's acres had their work cut out for them. The trees, in sore need of pruning and propping, hung heavily with Red Delicious apples not yet ready for picking. As she emerged from the orchard, she noticed the house needed as much work as the orchard. Its white paint was peeling and faded, the porch roof drooped, and a side window was cracked and needed replacing. Lois knew Herman had been ailing for years, and the condition of his property confirmed it. She pulled her car to a stop near the house, honked her horn, and waited. When no one appeared, she climbed out and walked to the house. The steps creaked and wobbled beneath her feet, but she managed to make it to the front door and knock.

As she stood at the door, she heard a purr and felt something soft brush against her legs. She turned to find a fat calico cat and bent to pet him.

"Aren't you a pretty thing." She scratched his ears as he continued to rub against her legs. "Friendly, too, aren't you?" She laughed as the cat demanded more attention. Not seeing anyone, but reluctant to leave without delivering the groceries, she sat in a wooden porch swing and glanced around for movement. As she did, the calico jumped to her lap and purred loudly.

"Are you here alone, kitty? Where are your people?" she asked as she scratched and pet.

"I'll be damned," an amused voice said, causing Lois to nearly jump out of her skin. "How did you do that?"

Lois looked up and was startled to see Nate leaning on the porch post.

"Do what?"

"Get that sour old cat to sit in your lap." He laughed.

"I didn't do anything. I sat, and it jumped on me." Relaxed from being startled, she smiled. "So this is your unsociable calico barn cat who hates you?"

"Yeah. He sure likes you though. The cat has good taste." He walked up the steps, stomping dirt from his boots as he went. He was dirty from work, his gray work pants and blue shirt covered in dirt, and his cap had seen better days. "Sorry I wasn't here when you drove in. Mr. Sloan didn't know what time I should expect his delivery person. I figured he'd send his boy later today. You sure are a surprise."

She blushed at his pleased smile. "That's okay. It's only

been a few minutes." She set the cat on the porch and stood. "I'll get your groceries from the car."

"No rush. I need something to drink. Would you like a glass of lemonade? Just made this morning." He looked at her with hopeful eyes.

"I shouldn't."

"Why not?"

She frowned, trying to think of a reason other than the fact she was a married woman and she was finding him too attractive to be appropriate. "I, um, should be getting back to work."

"It'll just take a minute. It's already made." He glanced at his watch. "It's lunchtime anyway. Stay for a few minutes, please."

There was something in his eyes, sincerity she supposed, that caused her to reconsider. She glanced at her watch. "I guess it is lunchtime. Lemonade would be nice. Thank you."

"Have a seat. I'll get washed up and be right out." He smiled as she returned to the porch swing. "The cat will keep you company until I get back."

"What's his name?" she asked, leaning to scratch feline ears again.

"I'd better not tell you what I call him. It's unflattering. Maybe you could come up with a name for him?"

"I'll try," she said as he disappeared into the house. The calico jumped into her lap again. He was huge, she noted as he stretched possessively across her lap and kneaded her skirt with his claws. "Hmm. I don't think a cute name will do for you. You aren't a Puffy or Sweetie Pie, are you?" She could have sworn the cat looked disgusted at the thought. "Something tough or courageous, maybe? King Arthur fits you, since you act like you own the place. Maybe Caesar? John Wayne? Hmm." She ran her hand across his back. "You're a huge brute." She scratched his ears. "How about Hugo or Brutus? That's it. Brutus. It fits you." She heard a chuckle from the door and looked up at the smiling man, feeling embarrassed at being caught talking to the cat again.

"Brutus, huh?" Nate pushed the screen door open with his hip. It closed with a slap behind him. He set a tray laden with two glasses of lemonade, sandwiches, and cookies on a rickety-looking table that, like everything else on the place, had seen better days. Opposite the swing, he sat in an old wooden chair that creaked under his weight. He'd cleaned up and changed into fresh clothes.

"I think it fits. He's a big beast. I can't see calling him Cuddles or Pookie, can you?"

"I can honestly say the thought of calling him Pookie would embarrass me." He looked at the cat. "And I don't think he'd like it much either."

"Probably not. Brutus it is then?"

"Works for me." He handed her a glass of lemonade. "Hungry? I fixed sandwiches."

"I shouldn't impose on you that way," she said with a negative shake.

"You aren't imposing. I'm enjoying the company. Unless I go into town, I don't see many people out here." He handed her a wet cloth for her hands. She smiled at his thoughtfulness.

"Okay then." She picked up a sandwich and took a small bite, nodding her approval. "I haven't seen you at the store lately."

"Been busy around here. I haven't been able to get away, so Mr. Sloan offered to make deliveries. I guess he figured I'd starve otherwise."

"It looks like you have a tremendous amount of work to do around here," she said as she glanced around.

"Don't be shy now. This place is a dump, and it'll take the rest of my life to get it in shape."

Lois frowned. "Mind if I ask why you would buy this place? Herman Ford really let it go his last few years."

"I didn't buy it," he said. "I inherited it. Herman Ford was my uncle. Did you know him?"

"Since I was a young girl. He was an interesting old man," she said politely.

Nate laughed. "Interesting? He was a cantankerous old coot. I didn't know him well, really. There were nine kids in the family. Herman was the oldest and my dad the youngest." He took a drink of his lemonade.

"If you didn't know him well, why would he leave this place to you?"

"He didn't have anybody else, I guess. His son died at Pearl Harbor, and my aunt passed away as well. The only thing Dad could figure out was, I was the only nephew left who hadn't settled down yet. No doubt about it, this place will settle a person down." He bit his sandwich and stared off into the overgrown orchard, and she assumed he mentally calculated the amount of work to do before the orchard ceased looking like a fruit-laden jungle. First, the harvest, and then the winter pruning followed by smudging in the spring to protect the delicate fruit blossoms from the cold, months of irrigation, spraying, mowing, thinning, propping, and then he'd be right back to picking in the fall. Nature's cycle never ended.

"You said before, you're from the coast. Have you ever run an orchard before?" she asked.

"No." He shook his head. "I'm learning as I go. There are a couple of older guys from around the neighborhood who've taken pity on me and are teaching me how to do this. The field man from the warehouse comes out once in a while and puts his two cents in. The spray company sends a guy out too." He grinned. "I'm a work in progress."

"It must take quite a crew to get everything done around here."

He shook his head. "Just me so far. Uncle Herman left me the land but no money to run the orchards. I'm cash poor at the moment, so I can't hire any permanent help. Just occasional day laborers when I need them. I'm hoping to make enough from this harvest to get some things done around here, maybe hire a guy full time."

"What did you do before you came here?" She picked up a cookie and took a bite.

"My dad is a commercial fisherman, and I've always helped run his boats." He frowned. "I'm not sure if I like being landlocked this way, but I decided I should give it a try since Herman thought to give me the place."

She smiled. "I've always wanted to live on the coast, to be able to hear and see the ocean every day. Do you miss it much?"

He got a faraway look in his eyes as if remembering something pleasant. A half smile formed on his lips. "Imagine feeling totally free. Just you, a boat, and endless water, watching the sunrise over the shore while drinking a cup of hot coffee poured from a Thermos. Saltwater spray on your face, seagulls singing to you, the slap of water against the side of the boat, the pull of a big fish on the line." He refocused and sighed at the overgrown orchard. "You tell me, do I sound like I miss it?"

"You do sound homesick, but you'll stick it out here?"

"I'm trying it on for size. If this summer is anything to go by, I'm not sure. I can't do this alone, and I'm depending on a heavy crop to provide some cash, or there's no way. The ocean may win me back. I can always hear it roaring in the back of my mind."

"You'll need to find some things here to give you the same feeling."

"Like what?" He laughed. "When I look around, all I see is more work than I can possibly do, rocks, sagebrush, and rattlesnakes. What's here to compare with the ocean?"

Lois tried to imagine a comparison in the high desert farming community. She glanced around at the landscape she found so familiar, the Cascade foothills forming their valley, the lush valley floor, and the abundance of wildlife inhabiting the area. Nate's orchard climbed slowly up those foothills, ending abruptly where the slope turned to jagged rock.

"Imagine that same cup of hot coffee, steam warming your face while you watch the sunrise over the foothills. The sky goes from dark to crimson in a matter of minutes, turning the sagebrush and summer dried grass a soft pink as the sun slowly creeps up to start its day." She gazed into his orchard, so overgrown a person could barely walk through without hip boots and machete. "Imagine a warm summer day, perfect for a lazy walk through a freshly mowed apple orchard. Bees buzz from dandelion to dandelion, quail peck for seeds in the tree row, skittering quickly as you pass through. A young pup named Skip flushes a pheasant from a thicket."

"What kind of pup?" he asked with a smile.

"Does it matter?"

"It might. Hard to imagine a dachshund flushing a pheasant."

"Golden retriever?" she asked, and he nodded his approval. "Imagine standing on the edge of the river, fly-fishing rod in hand, casting so smoothly it's like a work of art. Fish are lining up for a chance at your hook. An eagle soars overhead, looking for mice to take back to the nest high in the nearby tree."

"I get it, but take it to the next step."

"Which is?"

"Imagine the lazy walk through that freshly mowed orchard, hand in hand with a pretty woman whose hair is the color of honey and sunshine." He looked at Lois, making her blush. "Her skin is tanned from a swim in that same river. Skinny-dipping, because she's sure no one is around to see. She has long legs, soft shoulders, and lips begging to be kissed." He continued to stare into her eyes as he spoke. "And that quiet orchard, freshly mowed of course, is the perfect place for that kiss."

A flush started in Lois' cheeks and worked its way down her body. She wondered what had come over her to begin this silly conversation. The way he'd turned it around was completely unsuitable. He noticed her reaction and laughed, apparently pleased he'd made her blush.

"I guess what you're saying, Lois, is I should make the best of wherever I am."

"Yes, something like that." She swallowed and fidgeted. "I should get back to work. Mr. Sloan will wonder what became of me." She jumped to her feet, forcing Brutus from her lap. Irritated, the cat wandered from the porch, stretching as he went.

"Don't rush off," Nate said as he stood. "I didn't mean anything. Just words, that's all. I'm having fun with you."

"It's not that. I need to get back to the store." She brushed past Nate and headed down the steps. Her foot caught on the unfastened board that had creaked beneath her weight earlier. She cried out as she fell to the ground.

"Lois!" Nate rushed down the steps, crouching near her. "I've been meaning to fix that. Are you okay? Let me help you up."

"I'm fine." She frowned as Nate held his hand out to her and pulled her up, his hand resting on her waist to steady her.

"Are you sure you're okay?" He looked her over, brushing dust and grass from her skirt. She pushed his hand away and brushed the remaining dust.

"I'm fine. Just a little startled."

Nate brushed dried grass from her arm, his hand lingering. She could tell by the glimmer in his eye what he wanted to do. She dodged away and slid behind the wheel of her car.

"Can I trouble you for my groceries before you run off?" he asked, trying to hold back a smile.

Lois' cheeks pinked, and she sucked in her breath. "Oh dear. I'm sorry. I forgot." She stepped from the car, folded the seat forward, and pulled the bag from the back. He took the bag, and she slipped back behind the wheel, safe.

"Thank you for the lemonade and sandwich. I enjoyed it." Lois gave him a quick wave and backed her car away. On the drive back to Sloan's, she chastised herself for behaving in such a shameless way. What would Joe think of her? Horrified, that's what. She vowed to stop this behavior and not allow Nate the opportunity to speak to her that way again.

A week passed, and Nate didn't appear at the store. Lois tried to tell herself she was relieved. As flattering as his attention had been, it was inappropriate, and she was better off not running into him. Unfortunately, Mr. Sloan again made arrangements for a grocery delivery to the Ford ranch. Lois hoped Mr. Sloan's son would be available, but he was busy elsewhere, forcing Lois to make the trip.

Her car packed with several grocery bags, she again drove to Nate's home, swearing to stay only long enough to deliver the groceries. She picked her way down the bumpy orchard lane, successfully avoiding the holes and rocks, and parked near the house. She honked and waited. The early September day was warm, stifling, and soon she had to get out of the car or succumb to heatstroke. She honked again. He still didn't appear.

Letting out an irritated breath, she grabbed a grocery bag from the trunk and climbed the newly repaired steps to the porch. She raised her hand to knock, when Nate swung open the door, dressed in a black suit, a white shirt, and struggling with a tie.

"I'm sorry, Lois. I didn't hear you. Let me take that." He grabbed the bag and took it to the kitchen, returning quickly. "Are there more bags?"

"Yes, but I can get them." She started down the steps. He followed at a quick pace, grabbed the two remaining bags from the trunk, and ran back to the house. He emerged moments later, looking frazzled.

"Could I ask you for a favor?"

"Depends on what it is," she said, unsure if she should agree.

"Are you any good at tying ties? I can't do it right." He looked at her with miserable eyes. Lois smiled. His request was harmless enough.

"I can handle that." She walked across the lawn and climbed the porch steps. "A little overdressed for orchard work, aren't you?"

"My aunt died." He lifted his chin, allowing Lois access to the tie.

"I'm sorry. Is the funeral today?"

"Tomorrow, and Dad just called this morning. When you live in the boondocks like I do, people tend to forget about you." He scowled. "She died a week ago, and no one bothered to tell me. So now I have to rush to Seattle, and I doubt I'll make it in time."

"Why not put the suit on over there?" she asked as she tried the tie, frowned, pulled the tie apart, and tried a second time.

"There's a family thing tonight, and I was told to dress properly." He rolled his eyes. "As late as it is, I won't have time to change. My mother will have a fit I haven't cut my hair, so I don't want to aggravate her over the suit."

"If it helps any, you are handsome even without the haircut." She gave the tie one last attempt and was satisfied with the results. Out of habit, she ran her hand down his chest to smooth the tie, an action she used when helping Joe, and when she looked up, Nate was staring at her.

"It helps a lot," he said before dipping to kiss her. Startled by the move, she let him. The kiss was slow, warm, and left her breathless. "Thanks for the help. I'd better be going." He backed away, giving her a long look. Lois stood rooted to the spot, not sure what to do next. Nate took care of the problem by running in the house and returning with his suitcase. "I'm sorry to rush you off like this, Lois, but I need to get moving."

"Oh, of course. I'll be going. I'm sorry about your aunt." She walked slowly down the steps, turning to glance at him. When she reached her car, she heard footsteps behind her and turned to find Nate standing close.

"What?" she asked as he placed his hand on her waist and pulled her gently to him. His other hand tangled in her hair as he kissed her. Soon, she found herself backed up against the car, his body pressed to hers as he continued the kiss. It was long and hot and made her heart feel as if it would pound right out her chest. When he finished and stepped away, Lois was shocked speechless.

"If I didn't have to leave, I'd finish that," he said with a grin and leaned to open her car door. "Good-bye, Lois. Think of me while I'm gone." He nipped her lips again. "I'll be back in a few days."

Numb, she climbed into her car and started the engine. As she drove away, she wondered just what he meant when he said he'd finish that.

She stewed about the kisses for days, debating whether to tell Joe or accept it for what it was, an innocent flirtation. Nate said he was impulsive at times, and this incident proved it. He was young and reckless. She decided to let it go and not place herself in a position where he could do it again. If Nate wanted another delivery, she would refuse. It would be as simple as that.

But it proved to be far from simple. Four days after the kiss, Mr. Sloan asked her to make another delivery.

"Where?"

"Ford's place. If you go now, you can take your lunch break while you're out," Mr. Sloan said.

"Couldn't Billy do it this afternoon?"

"No. He has a baseball game today."

"I don't have enough gas in my car." She shrugged apologetically.

Mr. Sloan dug out his wallet, extracted a dollar bill, and placed it in her hand. "That should get you four gallons or so. The order is put together and setting by the back door. I'll expect you back"—he glanced at his watch—"around one-thirty." He turned to speak with a customer, the situation settled. Lois let out a sigh as she walked through the store. She grabbed both her purse and the grocery bags and was on the road in minutes. The situation with Nate was getting out of control. It wasn't an innocent flirtation any longer. He was serious about her, and she needed to tell him she wasn't available. It would kill Joe to know another man had kissed her, so she would stop this before Nate tried again.

The country landscape flew by as she rehearsed her speech. She would apologize for her dishonesty and end it right there. He would be upset with her for not telling him sooner, but that was too bad. She would tell him she'd been going through a rough time and was confused. His attentions had flattered her, but it must stop.

Lois stopped her car in Nate's driveway and honked. As usual, he wasn't around to hear it. She sat for a moment, debating her next move, deciding to take the grocery bags and knock on the door.

Her arms loaded, she maneuvered the steps and knocked. No one answered. She considered waiting on the porch but changed her mind and opened the door.

"Nate?" she called as she stepped in the door. "Nate?" She stood near the door, her eyes adjusting to the darkened interior, and was pleasantly surprised. In direct contrast with the ramshackle outside appearance, the inside of the house was neat and tidy. The hardwood floors were polished to a shine. The sofa, chairs, and television set were arranged comfortably, and the oval braid rug in the center added a homey touch.

She made her way into the kitchen, another orderly room

with painted green cupboards, a table with chrome legs, and a mishmash of chairs. She set the bags on the counter near the sink. Thinking Nate was out working, she opened the refrigerator and began unloading the groceries. When finished, she filled a glass with water and took a long drink.

"You're early."

Lois spit the water back in the glass. She turned to see Nate in the doorway, no shirt or shoes, and his freshly cut hair was wet from a recent bath. She turned her back. "You aren't decent."

"I'm wearing pants. That's decent enough. I didn't expect you so early."

She heard his footsteps as he came into the room. "Obviously. How did things go in Seattle? Did you make it in time?" she said to the window over the sink.

"Yes, plenty of time. Everyone was impressed I learned to tie a tie properly. I've never been able to do it." He laughed. "You've improved my standing in the family. I owe you."

"I'm glad I could help. Will you get dressed, please?" Her voice shook, and she took a small breath to steady it.

"It's too hot." He stepped closer, nearly touching her. She could feel his warm breath as he leaned and kissed her neck. "I thought of you the whole time I was gone."

"Nate...I need to talk to you." His lips trailed up and down her neck. She shivered "Nate," she began, but he turned her and quieted her protests by placing his lips tenderly to hers. His hands framed her face. The kiss was seductive. Tender nibbles turned into a deep and devastating kiss. She needed to push him away but was stunned to inaction. When his lips left hers, he continued to hold her close, leaning his cheek to hers. She felt his heart beating in step with hers, jackhammer fast.

"I dreamed about you." His voice was husky. "You were here with me." She closed her eyes and swallowed. "Do you want to know what we were doing?" She shook her head. He laughed and continued anyway, his lips teasing her skin as he spoke. "This. Standing close, holding each other, kissing." He placed his lips to hers and demonstrated with a kiss more intense than the last. Lois was amazed by the sensations crawling through her body. "Want to know what happened next?" She shook her head. He trailed little kisses across her cheek, and his breath tickled her ear. "We were in my bed." He kissed her again with more determination. "Make love with me, Lois."

"Nate, we shouldn't be doing this." He kissed her neck, and she sucked in her breath. He made maddening motions across her back, resting his hands on her hips. He gazed into her eyes.

"Now is the time to say so, Lois. I want you. Right here. Right now. We're both adults, and it's a natural thing for adults who are attracted to each other the way we are. Stop me now, or I won't be able to stop later." He stared into her eyes, waiting for her response.

She debated...one heartbeat...then two... This was wrong—there should be no question. He needed to know the truth. Her eyes locked with his. The moment stretched and felt an eternity. Lois' heart pounded. She laid her hand on his bare chest to push him away.

And answered him with a kiss.

Chapter 13

It was crazy.

They were crazy.

Nate and Lois dove into each other as if starving, their bodies craving the other's touch. Clothing was shed haphazardly as they'd stumbled into Nate's bed, leaving a telltale trail. It was sheer madness.

After, Lois lay in a strange bed with a naked man sprawled across her who wasn't her husband. He breathed into her hair, sighing with contentment as he attempted to regain his breath. She lay frozen and controlled the urge to hyperventilate.

Lois began to cry. "Get off," she whispered.

"What?" Nate rose to his elbow and looked at her.

"Get off. Now." She swallowed hard as the panic overtook her. "Get off of me!" she screeched as she pushed him. "Get away. Oh god. Just get away."

"Okay, okay," he said as he rolled to his side.

Lois rolled over, curled into a ball, and cried long, wrenching sobs until the pillow beneath her head was drenched.

"Lois, honey. What's wrong? Did I hurt you?" He snuggled behind her, running his hand across her skin. "What's wrong?" She sobbed harder. "Did I do something wrong? You weren't a virgin—I know they cry sometimes." He tried to comfort her. "What's wrong, honey?"

Lois shook as she sobbed, trying to locate her voice. She finally found it. "I'm married," she whispered between sobs.

"You're what?"

"I'm married."

"No, you're not."

"Yes, I am. I'm very married." She trembled and began to sob again.

Nate grabbed her left hand. "Where's your ring? Married women wear rings." He dropped her hand.

"It's at the jewelers being repaired."

Nate laughed nervously. "You're kidding me, right? You're pulling my leg to see what kind of reaction you'll get, right?" He rolled to his back. "Okay, you've had your laugh. I'm panicking over here. Tell me you're kidding."

"I'm not kidding. I'm married."

Nate lay motionless. "This is not the time to tell me this. The time to say 'I'm married' was when I asked you out. Or maybe when I kissed you, or maybe, just maybe, before we did this." He rubbed his hands roughly over his face and groaned. "Shit. Married. Goddamn it."

"I'm sorry." She rolled over and looked at him.

"Oh, that's lovely. The nice married lady I had sex with says she's sorry." He looked at her with disgust. "Is this some little game you play? Things get boring at home with hubby, so you start looking around?" He sat up and looked at her. "I'm not playing, honey. I'm not some plaything for a bored housewife."

"It's not like that, Nate. I've never done this before. I don't know why it happened. Really, I don't."

"That's just dandy, Lois." He flopped back on his pillow. "You've killed me, you know that? I may as well be dead. Some irate husband is going to come after me and kill me. Probably castrate me first, but I'm a dead man, so it won't matter what body parts I'm missing. Thanks so much." He stared at the ceiling and took a deep breath, steadying himself. "I need to know something." He swallowed hard. "Who is your husband? I'd like to know who I should run from when he comes after me. And he will."

"Joe McKinnon," she whispered.

He rolled up on his elbow and looked at her, stunned. "No.

It can't be. You're Lois *McKinnon*?"

She nodded her head. Her lip quivered.

Nate jumped from the bed and paced the bedroom floor. "You're Joe McKinnon's wife? Joe McKinnon? You can't be. Not Joe's wife." He looked at her, completely stricken.

"You know him?"

"Yes, I know him. Who do you think has been helping me around here? Joe McKinnon. I have coffee with him a couple of times a week at the café. Yes, I know Joe McKinnon." He began pacing again. "Shit. Shit. Shit. You've killed me and cost me a hell of a good friend. What will I do now?"

"Will you put some clothes on, please?" Lois looked away from the nude, pacing man.

"It's a little late for modesty. You have to get out of here. Fast. Get your clothes on. Leave. Now." He collected her clothes where he'd tossed them earlier and handed them to her.

"Turn around," she said.

"Oh, for Pete's sake." Nate grabbed his pants from the floor and stomped from the room. Lois sat in the bed, sniffling, not believing she'd betrayed her husband. This would kill Joe. She crawled from Nate's bed and slipped into her underclothes and dress. Barefoot, she walked from the room, taking one last look at the bed before she went in search of her shoes.

Nate was slumped on the sofa, shirtless as before. Lois slid her feet into her shoes and walked to the door.

"You'll tell him, won't you?" His voice held as much spark as a wet match.

"I hadn't thought about it yet."

"You will, or it will sit in the back of your mind like a cancer." He sucked in his breath and rubbed his hands across his face. "You'll have to tell him because the guilt will force you to do it. And then you can get on with your unhappy marriage. I, of course, will be dead. But since you weren't concerned

about that before this little game started, I can't imagine
you'll care about me now." He looked at her and frowned.

"Nate, I'm sorry."

"Yeah, sure, great. You're sorry. Will you leave, please? If
anyone sees you here, I'll be dead that much sooner."

Lois walked to the door, turning to look at him as she
turned the knob. "Nate…"

"Go!"

She hurried through the door and didn't breathe until she
was in her car and moving down the orchard lane. The miles
flew by, and as she neared Sloan's Grocery, she realized returning to work was impossible. Her tears ran mascara down
her face in dark streaks, her hair was disheveled, and her
stomach churned. She found a pay phone near the movie theater. Somehow, she managed to control her trembling hands
long enough to deposit a dime and dial Mr. Sloan's number.
She nearly hung up the receiver before he answered.

"Sloan's."

"Mr. Sloan, this is Lois. I'm not going to make it back in
this afternoon."

"What's wrong? Are you ill?"

"Yes, that's it. I'm ill. A terrible headache hit me out of
nowhere, and I need to rest," she said. How easy the lies came
already.

"All right. I'll take care of things here. I hope you're feeling better," he said sincerely, making Lois feel much worse.

"Yes, thank you. I'll be in tomorrow." She replaced the receiver and stood still for a moment, staring off into space. She
couldn't go home yet. Joe would be in the house for lunch,
and she needed time to think about how to tell him. Nate was
right. She had to confess, even if it meant the end of her marriage. At that thought, she began to cry. Divorce was the last
thing she wanted.

Somehow, she made it to her car and drove. An hour later,
she found herself atop Lang's Hill, staring across the wide

valley. Hot tears streamed down her cheeks while she tried to place the blame on Nate. Damn him for flirting with her. Damn him for kissing her. Damn him for seducing her. But she damned herself most of all for giving in, for wanting to give in. She'd wanted Nate Ford, and her weakness allowed the situation to burst out of control.

Lois wept until her sides ached because she felt certain she'd do it again if the situation presented itself. She could still feel his kisses and his rough hands upon her body. She could still hear him calling her name.

It was irrational to want Nate when she loved her husband. She didn't want her marriage to end. Joe was wonderful, loving, and caring. He loved her.

But Nate made her feel alive.

She sat for hours, staring into nothing. Her eyes wouldn't focus on the blocks of fruit trees in the valley below the sagebrush-covered hills, nor did she focus on the hawk hovering overhead. A Hughes Airwest plane droned through the sky, and clouds followed the wind, but Lois acknowledged none of it. In her mind she saw her husband's trusting face. She had in Joe what most women longed for, and she threw it away for a passionate afternoon in a stranger's arms.

The car found its way to her house like a homing pigeon, its driver lost in a haze of tormenting emotions. Thankfully, Joe was still working when she arrived home, giving her time to freshen up and remove the trail of mascara-blackened tears from her cheeks. On autopilot, Lois fixed meatloaf and put it in the oven, tossed a salad, returning it to the refrigerator until mealtime, and then sat and waited.

Joe entered the house later, stomping dirt from his boots. Lois immediately jumped from her chair and busied herself with dinner preparations, wanting to stall the moment when she would break her husband's heart.

"Something smells great in here," he called from the mudroom.

Lois stared out the kitchen window to avoid his eyes. He walked up behind her, wrapped his arms around her waist, and kissed her neck, as Nate had. She stiffened.

"Something wrong?"

"No. Why?" Her heartbeat skidded.

"You're tense." He kissed her cheek. "I'll get cleaned up. Is dinner ready?"

"About five minutes." She relaxed when he let go and walked away.

"I'll be right out."

She hadn't any appetite and had to force small bites. As soon as he finished his dinner, she would tell him she'd spent the afternoon in another man's bed. A man whom he considered a friend, a man he had taken under his wing. A man Joe obviously thought a lot of. She looked at her husband, handsome, steady, wonderful Joe. He was such a good man, always helping everyone who needed a hand. Nate wasn't the first young orchardist he'd helped. When Norman Lombard died suddenly during spring smudging, it was Joe who had helped Norman Junior keep the Lombard pear crop from freezing until the worst of Junior's grief had passed. And when Jimmy Cain had a heart attack, it was good-hearted Joe McKinnon who worked double time to make sure the Cain's harvest came off successfully.

And because he had such a compassionate nature, he'd taken on Nate Ford, a man who innocently betrayed that friendship. Unfortunately, Nate's innocence wouldn't be believed. Joe would think Lois was trying to protect her lover.

She sighed and looked across the table for a last look at the man who loved her, because after her confession, she doubted he would love her anymore. He was still so attractive, she couldn't figure out why she'd strayed. At thirty-nine, his dark hair had begun to gray at the temples, and creases formed around his eyes from hours of squinting in the sun. But he was handsome. His smile was quick and easy, his laugh genuine.

He was her hero, her prince charming. Her shame overwhelmed her.

"I, um, need to talk to you, Joe." She dipped her eyes.

"That sounds serious. Are things okay at the store?"

"Yes. Just fine." She swallowed and hesitated.

"Oh. Before I forget." He sipped his coffee. "I have a surprise for you."

"What?"

"Just a second." He jumped from his chair and walked into the bedroom, returning a moment later with a velvet box. "Something special for you." He smiled as she looked at him with shock. "I've been close to exploding over this. While the jeweler had your ring, I asked him to add a few diamonds to it for our anniversary. And he had some earrings in the case I thought you'd like. Diamonds." He grinned at her. "I thought they'd be perfect for you. I know I'm late, but I couldn't get away sooner to take care of it."

Tears welled in her eyes. She sleeps with another man, and her husband buys her diamonds. What timing. "Oh, Joe. I don't know what to say." Tears spilled down her cheeks as Joe knelt beside her chair.

"You don't need to cry, honey." He wrapped his arms around her. "I love you and wanted to do something special. Adding additional diamonds to your ring seemed appropriate. My love for you grows with each year, and I thought this was a way to show you. I love you more now than the day I married you. I didn't think it was possible, but I do." He took her hand and gently placed the ring on her finger and looked up at her with love-filled eyes.

Lois thought she would die on the spot. "I don't deserve you, Joe. You are so wonderful."

"You are," he said with a smile while he held her. "What did you want to talk to me about?"

"Nothing," she said. "It was nothing."

A week went by, and the pressure built to the point Lois thought she would explode. The guilt ate at her, and she had no confidant. She couldn't tell Anne, and her mother would be horrified. She attempted to tell Joe on several occasions, but each time, she thought of his face as he told her about the diamonds and couldn't do it. Her guilt grew to mammoth proportions until she couldn't eat, couldn't concentrate, and thought she would burst. It ate at her, just as Nate said it would.

She'd been on her way to town to purchase new shoes when she found herself bumping down an orchard road, dodging rocks and rain-filled potholes. Her car stopped, and Lois stared at the little white house needing paint and a new window on the side. The sky was gray. A slight drizzle dropped from the clouds. She didn't honk or open the car door, just sat quietly.

Nate opened the front door and leaned on the frame, eating a cookie, staring back at her. Lois opened her car door and stepped into the rain. She stood motionless, rain dripping down her face.

"What are you doing here, Lois?" Nate asked.

"Shoe shopping," she said, wiping the rain from her eyes, smearing her mascara.

"I don't sell shoes."

She nodded. "I know. I was on my way into town to buy shoes, and for some reason, I'm here."

"You shouldn't be here."

"I know that too." Warm tears ran down her face, mingling with the cool rain. "I don't have anyone else to talk to. I can't talk to Anne or my mother. I'm going crazy because I don't have anyone to talk to." She wrapped her arms around her waist and cried in earnest. "There isn't anywhere else to go."

Nate took a step away from the door. "Did Joe throw you out?" He moved down the steps and stopped in front of her.

She shook her head. "No."

"Does he know?"

She shook her head. "I tried to tell him and couldn't. He bought me diamonds, and I couldn't tell him."

The clouds opened, drenching them. Her hair was quickly plastered to her head, her blouse stuck to her skin. Her lip quivered. Rain ran down her face in rivulets.

"That explains why he hasn't pounded me yet. You can't stay here, Lois. Think about what you're doing." He stepped closer, wiping the rain from his face as a flash of lightening ripped through the sky. Lois jumped.

"I can't think straight." Her teeth chattered from the cold and wet.

"Then I'll have to do it." He put his hands on her shaking shoulders. "Look at me, Lois." She wouldn't. "Look at me. You have to leave. Now." She shook her head.

"I can't."

"Why not?"

She drew in her breath. "Because I need you. I don't know why, but I do. Don't send me away, Nate. Please."

He looked at her for a long moment, her teeth chattering from the cold, her eyes pleading. His hands dropped from her shoulders, and he blew out a breath. "Come inside before you freeze. We'll talk where it's warm." He took her hand, and they walked in from the rain.

She settled on the sofa while Nate added wood to the fire in the stove. Her clothes were soaked, and she shivered. He grabbed a blanket to cover her and frowned at her soggy condition.

"The blanket won't help much if your clothes are soaked. You'll catch your death." He left, returning with a flannel shirt. "Put this on, and I'll hang your clothes up." She took the shirt into the bathroom and returned a few minutes later. He wrapped her in the blanket, snug around her neck. "Sit down, and I'll make some tea." He left her to warm by the stove. She listened as he filled the teapot and put it on to boil. Shortly after the teapot's whistle, he returned with a steaming cup. She sipped, watching while he laid her damp clothes on a chair near the stove. When he finished, he stood in the center of the room.

"You know this is a terrible idea, don't you? Coming here?"

She nodded. "I know it is, but I couldn't think of anything else to do. Will you sit down? I can't talk to you like this." He frowned and sat at the end of the sofa.

"That's better. Thank you."

They sat stiffly, eyeing each other until he broke the silence. "You said you tried to tell him. What happened?"

She laughed, looking at the ceiling as she shook her head. "He had extra diamonds added to my wedding ring." She held her hand out for him to see. "And he bought me a present. Diamond earrings to match. A late anniversary gift. Can you believe the timing of it? I told him I needed to talk to him, and he interrupted with a present."

"Are you planning to tell him?"

"I can't do it. He's so good. I can't hurt him that way." She sipped her tea, looking at him over the brim. "It will have to be kept a secret. No one knows except you and me. You won't tell him, will you?"

"Not likely. It would be pretty stupid of me to say, 'Oh, Joe, by the way, I was in bed with your wife last week.'" He frowned at his own poor humor attempt. "But eventually, Lois, the guilt will get to you, and you'll tell him. You said you were here now because you needed someone to talk to. The guilt will get you. It's better if you tell him now. Tell him it was an accident, poor judgment, whatever. Blame me if it helps. But the longer you wait, the worse it will be."

"I'm not blaming you. We both did it. I'm talking to you now, and that relieves the pressure." She gave him a tentative smile, her first in days. "Be my friend, Nate."

He shook his head, frowning. "We can't be friends. Too

much has happened. You have to leave and either tell Joe or act like it never happened. But you have to stay away from here. From me."

She set her cup on the nearby end table. "But I need you, Nate."

"You keep saying that. You're married to a wonderful guy, so why do you need me?"

She thought for a moment. Rain dripped from the porch, hitting the steps, drawing her attention to the window. "Because you have no expectations of me. I can't disappoint you."

Nate frowned but remained silent.

"I can't give him what he wants, and it's driving us apart."

"What does he want?"

"What every man wants. Children. A son to carry on his name, a boy to throw a football with and wrestle on the living room floor. A child to take fishing and teach to bait a hook." Tears pooled in her eyes. "We've been married ten years, and I haven't been able to get pregnant. Ten years. I'm an absolute failure to him."

"He said that?" Nate leaned forward.

"Not in so many words. Joe is wonderfully kind. He says it's okay if we don't have children. He's happy with our life."

"But you don't believe him?"

The tears spilled down her cheeks. "No, I don't. Actions speak louder than words, don't they? I watch him at picnics and family get-togethers. He'll talk with the adults through dinner, but as soon as the meal is over, Joe always disappears."

"Where does he go?"

"I usually find him in the middle of the kids' baseball game, pitching or catching. Or maybe he'll be showing a boy how to bat. Sometimes he invites his nephews to go fishing with him. He's always looking for kids because he doesn't have any of his own." She wiped the tears from her eyes and took a ragged breath. "I'm his wife. I'm supposed to give him children, and I can't." The flood broke, and she shook with grief. Nate watched, obviously torn between his affection for Lois and his loyalty to Joe. Affection won, and he slid down the sofa and wrapped his arms around her as she cried. "Don't cry, honey. Don't cry, please." He held her tight, crooning in her ear. His hand ran gently across her damp hair. Lois snuggled in tight, her head nestled against his shoulder.

"I'm sorry," she whispered.

"For what?"

"Involving you in my problems."

He sighed. "I got myself involved. You tried to push me away, but I kept coming after you. You're as addicting as chocolate bars, Lois McKinnon." He kissed her temple.

She looked up at him with tear-soaked eyes. "I am? How is that?"

"The most obvious reason is you're beautiful. And when you cry, I want to hold you and make everything better. Am I helping or making it worse?"

"I'm better." She poked her hand from beneath her blanket and rested it on his chest. "You're wet."

"Farmers spend their life being drenched from one thing or another. I'm all right." He shrugged.

"No, you aren't. You're soaked. You need to get those wet clothes off," she said.

"That isn't a good idea." He shook his head. Lois ignored him and began to unbutton his shirt. He grabbed her hands and stopped her.

"This is a big mistake, Lois."

She shook her hands free and continued with the buttons and pushed his shirt from his shoulders. "Take off the wet pants too," she ordered. "Then you can warm up with me."

"Lois..." He attempted again, but she ignored him and began to unfasten his pants. Undaunted by his protests, she managed to pull his pants from him, leaving him in his underwear. He looked miserable.

Tears forgotten, Lois wrapped the blanket around their shoulders and snuggled him.

"This is a mistake. You're getting us in deeper." He moaned.

"Maybe, but you feel cold. I can't let you catch your death, can I?" She looked up at him with owlish eyes. "Is being wrapped in a blanket with me so unappealing?"

He let out a frustrated breath. "There is nothing unappealing about you."

"Fine. We'll sit here and warm each other up." She ran her hand across his chest.

"You're playing with fire, Lois, and we'll both get burned." He looked at her and swallowed hard. "I can't sit here like this and not want you." To prove it, he kissed her.

"You had better go to the other end of the sofa real fast."

"I don't want to." She returned his kiss.

"We have to stop, Lois." He pulled her to him and kissed her harder.

"I know."

"Then stop."

"I can't," she said between kisses.

"Me either," he muttered as he laid her back on the sofa and kissed her until they were both senseless and out of control.

Later, they lay on the sofa, wrapped tight in Nate's blanket. He planted tender kisses across her cheek and brushed his fingertips along her arm. The rain had slowed to a trickle, and the sky lightened as the sun fought to reclaim its space.

"Do you know what we've done?" he asked.

Lois giggled. "I have a good idea."

"Seriously. Do you know what we've done?" He rolled to his elbow and looked at her. She shrugged. "You can no longer say it was a one-time thing or an accident. We've been together twice now. It's premeditated. You lied to Joe to come over here."

"Shh." She pulled him into a kiss. "I don't want to think about that. I want you to kiss me again."

He laughed. "You're shameless. You know that?" He bent and kissed her.

"No, I'm not, actually." She frowned. "I'm filled with shame, and there are days when I feel I'll explode from the guilt."

"Then why?"

"Because for some reason I can't fathom, I need you. I've been feeling hollow and lifeless. When I'm with you, I can forget my faults and shortcomings and be happy with you."

"Even though it's wrong?"

"Even though it's wrong." She held him tighter. "And sometimes the guilt takes over, and I think I'll blow up. You're the only person I can talk to about this. I need you."

They snuggled in tighter, like two survivors of a tragedy, clinging to each other after a shared experience, growing closer because no one else would understand.

He blew out his breath. "It's getting late. Joe will be worrying about you."

"I know."

"What will you tell him?"

"About us? Nothing. He's better off not knowing."

"I mean about the shoes." He smiled.

"What shoes?"

"The shoes you were supposed to be shopping for today. Your excuse to be gone."

"Oh, I'll tell him I couldn't find any." She grinned. "And I'll need to go shopping again." She ran her hand over his bare hip. "And again."

Nate frowned and climbed over her to the floor. He tested her clothes and found them dry. "You need to get dressed and go home."

"All right. But it wouldn't hurt to stay a little longer."

"No. You'd better go. If Joe starts to worry, he may come looking for you. I don't want him finding you here." He handed her the dress and underclothes.

"Your house is far enough from the road, and the apple trees block the view completely." She stepped into her panties with no sign of embarrassment this time. "Has he been to your house before?"

Nate slipped into his pants and nodded. "A couple of times. He stopped by when I first moved in and gave me some ideas on what needed to be done around here. He's been a big help." He sighed. "You know you can't come back, right? Too much is at stake. Your marriage. My friendship with Joe. Our sanity." The look he gave her said he didn't want it to end, but logic and integrity demanded it.

"I know." She slipped her dress over her head and turned her zipper toward him. With gentle hands, he pulled the zipper and kissed her neck. She turned and snaked her arms around his neck. "Oh, Nate. I don't want to let you go. I need you." He held her tight and stepped back, his hands resting on her shoulders.

"No, you don't, Lois. You have a terrific husband who loves you. Go home to him. Tell him how you feel about things, and work it out with him." He kissed her forehead. "Go home to your husband and forget about me."

Lois stepped away from him, found her shoes near the door, and slipped her feet into them. Tears filled her eyes as she turned the doorknob. "Bye, Nate," she said before walking into the drizzling rain.

...Walking away from Nate was the most difficult thing I've ever done. How will I bear not seeing him again? He's right, so I must be strong and resist the urge. Lord help me...Lois

Chapter 14

Logan

Logan tossed the journal to the foot of the bed and looked for something to punch. She'd had an affair. His mother, Lois McKinnon, had cheated on his father with another man. Max's words came back to haunt him—"You may find out something you don't want to know." Damn the guy for being right. This was something he didn't want to know, but it was too late now.

He grabbed his cell phone from the nightstand and speed-dialed his home number. Melissa answered on the third ring.

"She had an affair."

"Logan? What are you talking about? Who had an affair?"

"My mother. Lois Goddamned Dishonest McKinnon. She had an affair. She cheated on him."

"Slow down and let me catch up. Are you reading her journal again?"

"Yes. September 1961. She had an affair with a jerk named Nate Ford. Goddamn her. How could she do that to Dad?" He leaped from the bed, too agitated to sit, and began pacing the floor.

"Are you sure?" Melissa asked.

"Positive. It's all there in black and white. She took a job at the grocery store and met him there. Goddamn her."

"Calm down, Logan. You're pacing, aren't you? You need to relax. There could be a perfectly reasonable explanation for this."

He stopped pacing, embarrassed she knew him so well. "Why would she write it in her journal if it hadn't happened? It's all there from their first meeting in the cat food aisle all the way through to them doing it on the sofa in his living room. Every freaking detail." He paced again. "I think I'm going to be sick."

Melissa laughed. "You are not. Calm down. I can't imagine prim-and-proper Lois having a hot affair. She gets embarrassed when a condom commercial comes on TV. There has to be an explanation."

"Like what?"

"Maybe it was just a fantasy."

"Why write it in her journal this way? There are dates and details."

"Maybe its fiction," she suggested. "Maybe your mother wanted to write."

"Mom? A writer? I don't think so. She never did, that I know of."

"You didn't know she kept a journal. Maybe she was a closet fiction writer. Maybe this journal started out as a diary, and when her own life was boring, she made stuff up." She laughed. "To be honest, I'd have a difficult time filling a journal with what goes on in my life too. Some days are too average. Maybe she made things up to make it more interesting."

"I don't know. It all seems so real, Mel. Dates, locations, everything." He sat on the edge of the bed.

"Maybe your Uncle Larry would know if she wrote stories. Call him and ask."

"That's a good idea. I think I will. I'll call you later and tell you what he said." He disconnected the call and dialed his uncle's number.

"Hey, kiddo," his uncle said when he heard Logan's voice. No matter his age, to his Uncle Larry, he'd always be kiddo. "How are you getting along with that sister of mine? We've been worried about you."

"I hired a nursing service to help out during the day. Mom is a real handful and was exhausting me. But it's better now." Logan relaxed on the bed, leaning on a stack of pillows. "Can I ask you something?"

"Shoot."

"It's about Mom. Do you know if she ever did any writing? Like fiction writing?"

Larry was silent for a moment. "All I know for sure is, she kept a diary. Your grandmother gave her a little white diary when she was a girl. Told her it was a place to keep all her secrets. It had a lock and key for extra security." He laughed. "I tried breaking into the thing a few times when I was a kid but couldn't figure out how to get it open without ruining it. I was sure she was writing all kinds of nasty stuff about me in it. Why do you ask?"

Logan hesitated, debating what to reveal. "It's nothing, really. I found a box of stuff, and it had what looked like journals in it. Some of the stuff was pretty farfetched, so I wondered if she ever dabbled in fiction."

"If she did, I didn't know anything about it. She did have a terrific imagination though. Sometimes she'd tell creative stories. I wouldn't be surprised if she wrote some of them down. Did you find the little white diary?"

"Yeah, and you're right—it's full of all kinds of nasty stuff about you." Logan laughed.

"Really?"

"No. Just kidding you, Uncle Larry. Actually, she thought you were okay for a brother. There was a story about you two sitting in the barn together after your grandpa died. She decided she liked you fine after that."

"I remember that. She was hiding in the barn crying about

Grandpa, and I found her."

"She said you needed a place to cry where no one could see you," Logan added.

"Yeah, I did. I was eleven and had been real close to my grandfather. I blubbered like a girl. She never told anyone either. I guess she was okay for a sister." He chuckled. "Is she doing okay?"

"Not really. I mean, she's doing better now that Max, the nurse, is here. He's doing a great job with her, and she's calmed considerably. I've been able to leave the house during the day and get some of the legal stuff taken care of."

"Would it help if we come for a visit?"

"I don't know. It might stir her up. I'm hoping to have her moved into an Alzheimer's care facility in a few weeks. Maybe you can help with the move? It might be easier with two of us."

"Sure, kiddo. Let me know what you need, and I'll be there."

"Thanks, that's great." Logan thought for a second. "Can I ask one more thing?"

"Sure."

"Do you remember a guy named Nate Ford? He would have lived in Henley in the early sixties." Logan held his breath waiting for the response.

"Nate Ford? Hmm…oh sure, I remember him—Herman Ford's nephew. Haven't thought about him in over forty years. When old Herman died, he left his place to him. Tall, good-looking kid but not much of an orchardist." Larry laughed.

"What makes you say that?"

"The place was in bad shape when he moved in, and it didn't improve much. Herman had let the place go to the dogs the last few years, and it would have taken a real experienced orchardist to turn it around. That wasn't Nate. Your dad took a shine to him and decided to help him out, probably because of old Herman. Anyway, the kid didn't know anything about fruit, and Joe was always giving him advice on what to do. From what I hear, he didn't have any money to spend on the place either, so he had to do all the work himself. The first few months he worked like a son of a gun, and then by fall he started slacking off."

"Why was that?"

"Rumor was he had a girlfriend keeping him occupied. Nobody ever saw him with her, so I don't know who she was, but apparently she kept him pretty busy in the afternoons. The lack of work being done in the orchard proved he had more important things to do, if you know what I mean."

Logan swallowed hard. "Yeah, I suppose it did. But nobody knew who she was, huh?"

"Not that I knew of. Kept it all pretty close to the vest. He never took her out in public. Rumor was she was a married lady and they met on the sly." Larry laughed. "Sounds like Peyton Place, not Henley, Washington. Rumors flew around about it for a while and then died when he sold the place and moved away. If it was true, I'm not sure why he would've been seeing a married woman when all the single gals swooned when he walked by. The waitresses at the café nearly fought each other to wait on him. He was considered a hunk back then, I guess."

"Why did he sell?" Logan's mouth was dry.

"I'm not sure about that either. Some said he got homesick and moved back to the coast. Others said the lady dumped him, and he was heartbroken. Maybe he had a tangle with her husband. I saw him in town one day with a beautiful shiner. Looked like somebody cleaned his clock. I didn't know him well enough to ask. Why the interest in Nate Ford?"

"It's just a name that popped up in a conversation, and I was curious. I better let you go. It was nice talking to you."

"You too, kiddo. Call anytime."

Logan disconnected the call and stared into space, his

emotions churning. Nate Ford existed and had possibly had a fling with a married woman. His mother. It had to be true, and his father must have discovered the affair and pounded the guy. Good for him, Logan thought. It made him feel better to know his father had beaten the guy up. But what about Lois? How did he feel about her? If it was true, she wasn't exactly unhappy in her marriage. She seemed to suffer from some sort of self-induced guilt over not bearing a child in the early years of her marriage.

As much as it made his stomach churn to think about it, he wanted to know more. Had his father found out and pulverized Nate Ford for messing with his wife? Did she confess her infidelity to Joe, or did he hear the same rumors Uncle Larry heard and found out for himself? Logan was sure that would have crushed him. He'd never met a more honest and loyal man than his father.

Despite his reservations, Logan had to know.

Chapter 15

Lois

August 1961
It's been a week since I've seen him. He doesn't come
into the store anymore and I know I'm the reason. He's
being gallant and staying away from me, and I've never
known such misery. He said the guilt would eat at me
until I exploded but it isn't guilt eating at me, it's long-
ing for a man I can't have. Is it possible to love my
husband while wanting another man? My thoughts drift
to him constantly...

The pear harvest began with a bang. More migrant pickers
flooded the area, joining those already in the valley for the
peach harvest. Lois made a Pickers Wanted sign with bright-
red tempera paint, and Joe stood it on the road near the driveway. The workers poured in. She spent her days between the
grocery store and riding a tractor, monitoring the pickers. At
the end of each day, she sat at a table made of two overturned
fruit bins and a sheet of plywood, counting picking tickets and
paying the day's wages.

Lois enjoyed the harvest. Many of the workers were familiar from previous years, and some of the older workers had
picked her father's crops as well. At the end of each day, she
fell into bed exhausted, satisfied. But invariably, she woke in

the night thinking of Nate and wondered if he ever thought of her.

Two weeks had passed since she'd seen him. It was getting easier. Thoughts of him came less frequently, and she believed, eventually, she wouldn't think of him at all.

It was Thursday, a hot and balmy summer day, typical for Henley in August. As a rule, Lois didn't work Thursdays, but Mr. Sloan was ill, and his wife called asking if she could open the store. She was working the cash register, chatting with old Mr. Dobbs about his grandchildren, when Nate wandered in.

She wasn't sure which of them was more surprised. Most likely Nate, from the look on his face, and she wondered if he'd been shopping on Thursdays to avoid her. He skirted the counter at a safe distance, his eyes averted. Lois continued to check the remaining customers' groceries, smiling absently, watching for Nate.

When the customers cleared, he appeared at the register with a small basket of groceries.

"Did you find everything you need?" Lois asked with brisk formality.

"I did. Thank you, Mrs. McKinnon, for asking." He swallowed and looked away. Lois rang up his items and completed the sale, bagging his groceries swiftly.

"Thank you for shopping at Sloan's." She handed him the bag, and her hand brushed his.

He stared at her. "I didn't know you'd be here today, Lois. It's Thursday."

"Mr. Sloan is sick."

"Well." He cleared his throat. "It was nice seeing you."

"You too."

Lois thought her knees would buckle as she watched him leave. She'd thought she was over him but obviously wasn't. She walked to the door and hung the Be Back in Ten Minutes sign and ran to the back room to catch her breath. A minute passed and she heard footsteps in the store. She stood still, wondering who would ignore her sign and come in anyway. She waited to see if the person left the store and caught her breath when Nate walked into the back room.

"Nate…did you forget something?"

His Adams apple bobbed with a heavy swallow; he shuffled his feet. "No. I don't know." He frowned, shuffled his feet again, and stuffed his hands in his pockets. "I don't know why I'm here."

"Oh." Tension radiated between them, palpable as electric current through the power lines.

"I've been doing pretty good, not thinking about you, that is. Since you don't usually work Thursdays, I thought this was a safe day to come in. Apparently, it isn't."

She stared at him, wishing he would leave, hoping he would stay. "It's like I said, Mr. Sloan is home sick today." Her hands knotted together. "You shouldn't be here."

"I know that." There was an irritated clip to his voice. "I know." He frowned and turned to leave, turning back to give her a last look. "I miss you, that's all." With his shoulders in a dejected slouch, he walked out the door.

Lois watched his retreating back and felt as if she would crumble to pieces. "I miss you, too," she whispered.

He stopped and turned to her, his face a mask of agony. "I'm miserable."

"Me too."

"But this is wrong. Joe…"

"I know." She nodded.

They looked at each other, debating. Lois made the first move, a small step toward him. He closed the gap, framed her face with his hands, and kissed her. All thoughts of impropriety flew from her head. Right or wrong, she wanted him.

He ran his hands possessively down her back and to her hips, and she didn't protest when he pulled her tightly to him. The rightness of her feelings for him propelled her down the path to possible destruction, but she didn't care. Right then, all she wanted was Nate pressed to her, his hands touching her. When he pressed her against the wall and pulled her blouse loose from her skirt, reason returned and Lois stopped him.

He took a deep breath and leaned his head to hers. "Right. I know. Not here. But..."

She ran a finger down his cheek, savoring the feel of his freshly shaved skin. "I know," she whispered and wrapped her arms around his neck. They held each other tight, unable to let go until a voice called out from the front door, forcing a break.

"Are you open yet?"

"Just a moment! I'll be right out!" Lois called, and then she spoke to Nate in a hushed voice. "You have to go. Out the back door, Nate, please."

"Why? I was shopping."

"It'll look funny if you come out of the back room while I was closed for my break. We can't allow rumors to start." She rubbed her fingers across her lips. "Is my lipstick smeared?" she asked as she wiped a red smudge from his lip.

"No." He smiled as he brushed his thumb across her lips. "You're perfect. Absolutely dazzling." He leaned down, attempted another kiss. She gently pushed him away before he found success.

"Get out of here." She gave him a shove toward the back door. "Please."

"Okay, but only if you'll come see me."

She didn't hesitate. "I'm off work tomorrow. Go." She gave him a peck on the lips and ran from the room.

⁂

The affair continued. Once a week, Nate ordered grocery delivery, and Lois took her lunch break with him. A second day each week, Lois made an excuse to be away from the house—one day it was shopping for a baby gift for a friend, another it was a luncheon. Whatever the excuse, it allowed her a free afternoon with Nate, not just the quick hour when she delivered groceries.

By October, they were firmly entrenched in their clandestine routine. Twice a week without fail, Lois and Nate were together. She was content. He wasn't.

It was Thursday. Lois was again shopping for shoes. This time, she'd told Joe she needed dress shoes and would be gone most of the afternoon, possibly needing to drive to a nearby town. She'd stopped feeling guilty at some point along the way. She needed Nate and decided the guilt was unnecessary. If Joe ever found out, she would muster up her guilt. For now, she enjoyed every clandestine minute with Nate.

They lay together in Nate's bed, his head resting on her shoulder. A light autumn breeze drifted through the open window, brushing their sweat-slicked skin. It was always the same. He met her at the door, and they kissed as they stumbled to the bedroom, clothing falling willy-nilly. After, they talked and laughed.

Nate appeared serious this time. She tried to joke him out of it, but his seriousness remained. He looked at her, his eyes boring into her with intensity.

"Do you think Joe suspects anything?"

"I don't want to talk about him, Nate. You know I don't."

"We have to." He lifted to his elbow and stared at her. "I love you."

"So you've said before." She evaded, as she always did.

"It's true. I love you, and I hate it when you leave me to go home to him. I lay here at night and think about you sleeping with him."

"Nate, stop." She placed her finger over his lips. "I don't want to talk about him."

"I do. It bothers me to think of you making love with him."

"He's my husband."

"Leave him and marry me, Lois." He took her hand and kissed it.

"I can't leave him, Nate. Don't ask me to." She sat up and stared at him. Lois hated these conversations, absolutely hated them. When Nate mentioned Joe, the guilt threatened to climb from its hidden place and thrash her.

"Why can't you? You come to me twice a week. How can you stay with your husband when you want to be with me? I love you. Marry me."

She crawled from the bed, glaring at him. "Don't." Push down the guilt, she thought. Shove it down.

"Why not?" he said. "You can't be happy with him anymore. You make every excuse to come here to be with me. Damn it, Lois. What do I have to do to convince you?"

"Nothing. There is nothing you can do." She picked up her panties and stepped into them, tugging them over her hips. The guilt crawled higher, threatening to grab her. She walked to the door, searching for her skirt and blouse, which had been tossed carelessly. If she could get away quick, the guilt would stay down.

"What are you doing?" he asked as she slipped on her skirt.

"Leaving. You're being unreasonable and childish, and I can't stay here." She picked up her blouse.

"But it's early yet." There was a hint of panic in his voice. He jumped from the bed and stood in the doorway, blocking her exit.

"I don't care for the direction this conversation is going. You know the way it is, Nate." And knowing the way it had to be killed her, knowing how unfair it was to Nate. Sweet Nate. She slipped her hand into her sleeve.

"I know the way it is. You hold all the cards. Everything has to be your way, Lois. What about me?" He tried to reach for her, but she dodged away.

"This is what we have, Nate. Just this."

He looked at her with hurt eyes, swallowed hard, and appeared resigned as he turned away. Lois wished he'd say it wasn't enough and break it off. The next second, she prayed he wouldn't.

"Okay," he said, his voice deflated. "This is what we have." He turned back and reached for her hand. "I'm sorry. Don't be angry. We have so little time. Don't waste it being mad." He cupped her face with his hands and kissed her. As usual, she couldn't stay mad. He pulled her back to the bed, pushing her clothes from her as he kissed her, trying to take her mind from their argument. He was successful, and soon they were kissing and laughing. With his warm body next to hers, the guilt crawled back to its hiding place, waiting for another day.

"Joe will be gone for a week," she said. "He's going hunting with some friends like he does every year."

"I know."

"How do you know?" she asked, surprised.

"He asked me to go along." He smiled at her stunned expression. In order to allay suspicion, she knew Nate had continued his friendship with Joe, hating the duality but not willing to give up Lois or his friendship with Joe. Twice a week he met Joe and his buddies for coffee and pie. Two other days a week he slept with his best friend's wife. To keep his conscience somewhat clear, he never did both on the same day.

"Are you going? He hasn't mentioned it."

Nate lay back on the pillow and laughed. "Hmm. Let me see—me, my lover's husband, and a loaded rifle in the woods. Would that be wise? I don't think so. If he suspects, it would be too easy for him to shoot me and call it a hunting accident." He rolled over, landing on top of her. "Besides, I'd rather stay home and play with you. Will you stay with me while he's gone?"

"Not the whole time but part of it. I'll need to feed the cats and make it look like I'm home."

"But you'll spend a few nights with me? I want to know

what it's like to wake up with you in the morning. I want to know what it's like to make love with you at sunrise."

"Okay. I will." She smiled and made her plans.

Two days later, she nearly canceled her plans as well as her connection to Nate Ford.

"Lois!" Joe called from the kitchen door. "Are you in here?"

"Yes!" she called back from the laundry room.

"There's somebody here I'd like you to meet. Can you come out for a minute?"

"Okay! I'll be right out." Lois added detergent to the washing machine and turned it on. She stopped in front of the hall mirror, straightened a stray piece of blonde hair, grabbed her jacket, and hurried out the door.

Joe stood in the driveway talking to a man whose back was turned to her. Joe smiled as she walked up. "Here she is. Honey, I'd like you to meet a friend of mine." He wrapped his arm around Lois as he spoke. "Nate Ford."

She tried to control her shock at being introduced to her lover by her husband. A slow smile crept across Nate's face.

"Nate, this is my wife, Lois," Joe continued, oblivious to his wife's discomfort. Nate held out his hand to her. She shook it reluctantly.

"I think we've met," he said. The amused expression remained on his face.

Lois wanted to claw it from him.

Joe looked at Lois with surprise. "You have? Lois never mentioned it."

"Well," Nate said, "we've never been formally introduced. I see your lovely wife at Sloan's when I'm shopping. I hadn't realized she was your wife."

"Yes, I remember you," Lois said. Her heart felt as it would jump from her chest. "It's nice to see you again."

"Nate is Herman Ford's nephew. I've been giving him a

hand on Herman's old place." Joe laughed. "I'm trying to teach a fisherman to raise fruit. Can you believe that?"

Lois' laughter was strained. "No, I can't."

"Maybe I'll make a trade and take you salmon fishing sometime," Nate said. His manner was easy, as if this conversation were perfectly normal. Lois thought she would explode from the tension building inside her.

"That would be great." Joe gave Lois a squeeze. "We'd better get the stuff you need, Nate. Would you like to stay for coffee? Lois could put on a pot while we're in the shed."

Nate glanced at Lois and must have seen her horror at the suggestion. "Better not, Joe. Maybe I'll take you up on that another time. I'm running behind today."

"I won't keep you then. Let's head out to the shed and get you on your way." He released Lois from his grasp and waved for Nate to follow.

With Joe's back turned, Nate smiled at Lois. "It was nice meeting you, Lois."

She glared at him. "You too," she said for Joe's benefit.

Nate bit his lip to hold a laugh and followed Joe. Halfway across the gravel driveway, Nate turned back and mouthed "I'm sorry" to Lois, then disappeared into the dark shed on her husband's heels.

Lois ran into the house and slammed the bathroom door behind her. She sat on the toilet seat and tried to catch her breath. She felt as if she'd been punched. What kind of game was Nate playing with her? Was he angry she wouldn't do what he wanted and leave Joe? Was he trying to force a confrontation? Would he say something to Joe while the two men were alone in the shed? She wrapped her arms around her middle and took deep, gulping breaths. It didn't help the panic crawling through her.

Fifteen minutes passed, and she heard Joe's footsteps in the kitchen. She'd calmed her nerves and thought she could talk to Joe without raising suspicion. She unlocked the bath-

room door and walked slowly to the kitchen. Joe stood at the
sink, filling a glass with water.

"You didn't tell me you knew Nate," Joe said and took a
drink. Lois swallowed hard.

"I don't really know him. He's a customer at the store. I've
waited on him a few times." Calm, she thought, stay calm.
"We've never done more than say hello and general chitchat
about the weather and things like that." She felt her palms go
clammy, wondering if Nate spilled their secret.

"He's a nice guy," Joe said. "Doesn't know squat about
fruit, but he's a good kid and he's eager to learn."

"Why was he here?" She wiped her sweaty palms on her
apron.

"He needed to borrow some tools. The kid is as poor as a
church mouse, so I'm letting him use a few things until he can
get his hands on some cash. Herman really let the place go.
It's a horrible mess."

"Oh really," she said.

Joe finished his drink and set the glass on the counter. "I
was thinking we should have him for dinner sometime. He's
all alone and doesn't know anybody in Henley. He might appreciate a home-cooked meal and some conversation."

Lois swallowed her panic. Dinner with her husband and
lover. Together. How lovely. "That would be...nice."

"Maybe we could invite a few other people. Do you know
any single girls we could introduce him to? He's a nice-
looking kid."

"I don't think I'd want to play matchmaker, Joe. You
know how those things turn out." Her hands shook, and she
stuffed them in her pants pockets to control the tremor.

"You're probably right. He'll make his own way. I'd better
get back to work." He crossed the kitchen and gave her a peck
on the lips. "You look pale, love. Are you okay?'

"Fine. Just fine."

He kissed her again. "I'll be out in the pears for a few

hours." He walked to the door.

"Joe, I need to run into town for a while, but I'll be back in plenty of time to fix dinner."

"Okay, see you later." He grabbed his cap from the counter and disappeared out the door.

Lois didn't hesitate. She pulled her apron over her head, grabbed her purse, and had her Corvair on the road in moments. She drove with angry determination. Her nerves skittered and skidded like bald tires on a wet highway as she picked her way down the now familiar orchard lane. She pulled her car to a stop in front of the house and took a deep breath. If Nate wanted to play games with her, he'd better recheck the rule book.

Her car door slam echoed in the quiet afternoon, but Nate didn't emerge from the house. With a huff, she stomped up the steps and made her way through the house. When she'd exhausted her search of each room, she made her way to the machine shed, following loud banging and clanging.

Nate's back was turned when she entered the darkened shed. Sunlight peered through the cracks, highlighting dust in the air. He hammered and pounded dents from the surface of a disc blade, unaware of his guest until she kicked him in the butt. He swung around, fists bunched and ready for a fight, until he focused on who had attacked him.

"For Pete's sake, Lois. I just about punched you. I thought you were Joe. What was that for?"

"How dare you. How dare you come to my home. You deserve more than that!" She paced away from him, her hands clenched into tight fists.

"Lois, honey," he said as he walked to her. When he reached for her, she swung her fist at him. He ducked easily. "What's wrong with you?"

"What's wrong with me?" she shrieked and swung at him again. He ducked. "What's wrong with you? You came to my home. My home!"

He laughed as she swung again. "I thought we handled that well. He doesn't suspect anything."

Angered by his humor, Lois marched to the tool bench, grabbed a hammer, and threw it at him. He jumped aside without difficulty, and the hammer landed in the dirt with a thud.

"Lois!" He looked at the hammer and at her. "You could have hurt me with that."

"That's right," she said and looked for another missile to throw his way.

"Now, Lois, honey," he said as he worked his way to her. "I can explain." He ducked and backed up as a hunk of two-by-four sailed by his head and bounced off the wall. "Now cut that out!" He backed up again as she eyed the tractor disc blade he'd been fixing. "Now, honey, we can talk this out—" He jumped when she flung the disc at him, followed by a screwdriver that hit his thigh. "Ow! Lois...Lois...what have you got there?" He feigned left as she swung a scythe at him. It was too heavy and she dropped it, glancing around for another weapon. "Lois...sweetheart..." He gulped when she eyed his shotgun propped in a corner. "Don't be thinking that way. That's for gophers." Her eyes narrowed as she walked with purpose to the gun. "Lois, that is not a good idea," he said with a hard swallow as he took cautious steps across the shed. As she reached for the shotgun, he grabbed her arm and spun her around. "We need to talk. What's gotten into you?" He smiled cautiously and laughed. "You're acting like a crazy woman."

"Damn you." Her eyes narrowed. "Don't laugh at me. You had no right to be there." Her anger came to a head when she thought of him standing in her yard, and she charged him, punching and kicking him.

"Ouch!" he cried out when her shoe connected with his shin. "Lois," he said, dodging her next kick. He backed up a step, holding his hands out to deflect her fists. "Lois, stop. I can explain."

She swung at him again. "Explain? How can you explain being where you don't belong?" She came at him again, her anger giving her strength, and she shoved him hard. He hit the wall with a thud.

"Lois!" he yelled as she pummeled him. He covered his head with his arms to ward off her insistent blows. "Lois, stop!" He huffed out his breath and grabbed her, twisted, and slammed her against the shed wall, holding her immobile with his much larger body. When she tried to squirm free, he grabbed her hands and held them tight over her head.

"Let go of me, you bastard!" She wiggled and fought, but he held tight. His labored breath warmed her cheek. "Let me go!" She attempted to kick him in the shin with her heel, but he managed to wrap his leg around hers, holding her like an octopus.

"Are you ready to listen to me?" he said through gritted teeth.

"I don't care to hear anything you have to say, Nate Ford. You are despicable." She wiggled ineffectually. "I don't care to ever speak to you again."

He continued to hold her, his breathing settled down after the exertion of subduing a wildcat in stirrup pants. "It was his idea, not mine. I wouldn't have come to your house on my own, Lois. You have to believe me."

"Why?"

"Because it's the truth. I was having coffee with Joe at the café and mentioned I needed to do some work around here, but I didn't have the right tools. Joe offered to loan me some of his."

"You could have said no."

"I could have, but that would be stupid." He took a breath. "I've told you before, I don't have any cash right now. There's a ton of work to be done here, and I can't afford to buy the tools I need. I'd be an idiot to turn down Joe's offer."

"But…"

"But nothing, Lois. I needed the tools, so I took the chance. I didn't expect him to drag you out of the house for introductions." He chuckled. "The look on your face was precious."

"What if he suspects, Nate? I was so nervous."

"I noticed, but it would have been more suspicious if I'd turned down an honest offer from a friend. We did okay. He doesn't suspect anything."

Her nerves settled and she relaxed. "No, I guess he doesn't. He asked if I knew any single girls to fix you up with." She giggled.

"What did you say?"

"I refuse to play matchmaker. He thought you'd do well enough on your own anyway." She leaned her head into his shoulder. "You could, you know."

"What?"

"Find a single girl to date. You're a handsome man, Nate. There must be a lot of girls who want to go out with you."

"Maybe. I've got a problem though."

"What?"

"I've found I prefer older, more mature women. I'm not interested in girls anymore."

"You should be."

"What are you saying, Lois?" His voice was hoarse.

"That I'm married, and you should be looking for someone who's available. Someone you can make a life with."

"I have what I want right here. I don't need to look around, so stop."

"Okay. I won't mention it again." She turned her head and nipped his lips. "My arms are going numb. Could you let go, please?"

He released her hands and wrapped his arms around her. "My leg is going numb. If I let you loose, will you kick me again?"

"I won't kick you."

Nate unwound his leg but continued to hold her in his arms. Overcome by the prospect of losing her, he snuggled her, kissing her lips and neck. She returned the kiss.

"Can you stay for a few minutes?" he asked between kisses, his breathing increasing with each peck and nibble.

"A few."

"That ought to do it." He gave her a grin, picked her up, and carried her into his house.

⁓

Joe packed his gear, kissed his wife good-bye, and departed for a week in the mountains with his friends. For appearances' sake, Lois waited until late evening to go to Nate. The cats were fed, and she was free until morning.

The house appeared dark when she arrived, and Lois wondered if Nate had given up on her. She'd considered calling to let him know when she'd arrive, but her neighbor, nosey old Carlotta Newton, made a habit of picking up the phone to listen in on the party line. Lois didn't know how many times she'd heard Carlotta's poodle barking in the middle of her conversations. Wouldn't Carlotta love to find Lois making arrangements with her lover over the phone? It would be broadcast across the valley in a matter of hours. She decided not to take the risk and to surprise Nate.

She peered into the window, and realized the house wasn't completely dark. Candles flickered in the living room. She stepped inside, and while her eyes adjusted, she heard a click, the sound of a record dropping to the turntable, and the needle set down. Frank Sinatra crooned, and she saw Nate with a smile on his face, standing by the record player. As he walked across the room, he sang with the record, took Lois in his arms, and danced her smoothly around the room.

"You have a beautiful singing voice," she said.

"Thank you." He smiled and continued his serenade. When the song ended, Nate dipped her with a laugh and kissed her.

"I was worried you weren't coming," he said when she righted herself. "Did Joe leave late?"

"Shh." She put her finger to his lips. "None of that exists tonight. It's just you and me. There isn't anyone else in the world."

He smiled. "We'll pretend we're alone on a deserted island."

"No, my fisherman, we're alone on a boat. Sailing across the ocean. That's more romantic." She snuggled into his chest, and they continued to dance in the candlelight as Nate sang to her.

"I didn't know you could sing like that."

"There are a lot of things we don't know about each other." He snuggled his cheek into her hair. "I know where you like to be touched and kissed, but I don't know your favorite color."

"There hasn't been time," she said as they continued to dance. "Yellow."

"Yellow?"

"My favorite color. Yellow like sunshine and sunflowers. What about you?"

"Blue. Like water and sky. Favorite food?"

"There are so many," she said with a thoughtful look. "Homemade bread. You?"

"Orange marmalade."

"Marmalade isn't a food," she said with a laugh. "It's a condiment."

"Sure it is. Marmalade is a perfect food. I can eat it by the jarful." He licked his lips and laughed. "Okay. Lobster dripping with butter is almost as good as marmalade."

"You are a fisherman, aren't you?"

He shrugged. "Since the day I was born. Some of my earliest memories are of being on a boat with my dad and brothers."

"Do you ever wish Herman hadn't left you this orchard?"

"What, and miss out on this character-building experience? That's what my dad told me. This place will build my character." He laughed.

"Would you go back to the ocean if you could?"

"If I hadn't met you, yes, I might have gone home by now." He kissed her temple. "But I did meet you, and that changed everything."

Lois agreed. Meeting Nate had changed everything for her as well. She still felt she needed him, but sometimes she looked at Joe and wondered why she needed Nate. What was it about Nate that drew her in? Was her crisis passing? Had Nate helped her through her difficult time? If Nate decided to throw in the towel and go home, would she miss him?

He ran his fingers through her hair in a truly loving gesture, and Lois had to admit she would miss him a great deal.

How was it possible to love two men at the same time?

Somehow she did, and it amazed her there was equal room in her heart for two. They were both wonderful, and she dreaded the day she would be forced to choose between them. She and Nate were together because of time stolen from Joe, and she knew someday Joe would find out, and those hours would be repaid with guilt, pain, and sorrow.

The song ended, and Nate led her to the sofa and told her to stay there. He ran to the kitchen and returned with a bottle of white wine and glasses. He poured each a glass and made a toast to smooth sailing.

They sipped wine, talked, and flirted all evening until silly from drink. They fell into bed, laughing.

Lois woke with the sun, wrapped in Nate's arms, and was content until she thought of Joe. She always woke with Joe's arms wrapped snuggly around her. Nate sighed in his sleep, and she forced Joe from her mind.

The week went quickly. Lois kept up pretenses during the day, going to work, spending some time at home feeding the cats. But at night, she was all Nate's. It was the most romantic week of her life. Each night Nate surprised her with something new: candlelight dinners, walks in the moonlight, and glasses of wine in bed. He wooed her with more dances in the living room, champagne in the bathtub, and always he sang love songs.

Lois found herself falling deeply in love and wondering again how it was possible to love two men at once. She still loved Joe but had found space in her heart for Nate as well.

Months passed. November turned into December, and with it came not only the winter but also unexpected news. Lois was rocked to her toes, shocked and stunned, when the call came. There was only one thing to do, only one direction to turn. She jumped in her car and drove to Nate.

The afternoon was cold, and frost covered the lawn. Lois sat in her car, staring straight ahead until he stepped out on the porch and smiled, his breath white puffs in the air. He hadn't been expecting her but, as always, appeared pleased she'd arrived.

She climbed from her car, slamming the door behind her.

"This is a nice surprise," he called from the porch. "Shoe shopping again?" he said with a conspirator's laugh.

"What? No. No shoes today. I need to talk to you." She wrapped her arms around her middle and passed him on her way into the house. He followed.

"What's wrong, Lois?" Once inside, he tried to hold her, but she backed away, shaking her head. He frowned at her resistance. "Joe knows." There was a suggestion of panic in his voice.

"No." She shook her head and turned away from him. He stepped up behind her and attempted to put his arms around her again. She shook him off and stepped away.

"What is it, Lois?"

She turned to him, shaking as she formed the words.

"I'm...pregnant."

"What?"

"I'm pregnant."

His eyes went wide. "But you said you couldn't get pregnant."

"My doctor says I am, so I am." She closed her eyes and swallowed.

"That's wonderful."

She opened her eyes and stared at him with disbelief. He wrapped his arms around her. "As soon as you can get a divorce, we'll get married and raise our baby together."

She shook free of his normally comforting grasp and looked at him with horror. "What makes you think this is your baby? It could be Joe's."

"How far along are you?"

"Three months."

"Of course it's my baby, Lois. Think about it. We've been together nearly four months. It has to be mine."

"No, it doesn't. It could be Joe's. The only thing I know for sure at this point is, this baby is mine." She backed away from him, away from the temptation to agree, away from the possible truth. Oh, sweet Nate, she thought, don't make it worse.

"Lois, there is a good possibility—no, a certainty—this baby is mine, and you know it." His anger flared.

"I know no such thing."

"Yes, you do. What kind of game are you playing, Lois? Of course it's mine."

"There's no way to prove it." She looked at him, regretting the pain she now must cause. Sweet Nate, she thought, why do I have to hurt you? "I can't see you any more, Nate." The moment to choose had come, and it hurt so much.

"But you're pregnant with MY child. How can you say that?"

She turned to the door, needing to break away fast. "I

won't be coming back. This has to be over. Now. I won't expose MY child to scandal."

"Oh, that's all I am now? A scandal? I love you, Lois. I want to marry you. We can move away from here where no one knows us. We can be together."

"No. I won't leave Joe. I've told you before. I love my husband, Nate, and I won't leave him." It hurt so much to say it and even more to see the effect of her statement on Nate's face. Sweet Nate.

"What about me, Lois? Have you any feelings for me at all?"

She gave him a long look, searching for the answer she'd known all along. "Yes, I do. I love you, Nate. A part of me always will." Her eyes filled with tears, and her voice held a sob as she spoke. "But I love him more. I'm sorry. Stay away from me, please, for the baby's sake." She turned and ran from the house, not looking back.

She drove the country lanes from Nate's house to her own without conscious thought until the blare of a car horn jolted her back across the centerline. She told herself repeatedly as she drove that this was the only way. Nate had to understand his presence would complicate matters and cause tongues to wag. Chances were good the baby was his, but she pushed the thought away. Admitting the child was Nate's invited scandal. She'd be the subject of constant whispers, and her child would have the stigma of being Nate Ford's bastard. No, the child would be Joe's, and if she had her way, no one but she, Nate, and Joe would ever know the truth. Publicly, she would hold steadfast to the idea the child was Joe's.

Forever.

Lights shone brightly through the windows as she pulled into the yard. Joe was home early, and she wouldn't have the luxury of time she so desperately wanted. The moment had come for Lois to come clean and admit she'd been unfaithful.

She stood on the wooden steps leading to her front door, and all the guilt she'd shoved deep months before came roaring back to the surface with a vengeance. The power of the surge nearly knocked her to her knees.

Joe sat in his living room chair, listening to Walter Cronkite deliver the evening news. When she opened the door, he looked up and smiled. Lois soaked in that smile, wondering if he would ever smile at her again.

"You're home late. I was getting worried about you. The roads must be getting slick." He looked at her with those blue eyes she'd always found so comforting.

"Sorry," she said from her place near the door. Her feet felt rooted, heavy, and unmovable. "I need to talk to you." She looked at her feet.

"Is something wrong?" Joe leaned forward, leaned his elbows to his knees, and waited. Lois sucked in a jittery breath, held her shaking hands, and looked into his eyes.

"I'm pregnant." She watched the broad smile move across his face, and he jumped from his chair with a whoop, crossing the distance to her with a leap.

"Really? You're pregnant?" She nodded as he grabbed her and spun her around. "Oh, Lois, that's wonderful news." He wrapped her in his arms. She was stiff and shaky. "What's wrong? You're unhappy. This is what we've been hoping for, sweetheart. Why aren't you happy? Is something wrong with the baby?"

"No. The baby is fine." For a split second she considered not telling him the truth. Would it hurt to let him think the child was his? "It's just that…" She hesitated and looked into his wonderful eyes and began to cry. She couldn't lie. Not about this. Eventually the truth would come out, and it would be so much worse when it did.

"What is it, honey?" He backed up a step and looked into her face, searching for clues to her distress. "Talk to me, please. What's wrong?"

She steeled her nerves. "It's just that…" She swallowed hard. He waited patiently. "It's just I'm not sure if it's…yours." The news sat between them like a bomb waiting to detonate.

"Of course it's mine. What are you talking about?" His face fell at the realization of what she was saying. "Why wouldn't it be mine, Lois?" His voice was calm, but his body tensed noticeably. Lois began to cry in earnest.

"Tell me why it wouldn't be mine." His voice was hard as steel. He backed her up against the door roughly and forced her to look at him. "Tell me, Lois. I want to hear what you have to say." She cried harder.

"I was with someone."

Joe's grip on her arms tightened. "With someone?"

She nodded and winced when his grip tightened on her arms.

"When? How long, Lois?"

"Since September. I went to his house in the afternoons." She cried harder at the admission. "Please don't hurt me, Joe. I'm sorry. Don't hurt me."

With an anguished cry, he released her arms and backed away. She wasn't sure if the look on his face was pain or disgust.

"Why, Lois? How could you do something like that? How could you do that to us? Why?" He paced the floor like an incarcerated beast.

"I don't know," she whispered, and at that moment, she meant it. She couldn't remember why she'd felt the compelling need for Nate Ford. She'd already forgotten how she'd been so lonely and how Nate had filled that empty space. She saw her husband, wracked with anguish at what she'd done, and didn't know why anymore.

"You don't know? How could you not know? How could you sleep with another man and not know why? Sweet Jesus," he muttered as he turned his back to her. His shoulders shook with agony. "You've destroyed us, Lois. Filled yourself with another man's bastard, and you say you don't know why? Have I done something to cause you to hate me this way? What have I done, Lois?" He turned to her then, his eyes filled with tears, and she was struck by the full force of her guilt.

"I don't hate you, Joe. I love you with all my heart."

"You can't love me and do what you did. What was it then? Excitement? Thrills? What was it, Lois?"

"I do love you."

Joe shook his head. "No, you don't. I wish you'd told me you didn't love me anymore instead of sneaking around with another man. I feel like such a fool. Since September? I had no idea. How stupid am I?" He clenched his fists, anger building again. "It was all those shopping trips, wasn't it? I should've been suspicious when you went shopping and never bought anything. But no, stupid, trusting Joe McKinnon believed his whoring wife." He let out an angry growl and kicked the footstool across the room. Lois flinched when it bounced against the wall. He stood still, regaining his composure as much as possible. With an angry sweep of his sleeve, he wiped his tears.

"Who is he?"

Lois shook her head. He walked closer, causing her to cringe from him.

"Tell me, dear wife. Whose bed have you been crawling into?"

She again shook her head, staring at him, eyes wide with fear for Nate. He stepped closer, inches from her but not touching. His anger rolled from him in violent waves. Joe had never hurt her, but she wondered now if he was capable of it. She swallowed and stared up at him.

"Who is he, Lois? Is it someone I know? Is that why you aren't talking? Tell me. I deserve to know the truth. I deserve that much from you."

Lois wrapped her arms tightly around her waist and began

to shake. "Nate," she whispered.

"Who?"

"Nate Ford." She found her voice and instantly regretted telling him when she saw the hurt in his eyes.

"Nate?" he whispered.

She nodded and looked away.

"My god. After everything I've done for him, he would do this to me?" He swallowed and closed his eyes. "It started before he came here that day, didn't it? Did you laugh at me for introducing you? Stupid ol' Joe didn't suspect a thing." He swallowed hard, trying to suppress his anger, and failed. "That's why he wouldn't go hunting with us, isn't it? He was with you."

Lois nodded her head, unable to speak. Tears trailed down her cheeks. She turned her face to the wall and wailed. Joe straightened his shoulders and grabbed his coat from the closet.

"Where are you going?" she asked when he reached the door.

"What do you care?" he said and turned the doorknob.

"Where are you going?" she shrieked. He didn't say a word as he left the house, but she knew where he'd go. "Don't hurt him, Joe. It wasn't his fault!"

Joe climbed in his pickup truck and didn't look back at the nearly hysterical woman standing in the doorway. Lois collapsed to the floor, sobbing. She lay there on the cold floor, staring into space until she was chilled. Only concern for her baby forced her to get up. She wandered to her bedroom, removed her coat, and lay down. Exhaustion soon won, and she drifted into disturbed sleep.

She awoke a few hours later to the sound of the front door closing. She jumped from her bed and ran to the living room to see Joe standing at the door.

"What did you do?" she said. He was silent as he walked past her and into the bathroom. His knuckles were bloodied and his jacket splattered, but he said nothing. "Joe?" she called through the door. Water ran in the sink, and then he opened the door. "What did you do?" She didn't see any marks on Joe, so the blood was Nate's.

He gave her a long look before walking past her and into the guest room.

"What did you do?" she shrieked as she followed him, stopping at the door, afraid to enter. "It wasn't his fault! It was mine! What did you do to him?"

The door slammed in her face, and the lock turned. Lois stood staring at the door for a moment before retreating to the room they'd shared for ten years. She stared at her marriage bed, destroyed by her actions, and suddenly she knew what true loneliness was.

Chapter 16

A month passed. Christmas came bringing colored lights, tree ornaments, and goodwill toward men. But the McKinnon house remained locked in a torrent of hurt and anger. Joe would neither look at Lois nor speak to her. She quit her job at Sloan's Grocery and devoted her time to knitting booties and baby blankets and caring for a man who looked through her. She'd ceased to exist for him.

When Nate seeped into her consciousness, visions of Joe's bloodied and battered knuckles usually jumped to the forefront. There had been a fight, but Joe wouldn't speak of it. The week before Christmas, Lois attended a Friendship Club luncheon in hopes of hearing news of Nate and that he was all right. But no one spoke of him, and she dared not inquire. She had to assume he was lying low until his cuts and bruises healed.

Joe's hands healed, and by the end of the year, no signs remained of the fight except for Joe's silence and lack of spirit. She'd smashed him into mangled bits.

By New Year's Eve, Lois was unable to bear the silence in their home. Joe spent his days in the machine shed, supposedly making repairs for the next growing season. In the evening, he ate in silence and retreated behind the locked guest room door.

As the clock crawled into the new year of 1962, Lois decided the silence must end, and Joe would either forgive her or divorce her. It was up to him to cast her out if he chose to do so. She'd committed adultery, and any court would grant him a divorce on those grounds.

At 11:00 p.m., she crawled from her bed, rested her palm on her thickening waistline, and mustered the necessary courage. A decision must be made soon and their story set, because once she began to show, there would be no going back. Snug in her robe and slippers, Lois stopped at the guest room door and knocked.

"Joe?" She knocked again. Determined to have her showdown, she opened the door and found the room empty. She walked through the house, illuminated only by the glow of the moon. He wasn't anywhere in the house, and she wondered if he'd been leaving at night without her knowledge.

She almost gave up, when she heard a sound from her sunroom off the kitchen. It was her special place, a room Joe had built for her to grow plants, read, or spend time alone. She looked through the window and saw him sitting in the dark, elbows on knees, head in his hands, and his shoulders shaking. She opened the door and heard a sound she thought she'd never hear, and it tore her apart.

Joe was weeping.

A knot formed in her stomach, and she berated herself for reducing a fine man to this. "Joe," she whispered.

He looked up at her through red, tear-soaked eyes. "Go back in, Lois. Leave me alone, please," he asked with a catch in his voice.

"We need to talk."

"I can't." He wiped his eyes with the back of his hand and sniffed. "I can't look at you. How can I talk to you?"

"Some things need to be settled. Soon. Before I start showing," she said, laying her hand on her stomach.

"What do you want me to say, Lois? You're carrying another man's bastard. What do you expect me to do? If you're worried about your precious reputation, it's a little late now."

Lois' temper flared. "For starters, you will stop referring to this child as a bastard. I don't care what you say about me or what fowl names you want to call me, but you WILL NOT belittle this child." She shook with rage, shielding her baby like a mother lion protecting her cub. "Prosecute me for the crimes I've committed, but this child is innocent. If you can't accept that, I'll leave right now. At this point, we don't know who fathered this child. It may have been you."

He gave her a long look and nodded. "You're right. I'm sorry." He looked away. "You're right. Babies come into this world with a clean slate, wrapped in innocence. I won't punish the child for what you've done." He swallowed hard and stared out the window into the frosty night. Snow lay in drifts and ice hung from the eaves. "I've been thinking a lot about all of this, trying to figure out where I went wrong with you."

"Joe, don't. It's not your fault."

"I think it is. Maybe I'm too old for you. I wondered about that before we got married. You were so young and hadn't had a chance to experience life the way I had. I'd been through the war, lived in different places, and was ready to settle down."

"No, Joe, I wanted to marry you and spend my life with you."

"Yeah, well," he shrugged. "Maybe the fact I'm pushing forty has something to do with it." He rubbed his stomach. "I'm not in the kind of shape I used to be. I'm heading into middle age, and well, you're only thirty-one. Maybe you need something I can't give you." He frowned. "Nate's a lot younger."

"Not that much."

"I know how old he is. I bought him a piece of pie on his birthday in October. He's twenty-six. A lot closer to your age than I am."

"Age doesn't matter," she argued, but he waved her away.

"Whatever. A younger guy has a lot more stamina. The sex was probably better with him. I do my best, but I'm getting older."

"Joe. Stop this, please." She stepped into the room, wringing her hands as tears threatened to fall.

"Hitting too close to home, am I? I'm trying to figure it out, that's all." His voice was flat, devoid of emotion. "Are you leaving me, Lois?"

"Do you want me to go?" She watched his face closely in the moonlight for an indication of his true feelings. This was the moment she'd been dreading.

He shook his head. "No. But it isn't about what I want. Do you love him?" His fists clenched. "Honestly, Lois, if you are capable of honesty anymore. Can you tell me truthfully if you love him? I need to know."

"Honestly?" She hesitated and considered telling a lie to save Joe's pride. But he deserved better than that. "Yes, a part of me loves him, but…"

Joe closed his eyes, flinching as her words slammed into him like a fist. "But?"

"I love you more. I will always love you more. Please don't throw me out, Joe." Tears trickled down her cheeks and her shoulders shook. A sound resembling a gasp slipped from her lips. "Please."

"Throw you out? I've been praying you wouldn't leave me. I've been afraid to talk to you because I thought you'd say you were leaving." He took a deep breath. "You're the only woman I've ever loved, and I can't shut it off like a faucet. Maybe I'm a fool, but I still love you."

Lois closed her eyes and absorbed his words. He didn't want her to leave. "I don't want to leave. My life is with you. I never considered leaving you."

"Then why?"

She opened her eyes and looked at Joe, seeing everything she'd always wanted in the man she'd married, and tried to articulate an answer that would make sense to him. "I was mixed up, and he helped me through it. I don't know what else to say except I don't need him anymore. I want to work things out with you."

Joe gave her a long look. "I guess I have to accept that."

She laid her hand across her stomach. "What about the baby? Can you accept this baby as your own? We may never know for sure."

He hesitated and nodded. "If you stay, this baby will be a McKinnon. I promise you. What about Nate?"

"That's over, of course. I've already told him."

"What did he say?"

"He wanted me to leave you and marry him. I told him no, I would never leave you."

"How does he feel about the baby? You told him, didn't you?"

"Yes. He knows. He's positive the child is his."

Joe frowned. "That could be a real problem. We need to talk to him. He has to understand there isn't any way he can have contact with the child. The gossip..."

Lois tensed. "I can't talk to him." She shook her head. The last thing she wanted to do was see that hurt look in Nate's eyes again. Sweet Nate. She'd been so unfair to him from the beginning.

Joe sighed. "I can talk to him."

"You won't hurt him, will you?"

"No. I'll talk to him and explain what you want. It's what you want, isn't it? You want him to stay away, right?"

"I don't want to see him again, and I think it would be harmful for the baby to have him around. What would people think?"

"So we raise it as mine and never tell anyone any different. Agreed?"

She nodded. "Oh, Joe, I'm so sorry. Can you forgive me? I'll beg if it's what you want." She dropped to her knees and looked up at him as tears filled her eyes. "Forgive me, please." She closed her eyes and waited for his answer.

"Get up, Lois. You don't need to do this. Get up off the floor," he said softly, his voice hoarse. "Don't you ever do that again."

He held his arms out, beckoning her. Lois didn't hesitate. She crawled onto his lap and into his arms. They held each other close, sharing tears and forgiveness, and they began to heal.

⁓

Logan was shaking when he laid his mother's journal on the bed. He'd counted the months. If Lois was nearly four months pregnant on New Year's Eve 1961, the baby was born in June 1962. Logan's birthday was June 8, 1962. He was the product of his mother's affair with Nate Ford. Joe McKinnon wasn't his father. His stomach rolled and he ran to the bathroom to throw up.

He lay on the cool bathroom floor, staring at the ceiling. When his stomach stopped churning, his mind took over the task. There was a remote possibility this wasn't true. Maybe it was as Melissa said. Lois had an overactive imagination and chose to spice up her journal with a little harmless fiction.

But complicating the theory was the fact Nate Ford did exist. Uncle Larry already confirmed it. But maybe, just maybe, this was all a fantasy. Maybe Lois had a crush on this guy and had manufactured an affair in her mind.

But what about Uncle Larry's story about Nate Ford having a married mistress and the possibility her husband gave Nate the black eye? Lois had written about Joe returning with bloodied, battered knuckles. Logan moaned at the implication.

The mounting evidence couldn't be denied. Logan's mother had an affair in 1961, and he was the result of it.

"Goddamn it all to hell. Why didn't anyone tell ME?"

Logan's world tilted, throwing him off center. Everything he knew about his family and himself suddenly became suspect. Who was Logan McKinnon anyway? A man spends his life forming who he is. Everything goes into the mix—family environment, societal pressures, and heredity. It was like discovering a hidden adoption and not being sure of his identity, his heredity. He questioned everything. Had Joe McKinnon really loved him, or did he fear Lois would leave him? "Stop! Stop! Stop!" He grabbed his hair in handfuls and muttered. "He loved you. You know he did. Dad couldn't have faked that. Not for forty-three years. Nobody's that good." He let out a calming breath.

Could this explain why he didn't look like his parents? Joe was dark with blue eyes. Lois was honey blonde with blue eyes. He'd always thought he'd landed somewhere in the middle with his light-brown hair and brown eyes. His maternal grandfather had brown eyes. So did Nate Ford. He cursed his parents for their deception, for causing him to doubt everything about himself, and for the fact he had no one to ask for the truth. Why hadn't he been told when he could ask questions?

He pulled himself from the bathroom floor, washed his hands, and took a drink of water. The house was dark with only the light from his bedroom piercing the night. He made his way through the house, checking to make sure the doors were locked and Lois was safely in bed.

He stood in her bedroom doorway watching her sleep. Was it possible that prim-and-proper Lois had had an illicit affair? He wavered between belief and doubt, with doubt doing its darnedest to win. It was too fantastic to be true.

Okay, he thought as he closed her door. Maybe she had an affair, but did it mean, without a shadow of a doubt, Joe wasn't his father? Not really.

Joe was gone. He couldn't ask Lois, so he returned to her journals to confirm or disprove his paternity. Not wanting to take the time for detail, he skimmed the pages for clues, beginning with his own birth.

June 8, 1962
He has arrived, our beautiful baby boy. Joe named him
Logan Joseph McKinnon; Logan after Joe's grandfa-
ther and Joseph for himself, like glue to make a
permanent bond. He says this boy is McKinnon from
head to toe, and I am relieved Joe has embraced Logan
so completely. We've not spoken of the possibility of his
paternity and most likely never will. Logan is a McKin-
non, and I have never loved Joe more. This baby fills
our hearts...

Logan skimmed through the passages outlining his infan-
cy, toddlerhood, and preschool years. Not much was
mentioned of Nate Ford, and the journal became mundane.
Lois continually counted her blessings—her wonderful husband and beautiful son. Life was good and normal as it should
have been, just as he remembered it.

It wasn't until he was eight years old he found Nate's
name mentioned again.

September 1970
I looked at Logan today, really looked, and am shocked
by what I see. As he grows and changes, the boy has
begun to resemble his father more and more and I wor-
ry about how Joe will react. I watch Logan as he plays.
His movements and actions are so much like Nate. It's
difficult to pretend any longer. I thank God Joe loves
the boy so.

June 1977
Logan turned sixteen today and is excited to have his
driver's license. Early this morning Joe took him to the
DMV and of course, he passed with flying colors. He
does everything well. When they arrived home, Logan
almost cried when he saw the car in the driveway
topped with a bow. It was Joe's idea to buy the car. He
loves that boy so much. I can't help but wonder what
Joe thinks when he looks at Logan now. He has grown

*tall and lanky and bears such a resemblance to Nate. I
feel I must watch myself and my emotional displays toward Logan for I worry Joe may think feelings for Nate
remain. There is a fondness, a small space he occupies
in my heart, but it isn't love in the romantic sense. Only
Joe stirs my heart that way.*

June 1980
*Logan graduated from high school today, with honors
of course. He is so much to be proud of. He fills my
heart with joy. The ceremony was moving. Logan gave
an impassioned speech as valedictorian of his class. He
is an adult now, no longer my little boy but a man. As I
send him on his way to begin his life, I am sad. There
are so many things I wish to say, so many things to tell
him. But I remain silent for fear Joe will misunderstand
and be hurt. There is no longer any doubt Logan is
Nate Ford's son. There is little of me in him. Physically, he is a replica of his father and I wonder sometimes
if we were fair to Nate in denying him his son. What
does Nate think of him? He sold his orchard and moved
away before Logan's birth. I know Nate is aware of him
and wonder sometimes how much he cares. Is it fair to
Logan to continue this deception?*

Logan placed the journal in its box and closed the lid. The
bones in his family's closet rattled so loud, the roar deafened.

If what he read was true, he wasn't Joe McKinnon's son,
and everything he'd always believed was a lie. He didn't want
to believe it, wanted nothing more than to forget he'd ever
read those journals. But he couldn't, and first thing in the
morning he planned to do something about it.

He'd find Nate Ford and get some answers.

Chapter 17

Light drizzle soaked Logan's jacket as he stood across the street reading the sign fronting the dockside building.

Ford's Ocean Charters

Fishing Charters—Whale Watching Excursions

He'd spent the previous day searching the Internet for anyone name Nate or Nathaniel Ford and came up with five in the Internet white pages. They were scattered across the country like downed bowling pins—one in Florida, one in Montana, two in California, and this one, in Westport, Washington, only twenty miles from King's Bay.

Fear had rooted him to his chair as he stared at the computer screen. Curiosity drove him down the road. Adrenalin flooded his system. He wanted to know the truth.

Or did he?

He hesitated, unsure if this was the right thing to do. What if the guy was an incredible jerk? What if he wasn't? Then what? What if he liked him? Would that be a betrayal to Joe, the man who raised him as his own? But Joe had spent his life lying to Logan, so did he even matter anymore?

Logan continued to stare at the sign. He knew when he saw the building this would be the right Nate Ford. In her journal, his mother had mentioned Nate came from the coast. His family was involved in commercial fishing. He'd been homesick for the ocean, so it made sense he would come home to the coast after his affair with Lois ended badly for him.

He felt foolish standing in the rain, so he screwed up his courage and crossed the street. He walked slowly, delaying the meeting by studying the window display. Ford's Ocean Charters appeared to do a good business, if the pictures were any indication. Customers proudly displayed their salmon, halibut, tuna, and lingcod. Grown men and boys alike grinned like idiots. Logan studied the pictures, wondering if Nate was in any of them, but they all appeared to be customers. Nate probably manned the camera.

He blew out his breath, tried to calm his jittery stomach, and opened the door. A friendly, dark-haired woman near his own age, wearing jeans and pale-blue flannel, greeted him from behind the counter. Nate's daughter, maybe? Logan didn't want to think of that possibility yet.

"How can I help you?" she asked with a smile.

"I'm looking for Nate Ford." His heart pounded.

"He's in the office." She pointed at a door. "Go ahead and go back."

Logan felt glued to the spot.

"It's okay. This time of year he spends most of his time in there doing bookwork. Believe me, he won't mind if you interrupt." She laughed. "He hates bookwork. You know how fishermen are. They always want to be on the water." She waved him to the door.

Logan nodded. "Thanks." His feet finally moved, carrying him to the door and possible truth. He'd never been so scared.

He pushed the door halfway and peered into an office packed with fishing gear, shelves of books, and metal file cabinets. A battered desk faced the door and was littered with ledgers, pencils, and paper clips. Behind the conventional desk was a computer desk jammed with manuals and a computer so new the stickers remained on the tower.

"Goddamn it," the man sitting at the computer exclaimed. Logan stood still, staring at the man who could be his father. With his back turned to Logan, he hadn't heard the door open, allowing Logan a moment. Though the man sat, Logan concluded he was tall and lanky but still broad shouldered. His hair—straight as Logan's—was gray and fell over the collar of his green flannel shirt. His fingers worked the keyboard tentatively. The computer was new, and he'd obviously not mastered it yet.

"Goddamn it," he muttered again and smacked the keyboard with his hands. "I'd like to get my hands on the idiot who created this stupid program."

Logan couldn't help but smile. It was a McKinnon Software business program. He walked up behind the man and saw the problem immediately.

"Scoot over a second," he said to the man, who was so perturbed at the computer he did as told without glancing from the screen. "It's pretty simple. If you take this out"—he pointed to the screen and moved the mouse—"and put it here, it'll work." He moved the mouse to the top of the screen and clicked a help button. "There's a built-in help system to answer most of your questions, or"—he clicked another button—"if that doesn't do it for you, call this eight hundred number, and a qualified technician will walk you through it." He stepped back.

"I'll be a monkey's uncle. It does work." The man smiled as he admired the screen where all his accounting numbers lined up perfectly. "You know your way around one of these things, don't you?" He laughed.

"Yeah, well, I'm the idiot who created the program. It's one of my best sellers at McKinnon Software." Logan watched as the man turned and looked at him. He thought he saw a flicker of recognition on the older man's face, but if it was there, he hid it quickly.

Logan couldn't breathe as he stared at the man. It was like looking at one of those police aging programs, and he was pretty sure this face would be his in twenty-six years. His mother was right—Logan was a physical replica of Nate Ford. The reality of it nearly knocked out his breath.

"I thank you for the help. I just bought this thing, and I'm trying to transfer my accounts into it." He sat back and looked up at Logan. "What can I do for you? Not much fishing this time of year, but I could set you up with something later in the season."

Logan stepped back and around the desk, feeling his jitters return. He stuffed his hands in his coat pockets, calming the obvious tremor. "Fishing sounds great, but I'm actually looking for information and was hoping you could help me."

"Oh? What kind of information?"

"History, I guess you could say." He looked at Nate and swallowed hard. "Family history."

Nate frowned. "Family history? Don't know how I could help you there, but I'll try."

"Are you Nate Ford?" Logan asked.

"Yes, I am."

"Can I ask you a few questions?" Tension built between his shoulder blades.

"Sure." Nate shrugged and leaned back in his chair, appearing relaxed.

Logan swallowed. "Did you live in Henley in the early sixties?"

The man hesitated and looked at him seriously. "Yes, I did. I had an orchard there for about a year."

Logan nodded, swallowed again. "Did you know a woman named Lois?" He watched the man closely, but his expression remained passive. "Lois McKinnon."

"Yes. I knew a Lois McKinnon. Her husband, Joe, was a friend of mine for a time."

"But did you know *her*?"

"Yes, I did. Why do you ask?" Nate questioned, his eyes narrowed.

Logan took a shaky breath. "She's my mother."

"I thought you might be related to Joe and Lois when you mentioned the name McKinnon. But what do you need to know from me?"

Logan was tempted to leave and not ask the next question but decided he needed to know. He was positive this was the correct Nate Ford, but the guy wasn't giving any indication he knew where Logan's questions were leading.

"Do you know who I am?"

"Joe and Lois' son," he said. "You told me that."

"Do you know who I really am?"

The older man looked as if he was weighing the situation. His eyes never strayed from Logan, but he didn't speak.

Logan persisted, his need to know the truth driving him deeper. "If you are the Nate Ford who lived in Henley in 1961, then you had an affair with her." He watched for a reaction, but Nate remained still, neither denying nor confirming, which Logan took as a confirmation of sorts. An innocent man wouldn't allow him to continue his accusations without a vehement denial. He had to get him to admit the truth.

"You had an affair that produced a child. Do you know who I am now?"

Nate remained calm. "I know who you are, Logan."

Logan started at the use of his first name. He'd only mentioned McKinnon. His heart pounded violently.

Nate continued. "I knew who you were the second I saw you. Did they finally tell you?"

"That you're my father?" Logan tried to control his trembling hands.

Nate nodded.

"So it's true?"

Nate nodded again.

"No, they didn't tell me. I found out on my own." Logan paced as his agitation came to a head. It was true. He walked to the window overlooking the ocean, tried to calm his nerves, and failed. "If you knew who I was when you saw me, why didn't you say something? Why make me go through the motions?"

"Because it wasn't up to me to tell you. What if you didn't

know and I blurted it out? What a mess that would have been," he continued, not waiting for Logan to answer. "I've always wondered if they would tell you. I've been expecting you for years. Lois always had a problem handling secrets and guilt. Her conscience would get to her, and she'd have to talk to someone. For a while, it was me." He looked at Logan calmly. "It's true. So what do we do now?"

"I don't know. I wanted to know if it was true and hadn't thought beyond that. Dad, Joe, never gave any indication he wasn't my father. I need to know who I am. I don't know anymore." He frowned as he turned away from the window and looked at his truth staring back at him. "It's like everything I thought about my life was a lie. For forty-three years I thought I was Logan McKinnon. I don't know who the hell I am now."

"Now wait a minute." Nate stood. "That's pure foolishness. You're the same person you've always been. Knowing about me doesn't change who you are. Okay, maybe genetically you're different than you thought, but you're still the man Joe raised you to be. There's some truth to those sappy cards you see on Father's Day, 'Anyone can be a father, but it takes someone special to be a dad.' Joe was your dad. He raised you. I was nothing but the sperm donor."

Logan saw red. "Well, that answers a lot of questions right there. I'm sorry I bothered you." He turned to leave, not willing to waste another moment in the company of a man who didn't care he'd produced a kid. Sperm donor. That sounded real nice. He stopped in the doorway and looked back, unable to mask his disgust. "You know, Mom wondered if she made the right choice in staying with Dad and denying you your son. I guess she made the right decision after all." He started out the door.

"Logan! Wait!" Nate called to his son's retreating back. Logan gave him one last disgusted glare and walked out the door, moving quickly through the front office, wanting to put distance between himself and the louse who fathered him. He was across the damp street and digging in his pocket for car keys, his anger seething just below the surface, when Nate made it out the door.

"Logan! Wait! You don't understand!" Nate stood on the sidewalk, waiting for passing cars to clear before running to Logan on the opposite side.

"I understand all right." He slid the key in the lock and opened the door as Nate ran to him. "I understand perfectly fine how guys like you operate. Have your fun and ditch the responsibility. I got your number loud and clear, pal."

"That isn't how it happened," Nate said with urgency. "Let me explain."

Logan cut him off as he slid into the driver's seat. "There's nothing to explain. I've always heard about jerks like you, but I never thought I'd have the misfortune of being related to one. I don't need you. Joe McKinnon was my father." Logan slammed the door, started the engine, and drove off, leaving Nate staring after his receding taillights.

He drove north without a destination in mind, just a determination to distance himself from something he wished he didn't know. Ten miles up the coast, he pulled into a cliff-top view area. He slammed the car into park and gripped the steering wheel with both hands in an attempt to steady himself and try to catch his breath. The anger wouldn't subside.

"Shit." With effort, he took one breath and then another until his fury passed. A water bottle thrown carelessly in the passenger seat caught his eye, and he grabbed it, taking a much-needed drink as it all began to make sense to him. All those odd looks his mother had given him over the years suddenly made perfect sense. How it must have bothered her to watch as her son grew to resemble the jerk who fathered him. He imagined that maybe the affair hadn't happened the way Lois described. She was screwed up at the time, and this guy took advantage of her. Maybe he'd forced himself on her. She probably wanted nothing more than to forget the whole incident and then found herself pregnant with the guy's kid. It all began to make perfect sense. It was no wonder his mother hated him. After meeting Nate Ford, it all made perfect sense. Nothing but a sperm donor, he'd said. Yeah, it sure made sense now.

A light mist fell as he sat staring at the ocean. Gray waves repeatedly slapped against the rocky shore, steady and calming. Raindrops trickled in rivulets down the windshield. Logan relaxed and his mind wandered. This explained so much. All the hurt and rejection he'd endured as a child was so easily explained now. He always had his suspicions Lois hated him, and now it was blatantly proven true. How could she have loved him? How could she look at him and not be reminded of her disgrace and the man who'd helped her fall? If he thought about it, there were so many other instances where it was proven over and over his mother would have been happier without him. She was never warm to him, her flesh and blood. All her love was for Joe. He could see that now. They were the cohesive unit, Joe and Lois. Logan, the bastard child belonging to his mother's lover, was the outsider.

But when he thought of Joe, his dad, he had difficulty seeing him in a bad light. Joe was a superb father. If Logan needed something, Joe was the one who took care of it. Joe was the one who made him feel loved. Joe was the perfect father. Logan tried to emulate him with his own children.

But Joe was the one who lied to him for forty-three years and apparently felt no remorse. And maybe that hurt even more. To have that one perfect relationship tarnished with this truth. What else had he lied about?

The sky darkened as the storm progressed, throwing waves higher onto the rocks. The cooling temperature brought Logan back from his distraction. He started the car and drove the miles to King's Bay.

He arrived home shortly before 5:00 p.m. with just enough time to spare. The house was quiet as he shrugged off his wet coat and hung it in the bathroom to dry. Before finding Max, he detoured to look in on Lois and experienced a moment of uncertainly as he watched her sleeping. Could he blame her for her attitude toward him? Now that he'd met Nate, the sperm donor, he could understand Lois and her behavior. Logan closed the bedroom door and wandered into the kitchen to relieve Max, a heavy feeling weighing his heart.

Several days passed. Logan's attempts to put Nate Ford from his mind failed. Nate's words continued to horn into his thoughts. "You don't understand. That isn't how it happened," he'd said. Logan wondered if he was being unfair to the man. Had Lois' depiction of the affair been accurate? Had they been star-crossed lovers? Had they been in love? If the journals were to be believed, they loved each other a great deal. But she loved Joe more.

Logan couldn't put it aside and found himself driving the curved ocean highway to Westport. He wasn't sure what he'd do there but was compelled to go. He pulled into a gas station on the edge of town, filled up, and went inside to pay. A young woman at the register waved.

"Be right with you," she said as she continued to ring up a previous customer's purchase. The counter was filled with containers of bubble gum, chocolates, high school basketball team schedules, and a pile of local newspapers for sale. He read the headlines while he waited, surprised when he found Nate's name. "Local Fisherman Honored for Community Work," it said. Logan glanced through the article describing Nate's altruistic contributions to Westport's less fortunate— fish donations to the shelter, money to the Christmas fund for children, and his time to the high school FFA club.

"Pump number four?" the woman behind the counter asked.

"Yeah, and I'll take one of these." Logan handed her a newspaper and a fifty-dollar bill. "I'm thinking of doing some fishing," he said to the woman. "Would you have any recommendations? There are so many charter services, it's tough to decide."

She didn't hesitate. "Ford's. Nate's one of the best in the area. I'd give him a try if I were you."

Logan nodded. "Thanks for the tip," he said as he walked out the door. In the car, he opened the paper he'd purchased and finished the article on Nate. On its conclusion, he wondered if he'd been too harsh on the man. If his contributions in the area were any indication, he was a generous man with a big heart, not the creep Logan wanted to believe him to be. Even so, he continued his journey around town, asking at the grocery, the hardware store, and the ice cream shop: who ran the best charter service in town? Each time, Nate Ford was the fisherman of choice.

He stopped for lunch at a burger place down the street from Ford's Charter Service with the idea he'd wander that way. After, he walked the two blocks, peering into store windows along the way. A display of model boats caught his eye, and he considered buying one for Derek's collection, when a voice interrupted his thoughts.

"Do you like boats?"

Logan turned to find Nate standing next to him. A furrow of worry lines creased his brow. "My son does. He collects models." He stared at his biological father, emotions churning like a chocolate milkshake in a blender.

"We got off on the wrong foot, Logan," Nate said. "Sperm donor was an unfortunate choice of words."

Logan continued to stare at the remorseful man. "I'd say so."

"If I could, I'd like to make amends. There's something I'd like to show you." He looked at Logan, dark-brown eyes filled with hope.

"I don't know." Logan frowned.

"Please, Logan. I'd rehearsed that day in my mind for years, and I'm afraid I failed against the reality of it. That wasn't the way it was supposed to go. Please come to the office. It won't take long."

Logan hesitated. He'd come to Westport to learn what he could. Shouldn't he hear the man out? "All right."

Logan waited while Nate opened a closet door and removed a large cardboard box. It said Logan in bold print on the side of the box. Nate waved him over to the desk and opened the box as Logan peered in. Inside he saw scrapbooks, photo albums, and school Christmas programs. Nate looked at Logan with tears swimming in his eyes and spoke with a catch in his powerless voice.

"I want to get something straight with you before you go tearing out of here with the wrong idea again. I would have been your dad if she'd chosen me. But she didn't want me. It was her choice that I not know you. Not mine. It was never mine." Nate's hands shook, rattling the box he gripped. He turned away. "I promised your dad I would stay away from you, and I did. I've kept that promise for forty-three years."

Logan stared at Nate's back, stunned by the emotion. Nate had attempted flippancy with his sperm donor comment, but apparently, he cared deeply. Logan wasn't sure how to react.

"Was it her idea or Dad's?" Logan said quietly.

"Joe said it was hers, and I believe it. Lois never intended to leave him, and I'm sure she promised Joe she'd never see me again."

"But she broke her word to Dad and sent you all this stuff? She must have reconsidered her decision."

Nate's voice shook. "No. She never did. I haven't had any contact with her since she told me she was pregnant in '61."

"Then how did you get all this stuff?"

Nate turned to him, eyes wet, a small smile on his lips. "I

was there." He picked up a scrapbook and opened it to a picture of Logan's kindergarten Christmas program. "I was there. Standing in the back. I'd let my hair grow longer, had a mustache, and wore a hat so no one would recognize me. I bought one of those expensive cameras with a zoom lens so I could take pictures of you. I was there, Logan." He handed Logan the scrapbook and watched as Logan flipped through the pages of Christmas programs, basketball games, school plays, and high school and college graduations. "I never left you. Never."

Logan felt a lump in his throat. "Why? Mom said she wasn't sure who my father was. Why put so much effort into me if you couldn't be sure?"

"There was never any doubt in my mind. She and Joe had been trying to have a baby for ten years and couldn't. She's with me for nearly four months and gets pregnant. It doesn't take a genius to figure that out. When I saw you in your Christmas program, I knew. You looked like me at that age. I never doubted I was your father."

"Then why didn't you fight for your rights as my father? If you were so sure, why didn't you force them to acknowledge you?"

Nate laughed. "My rights as a father? I didn't have any rights. That's a modern phenomenon that fathers have rights. Back then she held all the cards. It was 1961. You have to think about the times we lived in. There hadn't been a sexual revolution or women's liberation. Having an affair was wrong, and the product of that affair would have been treated poorly. Would you have wanted to go through life as Nate Ford's bastard? I don't think so, and we wouldn't have done it to you." He sighed. "As difficult as it was, she did the right thing. If she had divorced Joe and married me, everyone would have known immediately, and Lois couldn't have borne the scandal. She was a respectable woman."

"How respectable was it to have an affair?" Logan countered.

"She fell, briefly. But she righted herself quickly enough when she found out about you."

"But was it fair to you?" Logan asked, trying to understand.

"It was as fair as the times allowed, Logan. People thought differently then. A family was a husband, wife, and baby. Not husband, wife, baby, and baby's father. There was no way to make it work in the framework in which we lived." He laughed. "If we did it now, some TV producer would have us move into the same house, fill it with cameras, and turn us into a reality show. But in 1961, people didn't have sex outside of marriage. Or if they did, it wasn't talked about."

"But you and Mom did," Logan accused.

"Yeah, Lois and I did. I didn't know she was married, or I'd never have pursued her. Yes, I seduced her and got her into my bed, but I had no idea she was married. She wasn't wearing a ring, and she didn't tell me. When I found out, I tried to stay away from her, but she came back. We were like a magnet and steel. You can hate me for that if you want, but you have to accept the fact that if we hadn't had our affair, you wouldn't exist."

Logan couldn't argue with that logic. "I don't think hate is the right term for what I'm feeling. Not today anyway. I really don't know what I'm feeling other than anger over being deceived all my life. Do you know what this is like for me? I have to believe *you* that this is true, and I don't want to. I don't want to think my mother was capable of cheating on my father and he could live with this kind of dishonesty. I don't want to believe it."

"But you know you have to. There is too much evidence to prove it's true. Just looking in the mirror gives you the confirmation. What we do about it, I don't know." He smiled at Logan. "All I can say is, having this conversation with you is a dream come true for me. For forty-three years, I've wished for the day you would walk in my door and I could talk to you. I'm sorry if that upsets you, but I've lived with this for a long, long time. And if you leave here today and I never see you again, well, I'll live with that as well. At least I've had this conversation with you." Nate plopped down in his desk chair and relaxed. "Have a seat. I could make some coffee, if you like."

Logan sat in the chair opposite the desk, his tension settling down to manageable. "No thanks on the coffee." He glanced at his watch. "I have to be getting back soon."

"Oh." Nate was obviously disappointed. "Since we've got things calmed down a bit, I was hoping I could buy you dinner."

Logan found he was disappointed as well. He'd come here wanting to hate this man and found it difficult. "That would be nice, but I have to be back at Mom's by five."

"How are your folks? I lost track of them when they sold their property."

"After they sold the orchard, they moved to King's Bay. Dad passed away last month, and Mom has Alzheimer's disease. I'm staying with her until a spot opens up in a care facility near my house in Vancouver." Logan watched as emotion ran across Nate's face.

"When you say you have to believe me, you mean that quite literally, don't you? You have no one else to ask. I'm sorry, Logan. All of this must be difficult for you. Losing Joe, finding out about me, and dealing with Lois' illness."

"It all came at me at once, but it's better now. I have a nursing service with Mom during the day, but he leaves at five."

"Alzheimer's. Poor Lois." He thought for a moment. "You said your parents didn't tell you about me. How did you find out? As far as I know, no one knew but the three of us."

"Mom kept a journal starting when she was six years old. I found a pile of them stored in the closet a couple of weeks ago."

"Oh? I didn't know she did that." He appeared uncomfortable with the thought. "What kind of things did she put in this journal?"

"Everything. Details of everything."

Nate raised his brow. "Everything? So you already know a great deal about all this."

Logan nodded. "A lot, but there are holes I wouldn't mind having filled in. She wrote about everything that happened to her though." He couldn't help but smile at Nate's discomfort.

"Like what?"

"Oh, let's see. Cat food, for one."

Nate laughed. "It's how we met. The cat food display at Sloan's Grocery. I had this big, stupid cat that hated me. He was a lousy mouser, so I had to buy tons of cat food for him."

"There was also something about skinny dipping in a river, kissing in the orchard." Nate started to look uncomfortable again, but Logan continued. "You were a sly dog. She didn't have a chance."

"All's fair in love and war." Nate smiled. "Okay, so you know all my secrets. I already said I seduced her." He laughed. "She was such a beautiful woman, I couldn't help myself. I saw her in Sloan's and decided I had to have her for my own. She wouldn't go out with me and wouldn't say why, so I assumed she was shy. I set out to seduce her and was completely stunned when it worked. If she had told me right off she was married, I wouldn't have done it, but I thought she was just a pretty girl who turned me upside down every time I looked at her."

"It was pretty tricky of you to request grocery delivery to get her out to your house."

"That," Nate said defensively, "was purely coincidence at first. Old Mr. Sloan was the one to suggest the grocery delivery. A new store had opened across town, and he was worried about losing business. I mentioned I was working my place alone and had a tough time getting into town, so he said he'd have his kid bring the stuff out to me. I thought it was a great idea. I had no idea he would send Lois, and when he did, I guess I took advantage of the situation. I can't say I'm sorry I did."

"But didn't you think it was wrong to continue seeing her after you found out she was married to your friend?" Logan asked, trying to get a handle on the guy.

"Of course it was wrong. The whole damned thing was wrong from start to finish, but I couldn't help myself. By the time I found out she was married, I was already half in love with her. In my own defense, I did try to call it off after the first time, but she came back. Told me she needed me with these big ol' tears running down her face. I was putty in her hands. You're married?"

Logan nodded.

"Imagine falling in love and not being able to be with her. Imagine she is living with someone else, sleeping in his bed every night. It's tough, isn't it? But I had some stupid idea she would leave Joe and marry me. I asked her frequently, but she always said no. I thought when you came along, she would see it my way and leave him, but she wouldn't. She loved Joe too much. Hell, I loved Joe. He was a wonderful guy."

"He was." Logan looked at his watch and frowned. "I have to get back." He stood and held out his hand to Nate. "Thanks for your time. It's been interesting talking with you."

Nate stood and took his hand. "Can you come back sometime? I don't want to pressure you, Logan, but I would enjoy talking with you again. Maybe I can fill in some of those holes for you." He looked at Logan hopefully.

Logan thought for a moment as feelings of guilt crept in, feelings of betraying Joe. "Okay," he said, his curiosity getting the best of him. "I may only be around here for a few more weeks. As soon as Mom's place opens up, I'll be moving her."

"Maybe you could come back for lunch tomorrow? There's a great chowder place down the street. My treat."

Logan nodded. "Sure. Lunch tomorrow. Thanks. I'll see you then." He left Nate Ford with a strange feeling of kinship he hadn't expected and actually looked forward to lunch the following day.

⌒≈

Logan spent the following morning doing laundry. Lois wanted to help but couldn't quite put the laundry pile together with the washing machine, so Logan demonstrated the procedure. Together, they sorted the clothing into colored piles, and she helped dump them in the washer. She proved an able helper if he told her what to do and was pleased with the activity. As long as he remembered she had the mental abilities of a young child, they got along fine.

He thought about her journal entries while they worked and found he had a newfound patience with her. Knowing she had been proud of him and had loved him made a tremendous difference in his responses to her, and Logan wished he could talk to her about the things that pulled her away from him at an early age. He understood now.

Shortly before Max's arrival, Logan brewed tea and sat at the table with his mother. He helped her spoon the sugar into the cup and cut a banana in half for them to share.

"Mom, do you remember Nate Ford?" He'd decided to ask to see what she said. If it upset her, she'd probably forget about it in five minutes anyway. She looked at him with blank eyes, and he assumed she was off somewhere and wouldn't be able to answer.

"Nate," she said with a smile.

"Who was he?"

She frowned as if unable to put the thought together and shook her head. "Joe hurt him." She looked at her hands and wiggled her fingers. "Bloody hands."

"Why did Dad hurt him?"

"My fault." She looked at Logan thoughtfully, and he wondered what was going on in her mind. Her thoughts were usually such a jumble, words transposed and misused, but occasionally she spoke with clarity.

"What did you do?" he asked, watching her closely and waiting for her response. She sat still as if considering her words, and when he thought she'd trailed off completely, she knocked him for a loop. With a girlish giggle, she gave him a smile.

"We made a baby."

Logan sat in the chowder house awaiting Nate's arrival. He'd purposefully arrived early to allow time to think. It was an undeniable fact he was Nate's son. Nate confirmed it, and now Lois, in her vague way, confirmed it as well. It didn't matter if he liked it or not, it was the truth. He supposed they could have DNA testing if he wanted scientific substantiation, but the fact he was the spitting image of Nate made it unnecessary.

The waitress seated him near the large windows, and he gazed out at the pier and marina. The previous day's clouds had cleared, and sunshine glinted from the waves as his mind wandered. If Nate had raised him, he wondered, would he have grown up here? Would he have spent his time on fishing boats? Or would Nate and Lois have stayed in Henley? Most likely, he'd have grown up on the water and would be a fisherman like Nate instead of a computer programmer. The idea wasn't unappealing, and he again felt guilt. Was he being disloyal to Joe?

"Hey, Logan, you're early," Nate greeted him with a wide smile as he sat in the seat opposite Logan. The waitress set menus before the men, looking from one to the other.

"Gee, Nate. You two must be related or something," she said, looking back and forth.

"Yeah, something like that," Nate said with a grin.

"I'll be back in a minute for your order," she said, stepping from the table.

Logan laughed at Nate's pleased expression. "That comment makes you happy?"

"Thrilled. I've always seen it. It's nice to know other people do too."

The waitress returned for their orders, and the men settled in with coffee, looking at each other across the table.

"I don't know where to start," Logan said.

"Which holes do you want filled? I don't know what your mother put in her journals. Fill me in, and we'll take it from there."

Logan gave him a rough outline. Nate nodded as he spoke. "All true. But you want my perspective on things." He leaned forward on his elbows, his gray hair flopping across his forehead. He smiled as he thought. "She knocked my socks off the first time I saw her. She was pretty, built nice, and all I wanted to do was kiss her." He looked at Logan and laughed. "Maybe I should tone down the physical references when talking about your mother."

"I know she was attractive, but I'm having a hard time imagining Mom as a hottie." Logan laughed and found himself relaxing.

"She did it for me. After the first time I saw her, I started making excuses to shop at Sloan's Grocery. Stopped in several times a week whether I needed something or not." He chuckled. "I had the best-stocked cupboards in Henley. But it was worth every dime I spent to see that pretty lady. I asked her out every time I saw her. Never failed, every time I approached her, Mr. Sloan showed up and interrupted. She never actually said no, so I kept trying. The first time she arrived with my groceries, I thought she was a gift from heaven. I was so doggoned lonely in that orchard by myself I could hardly stand it. So I talked her into staying for some lemonade, and we talked and talked. One thing led to another, and we ended up in bed a few weeks later. Sorry, Logan, if that makes you uncomfortable to hear, but it's what happened. Anyway, after the fact, she tells me she's married—and to a guy I'd become good friends with." He sighed. "I'd arrived in Henley as green as summer grass. I didn't know an apple tree from a cherry tree, and I had eighty acres of fruit to take care of. I was in the local café for a late lunch one day and heard some guys at the center table talking fruit, so I eavesdropped. One of the guys was talking about what he needed to do in his orchard, and it was something I'd never heard of, so I interrupted and asked him about it. They invited me to have a cup of coffee and taught me what I needed to know. Twice every week this bunch got together for pie and coffee, and they accepted the greenhorn into the group. One of them was your dad. Joe took me under his wing, stopped by my place a few times, and gave me direction."

"When I found out I'd slept with his wife, I about died on the spot. I knew his wife was named Lois, but I'd never met her, so I didn't know THIS Lois was HIS Lois. Needless to say, I was devastated. I was in love with this woman already, and there was no way I could have her."

"Had Dad ever mentioned they were having problems?"

"No. Never. When he talked of Lois, it was all sweetness and sunshine. He loved her to distraction, and it was obvious. But from what Lois told me, they'd been growing apart for several years. She hadn't been able to conceive a child, and it weighed heavily on her. It wouldn't be a big thing now, but back then it's what a woman was supposed to do. Keep the home, raise children. Lois couldn't do what every other woman could do easily, and it didn't help that June Cleaver was on TV every week being the perfect mother. Poor Lois was caught in an era where a woman without children didn't feel like a woman. There were no local sperm banks, fertility clinics, or surrogate mothers to help her out. I guess I came along at a particularly low time for her. Her friend Anne had four children already, and it distressed her."

"From what I understand," Logan said, "Dad accepted it and was comforting."

"And that irritated her more than anything," Nate said. "She was devastated every month when she realized she wasn't pregnant, and good-hearted Joe was comforting. She wanted him to be as upset as she was, and he was comforting. Poor guy couldn't win." He sipped his coffee. "Anyway, I watched Lois drive out that day and honestly thought I'd never see her again. I wouldn't do that to Joe. But a week later, she came driving in, cried those big tears, and said she needed me. I held off as best I could, but I have to say, the second time, she seduced me. I fought it but had to give in eventually. She's a determined woman when she puts her mind to it. And I'm only human, after all."

Bowls of hot chowder and a basket of rolls were brought to the table. Both men dug in as Nate continued.

"I told her every time she came over we had to stop seeing each other. She agreed every time but still came back. Each time she left, I fully believed she wouldn't be back. Eventually, we stopped saying it and settled into a regular routine. I'd order groceries once a week, and she'd lie about a shopping trip or an appointment a second day each week. The most time we ever had together was the week your dad went hunting, and she spent most of the week with me. She'd go to work and run home to feed the cats, but for the most part, she was with me all week." He took a bite of chowder and grabbed a roll from the basket. "A short time later, she told me about you. At first I was elated. I knew you were mine, and I was sure Lois would leave him and marry me. When she walked out the door for the last time, I thought I would die…"

Chapter 18

Nate—December 1961

Nate stood still as death as Lois walked out the door. He'd always maintained the fantasy she'd leave Joe and marry him, and now she made it perfectly clear it would never happen. She'd go back to her husband, confess, and get on with raising the child.

His child. He knew without a doubt it was his.

He wasn't sure how long he stared at the door, his mind devoid of thought. He stumbled to the sofa and fell flat on his back, his eyes fixed on a crack in the ceiling he needed to repair. Could a broken heart be felt physically? He wondered as a slow ache spread through his system. He shouldn't be surprised she left him. She'd never been his to begin with.

She belonged to Joe.

She'd always been Joe's.

She wouldn't marry Nate and had never considered it. How many times had he told her he loved her? Countless times, as if saying it over and over would make her love him. She'd said it once. Just once as she told him she was leaving and wouldn't be back. And the one time she had said it, she'd followed it with those heartbreaking words: "I love him more." Nate groaned as the scene replayed in his head. He'd been such a fool.

It was only a matter of time before Joe would come after him. For all Nate knew, she was confessing her sins at that moment, and knowing Joe, he wouldn't let it go. He'd require justice, and Nate was pretty sure that meant pounding his wife's lover into the ground.

Hadn't he known it would come to this when it all started? He'd known the first day when she'd sobbed about being married that one day a furious husband would come to seek revenge. A guy couldn't expect to get away with a thing like that. If the roles were reversed, he'd want to do some pounding too, and he'd take great joy in it.

Headlights bouncing down the orchard road brought him from his lethargy, and Nate knew she'd confessed and the headlights were Joe's. Nate looked at the wall clock and noted calmly she'd been quick about it. Only ninety minutes had passed since she walked out his door.

Nate watched with passive resignation as the pickup truck stopped in his driveway, and Joe climbed out radiating obvious rage. He could see it in Joe's face and tense shoulders. Nate walked out his door and stood on the porch that was slick with ice he hadn't cleared. He patiently awaited his sentence as his judge, jury, and executioner stepped away from the truck.

"Nate," Joe said as he neared the steps. He nearly vibrated with fury.

"Joe."

Joe stood at the base of the steps, visibly attempting to contain the ire crawling through him. "You filthy son of a bitch." His voice shook. "You know why I'm here?"

Nate stood stone still. "Yes."

"Do you deny it?"

"No."

"So you admit you touched my wife? That you trespassed on what is mine?"

Nate nodded. "Yes." He was too heartbroken to try to defend his actions, so he stood and waited for the beating he knew would come. "I love her," he said quietly.

"She's not yours to love. She's mine!"

"I know that now. I didn't when it started," Nate said

Joe climbed the steps. The first punch came fast and took Nate by surprise. Joe's fist connected soundly with his jaw, sending him backward into the door. The next one crunched his nose and blackened his eye. Blood dripped to his shirt. Successive blows knocked the wind from him, bruised his ribs, and had him sucking for air on his knees. The kick to his stomach sent him sprawling onto the icy porch, and he considered himself lucky he'd fallen before Joe could put his knee in his groin. Nate did nothing to defend himself against the onslaught. He knew he deserved every bit of it.

"You slimy little bastard," Joe said as he stood over him, his boot on his back holding him down, forcing him to lie in his own blood. "What do you have to say in your defense? You seduced my wife. Is that how you repay my friendship? I wish I'd never laid eyes on lowlife scum like you."

Nate had taken everything he could and broke down and wept. "Just kill me, Joe. Put your boot on my head and crush my scull." He sobbed. "If I can't have her, there's no point to anything anymore. I love her. You should understand that. I love her!"

"You stay the hell away from her. Do you hear me?" He removed his foot from Nate's back and backed away. "If you so much as speak to her again, I will kill you. I promise you that." Joe walked away, leaving his wife's lover bleeding on the porch.

Nate laid on the cold porch long after Joe's truck retreated down the orchard road. He ached from head to toe and wasn't sure if he could get up. He lay inert until the temperature dipped low enough to reach his numbed consciousness, and his tears froze to his cheeks. He pushed up to his hands and knees and managed to open the door and crawl inside.

He woke the following morning in the center of his living room floor. The blood from his nose had caked, his eye had swollen shut, and his stomach felt like a truck had driven over it. He rolled to his back with a groan and stared at the ceiling, filled with despair.

How would he go on? His life was suddenly hollow, devoid of anything of substance. He'd lost Lois and the child he knew belonged to him. Joe, the friend he'd betrayed, would have it all. Lois, the child, everything.

Or would he? Would Joe be unable to forgive Lois for her infidelity? Would he be unable to accept a child who wasn't his own? Maybe Joe would cast her out, and she would come back to him. Nate was filled with a strange kind of hope.

On New Year's Day, that train of thought was swiftly derailed when Joe's pickup again bounced down his orchard road. Nate tensed at the sight. His nose was healing nicely, the black eye was fading, and he didn't think Joe had the right to pound him a second time. He toyed with the idea of grabbing his shotgun but resisted when Joe stepped from his truck and stood uncomfortably in the driveway.

"I think I got the point the first time, Joe," he called from the safety of his porch. "Get off my land before I call the sheriff."

"I need to talk to you," Joe called back. "For Lois."

"How do I know you speak for her?"

"You have to take my word for it. I'm not the one with a credibility problem here. You can trust my word. Can I come up and talk to you?"

Nate hesitated, leery of letting Joe near him again. This could be a ploy to beat the crap out of him again.

"I'm not going to touch you, Nate. I'm here because Lois asked me to talk to you." He squinted toward the porch.

Nate frowned. "Okay. I just put on a pot of coffee." He turned and walked in the door, not waiting for Joe to respond.

Joe walked in and stopped in the kitchen doorway.

"Have a seat." Nate set a coffee cup on the table. The two men sat on opposite sides, each eyeing the other with caution.

"Why would Lois send you to talk to me?"

"She wants to know your intentions toward the child. Since there's a possibility it's yours, she wants to know what you intend to do."

"I'd say there's more than a possibility it's mine," Nate countered.

"That's true. It's a strong possibility. But you've got to think this thing through. She doesn't want to leave me. Think about the consequences if you want anything to do with this child. Tongues will wag. Gossip will run rampant."

Nate frowned and looked away. "So you want me to walk away from my child?"

"Lois does. She's terrified of the scandal. She wants this child raised in a clean atmosphere, not one where her child is called bastard or other filthy names. She doesn't want people whispering when she walks down the street." Joe looked at Nate intently. "You know it would happen as well as I do. You know how people are around here with their noses in everyone's business. It's a small town, and it wouldn't be long before everyone would know. Lois couldn't live with it."

Nate winced, felt his stomach churn. "What about you? How would you feel about raising my child? Would you treat it differently than you would a child of your own?"

"At first, I couldn't stand the thought the baby could be yours. But Lois and I talked about it, and she's correct in saying that no matter what her sins, this baby is innocent and doesn't deserve to be punished. I'll love any child that comes into my home, whatever the source. I don't have to say this, but I promise you that."

Nate frowned, running his finger along the handle of the cup while he considered his options. He couldn't have Lois. Did it matter so much about the baby? He knew she would have difficulties with the gossip if he tried to have a relationship with the child. How would it be explained?

He felt numb at the prospect, but he agreed. "I'll do it for her. If it's what she wants, I'll stay away." His eyes met Joe's. "I give you my word."

Joe nodded. "I'll have to accept that. Considering the situation, we can't do anything legal, so I'll have to accept your word you'll stay away from her and the child."

Nate nodded, frowned. "For her."

"And we'll never speak of this again. Not to anyone. That's Lois' request. No one can ever know about this, or it will cast suspicion on her and the child. Not even your family, Nate."

"No one will hear it from me." He felt sick at the thought of his parents not knowing their grandchild, but he knew they would be in Henley in a heartbeat demanding to see the baby. No, he'd keep silent.

For her.

"Then that takes care of it." Joe slid back his chair and stood. "We'll raise this baby right, Nate. You have my word."

Nate looked up at Joe and saw his sincerity. "I know you will, Joe. It's the only reason I'm agreeing so quickly. I know you'll do it right."

Joe turned to the door.

"Joe," Nate said quietly.

"Yeah?"

"I didn't mean for any of this to happen. I didn't know she was your wife at first."

"She told me how it happened. I might have been able to forgive you if it had ended after she told you. But you kept seeing her for months. As difficult as it is, I have to forgive her, but you are another matter entirely."

Nate was adrift. Not only had he lost Lois and her company, he also lost Joe and his guidance. Work needed to be done in the orchard, and he wasn't sure what to do or how to go about it. He was a fisherman, not a farmer. He thought about stopping at the café for a cup of coffee and a visit with the other orchardists who frequented the place, but he didn't want to run into Joe.

He knew he should be pruning but was afraid of doing it incorrectly. His orchard was horribly overgrown; any idiot could see it. His trees needed serious attention, so he headed to the library for books on the subject.

After an hour searching the stacks, Nate found several books with everything he needed to know. At the counter, the librarian issued him a new library card, checked out his books, and wished him a pleasant afternoon. He walked from the building, squinting against the bright sunshine, feeling more hopeful than he had on entering. As he rounded the corner, he ran squarely into two women chatting as they walked down the street, nearly knocking one off her feet.

"Oh jeez," he exclaimed as he reached a steadying hand to her. "Excuse me." They both saw at once who the other was and stared in horror. "Lo—" He caught himself. "Ladies, pardon me. I wasn't paying attention." He quickly backed away and walked around the two women, glancing back as he retreated down the street.

"Do you know him?" He heard one of the women ask. "He looked at you kind of funny."

"Him?" Lois responded coolly. "No. I've never seen him before. I think he was startled by running into us."

Nate walked down the street and ducked into an empty alley where he leaned against a brick wall and nearly hyperventilated. He dropped the books he carried on the ground, bent and put his hands to his knees, and caught his breath.

"Shit," he muttered. He couldn't do this. He couldn't bear the thought of running into her this way. It was too hard to see her swelling with his child and know he couldn't be a part of it. She'd be nearly six months pregnant now. He knew enough about pregnancy to know she'd feel little feet kicking. He'd give anything to put his hand on her stomach and feel one of those kicks.

When his heartbeat returned to normal, Nate walked with purpose down the street, turned into an office, and asked if an appointment was necessary.

"No, sir," a pretty receptionist said. "How can we help you?"

"I want to sell my orchard and house as soon as possible," he said without hesitation.

"Henley Realty is happy to assist," she said with a smile as she stood. "Come with me. Mr. Hancock will help you."

He signed on the dotted line, and two weeks later his property sold to an adjoining neighbor who had always wanted to expand. Nate Ford packed up and was gone before the first bloom of spring.

⁓

"I came back here," Nate said to Logan with a wave of his hand. "This is where I was raised. My dad had a commercial fishing operation—salmon, tuna, whatever was running—so I came home to work with him." He waved to the waitress who walked to the table. "Lisa, could we get a warm up on the coffee and maybe a couple pieces of pie? What do you say, Logan?"

"Sounds good. Apple if you have it," he said to waitress.

"Same here."

"Will do. I'll be right back." The waitress left, returning moments later to set plates of pie before the men and pour fresh coffee. Nate nodded his thanks.

"You said you're married?" Nate asked as he dug into his slice.

"Yeah. Twelve years. Her name is Melissa."

"Kids? You mentioned a son."

"Three. Two boys and a girl," Logan said with a proud

smile.

"That's wonderful. Three kids." Nate's eyes teared, and he wiped them away with the back of his hand. "Sorry. It's all this talk about the past. Stirs me up. I haven't talked about any of this in years."

"Does your family know about me?"

"I never did tell my parents. The fact they couldn't know you would have been too hard on them. They're both gone now. Besides, I gave Joe my word, and I never went back on it." He gave Logan a little smile. "My wife knew about you though. You were the reason we met. But I'll get to that."

"What did you tell your family when you came back?" Logan asked.

"They knew there was something wrong with me. I was lethargic and ill tempered. I was out working with my dad one day and about bit his head off over something stupid, and he slammed me up against the pilot house and asked me what was wrong with me." He chuckled. "I couldn't tell him about you, but I could tell him I'd been jilted by the love of my life. He could understand and sympathize with that. When we got back to the dock, he had the crew take care of the boat, and he hauled me off to the closest tavern and we got drunk together. I'd never seen my dad drink anything, and here he was buying me beers so fast I could hardly drink them." He laughed at the memory.

"Did it help?"

"The hangover didn't help much, but it brought things out in the open with my family. If I was in a bad mood, it was more understandable." He sipped his coffee. "I did pretty well for a while, tried not to think about Lois. I'd left all of that behind and was trying to get on with my life and forget completely about my time in Henley, but for some reason, I'd continued my subscription to the Henley newspaper by mail. I usually threw them in a pile and forgot about them. I'm not sure why, but my mother picked one up and read it. I about died when she said, 'Aren't these people friends of yours?' and pointed out a mention of Joe and Lois." He paused and looked out the window. "It was a birth announcement." He looked back at Logan with wet eyes. "I had a son."

June 1962
He wasn't sure what drove him to do it, but Nate threw some clothes in his car and hit the road. Destination, sure disaster if Joe found out. From what the article said, Logan Joseph McKinnon was already five days old and would leave the hospital in another day or so. Nate drove as if a cattle prod jabbed his butt and made Henley by evening. His hands shook as he signed the motel register and took his key.

A call to the hospital the following morning confirmed the nursery visiting hours—2:00 p.m., he was told. He killed time in his room throughout the morning, had lunch in the greasy spoon near the motel, and by two was parking his car in the hospital lot. He sat for a while, calculating the best way to see the baby without Joe knowing, deciding to go to the nursery and see how it went.

Carefully, he made his way through the hospital corridors, dodging lunch carts and swift-walking nurses. When he reached the nursery, he almost lost his nerve. If he were to run into Joe, this would be the place.

He looked up and down the corridor. Satisfied he was alone, Nate crept to the nursery window and saw six sleeping and crying babies. There were three boys and three girls, according to the pink and blue blankets in the bassinets, but he couldn't make out the name tags to know which infant was Logan.

"Which baby are you here to see?" a voice said from behind, nearly scaring him to death. Nate turned to see a young nurse in a starched uniform. "Sorry, I didn't mean to startle you."

"That's okay. Which is the McKinnon baby?"

She pointed. "Middle of the back row. He's a sweetie. Very mild mannered, doesn't cry a lot."

"Is he healthy?" Nate asked as he stared.

"Very. When he does cry, you know he wants something," she said. "Would you like to see him?"

"I couldn't do that," he said to the nurse's quizzical look. "See, he's my…cousin's baby, and well, we've had an argument, and he'd be mad to see me here."

"But you think enough of him to come see his baby? That is so sweet."

"Babies come into the world innocent, right? He shouldn't suffer for the sins of the adults around him."

"That's true," she agreed. "I may have a solution for this. Mr. McKinnon doesn't usually come in until late afternoon, so I don't think he'll see you. Come with me." She smiled and motioned for him to follow. They walked through a door down the hall from the nursery that appeared to be an examination room. "Wait here for a moment."

She left him alone, returning moments later with a baby in her arms.

"I have to stay here with you, but if you want to hold him, this is your chance. Would you like to?" She held the baby out to Nate.

He was stunned to see his son up close. "He's beautiful." He took the baby in his arms and thought him the most precious thing he'd ever seen.

His son.

"I'll be right over here if you need me." She moved to a small alcove, giving Nate privacy.

Nate was awed by his son, so perfect in every way. He pulled back the blanket and touched his little fingers with his own. Logan opened his eyes and looked up at Nate and yawned. Tears formed in his eyes, and at that moment, the reality of what he'd done hit him. He'd given away his son, and this would be the only time he'd be allowed to hold him.

222 · SHARLEEN SCOTT

Once Joe and Lois took him home, he'd never see Logan again. The pain hit him like a blast in his heart, and he wondered how he would live with it.

Not wanting the nurse to see his agony, he held back the tears and smiled at his son. It had to be his imagination, but he thought Logan smiled back.

"I love you, Logan. I'll always love you," he whispered as he kissed the baby's forehead. He breathed in deeply the baby scent of talcum powder and milk. Nate stood in the examining room, cuddling his son as long as the nurse allowed. When she placed her hand on his arm and announced the baby needed to be taken to his mother, Nate nearly refused to let go.

"I'm sorry," the nurse said softly. "But I need to take him now. Maybe you and your cousin will reconcile, and you can see him again."

Nate nodded and released his hold. He watched as she took Logan from the room and had to control the urge to chase after her and take him back. It was so unfair, he thought. Logan was his son.

He left the hospital in a haze, the scent of baby Logan still on his hands. When he reached his motel room, he dropped on the bed and sobbed for the child he wouldn't be allowed to know. The punishment for his sins had begun, and it would be a lifetime sentence.

Nate returned to the coast and never told his family why he'd taken off at a dead run and returned depressed. He threw himself into work, spending as much time on the fishing boats with his dad as possible, and tried not to think about how old Logan was that day. When it became more than he could handle, he'd disappear for a few days, leaving his family worried. Sometimes he went down the coast. Sometimes he drove aimlessly and found a motel room when he tired.

After a year of these wanderings, he started making trips to Seattle. He liked the larger city and enjoyed getting lost in the crowd. Not knowing anyone allowed him to meander and wallow in his depression. Nate wondered sometimes if Lois ever thought of him. Was she so involved with raising their son she could forget the man who'd given her the child? Did she ever think of Logan as a precious gift he'd given her? That's how Nate came to think of him, as a gift. He hoped Lois realized what giving her that gift meant to him. And what it cost him.

He wandered through the Seattle streets early that day, no destination in mind. He chose a direction and walked. It didn't matter where he went. Up a hill, around a corner, and then another, until he tired and turned back. He didn't come to Seattle for a fun time, but to think and sometimes flounder in self-pity. He was a champion in the self-pity department these days.

His walk took him through a residential area and into a neighborhood of small shops. The smell of baked goods, yeasty and sweet, caught his attention, and his stomach growled, reminding him of his skipped breakfast that morning. He wandered down the street, following the scent, and soon stood in front of a large bakery window. A wedding cake and birthday cakes filled the shelf, but it was the one in the center that caught his eye and sent the jolt through his system.

It was yellow—bright as sunshine and sunflowers—and trimmed with baseballs and bats. The words in the center read Happy Birthday, Slugger. Nate stared at the cake, his feet rooted to the spot, not realizing tears ran down his face until a hand squeezed his arm.

"Are you okay?" she asked softly.

"What?" he said, startled.

"Are you all right?" she asked again.

He looked down at the girl who spoke to him. She was slim and barely reached his shoulder. Her dark hair hung down her back in a fat braid, and her dark eyes looked at him with concern.

He sniffed and wiped at his eyes. "I'm fine. Thanks." He

stepped away, but she called to him.

"Are you sure? Maybe you'd like to come in for a coffee or something? We make pretty good coffee."

Nate wasn't sure why, but he turned back and followed her into the bakery. She seated him in a corner booth, poured a cup of coffee, and sat opposite.

"I'm Gracie," she said. "I run the counter here."

"I'm Nate," he said. "And today is my son's second birthday." He swallowed hard as he said it, unsure why he'd blurted it out that way.

"Do you want to buy a cake for him?"

"I would love to buy him a cake and a present, but I can't." He stared into the coffee cup, mesmerized by wisps of steam.

Gracie placed her hand gently on his. "Why can't you?"

"Because…he isn't mine to give gifts to anymore."

"Why?"

Nate blew out his breath, and blinked back the tears threatening to spill again, and began to explain everything to a total stranger, finding it easier than he'd expected. The story poured from him, beginning with meeting Lois in the store and ending with holding Logan in the hospital. Gracie listened to his story, asking occasional questions. He held nothing back, told her every detail, and then watched for her reaction. He felt the most tremendous relief at having shared his story, and he thought he understood Lois' compulsion to return to him over and over. Keeping a secret of this magnitude was nearly impossible.

"That is the saddest thing I've ever heard. How horrible it must be for you to not know your son. How do you bear it, Nate?"

"Not well, apparently. You saw me out front. I think of him until I'm about to go out of my mind. He's my son, and I can't celebrate his birthday."

Gracie reached across the table, took his hands in hers, and smiled. It wasn't a come-on gesture but one of true empathy.

"Wait here a minute, okay?" She released his hands and ran into the back of the bakery, returning minutes later with a small birthday cake, candles, and two plates. "Why can't we celebrate your son's birthday?" She grinned as she set the cake and plates on the table.

Nate stared at the little cake decorated with baseballs and bats, and smiled. "Why not?" he agreed.

Gracie poked two candles into the frosting and lit them. She sang "Happy Birthday" and encouraged Nate to join her.

"Okay," she said when they finished singing. "Make a wish for Logan." She stared at him with wide eyes. Nate closed his eyes and blew out the candles. He looked at Gracie and smiled.

"I wished—"

"It won't come true if you tell me."

"Okay," he said with a smile. More than anything he wanted this wish to come true. He'd wished to know his son someday.

They ate their cake and talked. Nate was surprised at how easy it was to talk with Gracie. He'd unburdened his troubles onto her shoulders, and she hadn't run. She was the most sympathetic and compassionate woman he'd ever met.

When they finished eating, Gracie's boss glared at her from the counter, and she had to excuse herself.

"Don't leave," she whispered. "I get off work in half an hour." Then much louder she asked, "Can I get you another cup of coffee, sir?"

"That would be great. Thanks." He sipped coffee and nibbled birthday cake, watching Gracie wait on customers until her shift ended. She removed her apron and grabbed her purse.

"Come with me," she said, and Nate followed, intrigued with the slim young woman. Gracie took his hand and pulled him down the street two blocks before turning into a small shop. Nate peered around the toy shop packed to the ceiling with every imaginable plaything.

"What are we doing here?" he asked her.

"Shopping," she said as if he were the silliest man she'd ever met.

"For what?"

"A birthday present."

"For who?"

Gracie blew out a frustrated breath. "Your son, silly. For Logan."

"But what's the point? I can't see him."

"They have a mailbox, don't they?"

"Of course."

"There you go." She grabbed his hand and pulled him through the store. When she'd finished, Nate held a brown teddy bear wearing a baseball uniform, and a train with clickity-clack wheels. She walked him to the counter to make their purchase. Nate paid for the items and looked at Gracie for guidance.

"Do you ship?" she asked the clerk.

"Certainly."

"Wrap these in paper a little boy would like and mail them, please. What's the address, Nate?" she demanded. He looked at her for a moment before giving the clerk Joe and Lois' address.

"Address it to Logan McKinnon, please," he said.

The clerk nodded. "We have a display of birthday cards over there if you'd like to include one."

Nate shook his head. "No card or return address. Just his name and address. She'll know where it came from."

They walked from the store hand in hand, and his mood lighter than it had in years.

"I wonder if they'll let him have the toys?" he said more to himself than to Gracie.

"Why not? They don't have to tell him where they came from."

Nate smiled and put his arm around her as they walked down the street. He'd known Gracie for a few hours, and already she'd done more to lift his spirit than anything else he'd tried.

"You aren't married, are you?" he asked with a sideways glance.

"No, I'm not." She looked up at him with a grin.

He laughed. "Just checking. Do you have any plans today?"

"No."

"Would you like to spend the day with me?" he asked with a smile. "I'd like to take you up in the Space Needle. I've heard you can see for miles." For the first time in two years, Nate was optimistic. With Gracie at his side, his bad times were beginning to fade.

For months, he made the trip to Seattle to visit Gracie. Eight months after they met, he proposed and they married.

Logan's eyes filled with tears as Nate told him the story of his second birthday.

"This is too weird." Logan wiped his eyes with the back of his hand, embarrassed.

A slow smile spread across Nate's face. "She gave you the toys."

"She gave me the toys," he said with a nod.

"What did she say about them?" Nate leaned forward, obviously excited to have the connection with his son.

"I was too young when those came, so she didn't say anything I can remember, but when I was older, these boxes would show up every Christmas and birthday addressed to me." He looked at Nate and noticed the pleased expression he wore. "She always wanted me to open them before Dad came in from work."

"How did she explain them to you?"

"She said they were from some relative of hers who lived

in Seattle. I thought it was strange, but I liked getting the gifts, so I wasn't about to say anything. I'd never met any relatives from Seattle and couldn't figure out why they would send me nice presents. And stranger still was the fact I never had to write any thank you notes to this relative. Mom was a stickler on thank you notes, but she brushed this off and didn't make me do it."

"So you got the bear," Nate said with a grin, unable to contain his glee. "Gracie and I debated for ages over which one to buy you."

Logan looked at him and smiled. "I still have the bear. My kids play with it. The train too. The little wheels still make the clickity-clack sound." He laughed. "And the G.I. Joe. I chewed all the gum and ate the candy though."

Pleasure glowed from Nate's lined face. "Oh, Logan, you don't know how much that pleases me. I always wondered what she would do with them. I imagined the boxes thrown in the garbage, unopened. When Gracie suggested we do that, I thought she was nuts. I couldn't imagine Lois letting you have anything from me. But she did." He laughed. "Hey, what did you think of the fishing gear? Catch lots of fish with that stuff?"

"Some. Dad and I spent a lot of time fishing, so the pole and creel came in handy. Did you make the flies?"

"I did." Nate couldn't stop smiling. "You used the fishing stuff."

"I used everything you sent. The nice pen sets in high school, the calculator, the turtle wax for my car." He laughed. "I thought that one was a little odd."

"Sixteen-year-old boys always have cars and love to polish them. Hey, how about the tapes?"

"Bruce Springsteen, the Eagles, Bob Seger, Heart—yeah, I listened to them and appreciated your taste in music. I took the old eight track player out of my car and bought a stereo with a tape deck so I could listen to them." He shook his head.

"Why didn't anyone tell me about this? All these things, all those years. There's probably a lot more if I start thinking about it."

"Promises were made, Logan. I kept my word. They kept theirs." He leaned forward on his elbows, looking at Logan seriously. "It had to be that way. You can look back as an adult, in the times you live in now, and think what a terrible thing we did to you. But imagine what you would've thought at twelve or sixteen. Most likely it would have messed you up and made you angry. No, as difficult as this was for me, it was best for you."

"I'm not sure I agree. Wouldn't it have been better for me to know you all along? Or at least know about you?"

"No, it wouldn't. You were allowed to grow up a normal kid in a normal family. If you'd known me then, everyone would have known about the affair, and it would have been a horrible mess. You have to remember the times we lived in. Today, this is talk show fodder and probably a boring one at that, considering all the weird things going on these days, but in 1961, the gossip would've killed your mother. No, it was best this way. It was best for both of you. Joe was your dad. He's always been your dad, and even now he's gone, I wouldn't try to take his place. It's his place, not mine. He earned it."

"So where do we go with this?" Logan asked.

Nate shrugged. "I don't know. When you left the other day, I doubted you'd come back. When you leave today, I'll wonder the same thing. You don't owe me the time of day, Logan. How this turns out is up to you. All I can say at this point is, I'm thrilled to have this afternoon with you. I never expected any time with you at all, so this is a delight for me."

"If I say I'm coming, then I'll be here. If there's a problem, I'll call." Logan frowned at the implication he'd leave Nate hanging.

"I don't mean to be insulting. It's just I've learned not to get my hopes up over the years. When you walked into my office two days ago, my heart nearly stopped. The last time I'd been close to you was when you were five days old and I held you in the hospital. I've waited forty-three years for the chance to talk to you, and it means a lot to me. You've known about me for what, maybe a week, and known me for two days. I know I don't mean anything to you, so I understand if you choose not to come back. That's all."

Logan's frown deepened. "I'm not sure what you mean to me yet. It's something I need to work on." He leaned back in his chair and crossed his arms. "I can't dismiss this. Like you say, if it weren't for you, I wouldn't be here. And the fact you were a peripheral part of my life means something too. You didn't bow out by choice like some deadbeat dad. You were there as much as you could be, considering the circumstances, and I have to factor that into this. One thing I'm having trouble with is being here with you somehow makes me feel disloyal to my dad. Joe McKinnon was the kind of dad every kid should have, and I can't help but feel I'm being disrespectful to him."

"I'm not trying to take his place. I knew Joe McKinnon too, and I could never walk in his shoes and wouldn't care to try."

Logan glanced at his watch. "I'd better be getting back to Mom's. Max needs to leave by five. There are still so many questions I want to ask. Can I come back again?"

"You think you have to ask after everything I've said?" Nate laughed. "Come back whenever you please. You'll always be welcome. Always."

Logan nodded.

"Maybe you'd like to come by the house? I could show you some things. We could look through the albums together. Maybe you would tell me some stories about you."

"I can do that. I'm not sure what's on my schedule for tomorrow. I'll call and let you know." He stood to leave. "You know, I'm not sure what I should call you."

"My name is Nate, not Nathaniel or anything fancy like that. Just Nate, and that works fine for me. If you choose something else, it's your decision." He stood. "Everything is your choice, Logan."

Logan left the chowder house feeling confused, and he generally didn't suffer confusion about anything. He was fairly straight forward, made his decisions quickly and decisively. His employees appreciated that fact. Everyone always knew where Logan McKinnon stood on something. But this kept him going in circles.

He drove back to King's Bay, rehashing his conversations with Nate. He'd have to call him Nate. Joe was Dad and always would be. Father sounded too formal, and he wasn't sure if he wanted to call him that anyway. Nate would have to do.

As details swam through his mind, he tried to organize them like a solvable business problem, but the more he tried, the more confused he grew. This couldn't be solved in an analytical fashion. He was too closely involved and too engrossed by the emotions of the situation.

There was Lois, the frustrated '50's-era housewife, depressed by her lack of children and steadily pushing her husband away from her. There was Nate, the innocent lover at first but then guilty coconspirator in an illicit affair. Then there was Joe, the wronged husband who did his best to right a situation he did nothing to create, the noble hero who forgave his wife and raised her lover's child as his own. And the last player in the tragedy was Logan himself, child of the illicit affair, raised in ignorance of his conception. Was that the only crime against him, and if so, had it hurt him? No, he thought, it hadn't hurt him. As Nate said, he was allowed to grow up a normal kid in a normal family. Actually, Lois and Nate had hurt themselves more. Lois grappled with guilt for many years until Alzheimer's disease robbed her of her mental ability. He didn't know if she was capable of guilt anymore.

And maybe Nate was the most tragic figure of all. Nate was cast from his son's life for the good of everyone involved. Nate wasn't allowed to know his son and was forced to watch while another man raised him as his own. Nate spent years yearning to know his child, knowing he never would. The three McKinnons had each other. Nate was shoved out in the cold.

As he pulled into his mother's driveway, he decided, at least for now, to give Nate what he wanted. He would spend time with him, listen to his side of the story, and tell him stories of himself. He wasn't sure if he could continue a relationship beyond that, but for now, he'd make the old man happy. It was difficult to walk away and say he had a father and didn't need another one. True, Joe had been a wonderful father, but was it fair to the man who'd fathered him to turn away?

"I'm back, Max," Logan said as he walked into the kitchen. "What are you doing?" He watched as Max took one last swipe across the kitchen floor with the mop.

"Not what you're thinking, so don't expect a weekly mop up." He laughed. "Lois and I were making a cake, and she forgot the beaters need to stay IN the bowl. She pulled them out covered with batter, and it went everywhere." He set the mop in the bucket. "I've about got it, and Lois is cleaned up and in bed. Dinner is in the fridge. Are you getting all your legal mumbo jumbo settled?" He leaned on the counter, relaxed.

"Yeah, it's perking along just fine. Actually, I've been taking care of something else today. I've been visiting with my father." He watched for a reaction from Max.

"At the cemetery? A lot of people do that sort of thing." He shrugged.

"No, not at the cemetery. In Westport." He chuckled at the confused look on Max's face.

"Come again? I thought your father died."

"That was my dad. My father lives in Westport."

"Oh, I didn't realize Lois had been married before."

"She wasn't. Remember the journal I was reading? Well, I found those closet bones you warned me about. I just spent the day talking with a guy I didn't know existed until a week ago. Joe McKinnon wasn't my biological father, and no one bothered to clue me into the fact."

"Whoa," Max said. "You don't seem too upset about it."

"I was at first, but as I get the whole picture, it's hard to be upset. Mostly I'm having trouble coming to terms with my parents keeping it from me. But I'm working through it."

"What do you think of him?" Max asked.

"I like him. I didn't want to, but I'm starting to like him, and that worries me. I have this feeling of being disloyal to my dad." He rolled his shoulders to relieve the tension building again. "I'm also worried I'm latching on to this guy because my dad is gone. Taking care of Mom has been a full-time thing, and I haven't dealt with Dad's death yet. Am I trying to delay my grief by hanging out with Nate? I don't know what to think." He frowned. "And I'm concerned about what Dad would've felt about it. In her journal, Mom speculated a lot on Dad's feelings about Nate, but they agreed to never talk about him. So I don't know what Dad would do right now."

"Your dad must have known you'd find out eventually and would want to meet your biological father."

"I suppose, but I doubt if he'd be happy about it. I imagine adoptive parents must go through this when their child wants to meet the birth parents."

"Question," Max said. "Does meeting this guy lessen your feelings for your dad?"

"Of course not. I loved him, and that will never change. He was one heck of a great dad."

"There you go. What would Lois think of you finding out?

If she were in a condition to care, that is," Max asked.

"It was her choice originally that Nate not be a part of my life. But later on she had second thoughts and wondered if she'd been fair to him. Now, she might think it was okay since Dad isn't here to be hurt by it." He chuckled. "I look just like him, which explains a lot. She's been calling me Nate and saying some weird stuff to me. I understand it now and wish I could talk to her about it."

"Have you finished her journals?"

"No. I skimmed through some of my early childhood stuff to find out more about Nate, but I didn't read it closely. There are still a few volumes written after I graduated from college I haven't tackled yet."

"Maybe you should finish them. It couldn't hurt anything at this point since you've already rattled the family skeletons. Maybe you'll find out if Lois wanted you to know him or not." Max pushed away from the counter and grabbed his jacket off the chair back. "You already know the guy, so it doesn't matter in that respect, but it may help ease some guilt." He clapped Logan on the shoulder. "I've got to be going, my friend. Have a good evening. I'll be back at eight."

"See you tomorrow," he said to Max's retreating back. "Hey, Max."

He turned. "Yeah?"

"Have you ever considered psychology? You'd make a great therapist." Logan laughed.

"Nah. I'll stick with what I'm doing. That way, if I screw with your head and make it worse, you can't sue me. Night." He waved as he wandered out.

Logan checked on his mother to confirm she was indeed sleeping, fished his dinner from the refrigerator, and warmed it in the microwave. With it and a glass of milk, he settled on his bed with his mother's journals.

Chapter 19

Lois

June 1967
Dear friend, another box arrived today. He has sent them twice a year for three years now and I can't help but smile. It is so like Nate to do something this thoughtful. Of course, I can't tell Logan who sends them so I've invented a childless uncle in Seattle. It's deceitful but Logan laughs so sweetly as he opens the box. Each gift is perfect for him and I know Nate is putting a lot of thought into his choices. I still wonder sometimes what became of Nate. Is he doing all right? Did he return to his family? Has he married and had children? I hope so. When the thoughts persist, I turn on the TV or read a book for distraction, but I look at Logan and the thoughts return. He looks so much like Nate already. I wonder how Joe feels about this but I dare not ask. We agreed to never speak of Nate again and I must abide by that promise. Lois

June 1972
My friend, Logan is ten today and this year's box contained fishing gear that has him hounding Joe for a trip to the river. He, of course, will comply, as he loves to go fishing nearly as much as he loves Logan. What a

pair. I can't help but think of Nate today, fondly as always. The fishing gear is so representative of the man who sent it. I remember the day he told me of his love for the ocean, a boat rolling beneath his feet and the freedom to be found there. Has he found his freedom or does he feel trapped by guilt as I do? As the years pass, I find the source of my guilt has shifted. Joe has forgiven me for my infidelity and we are stronger than ever. I love him so. Now, I feel guilt for Nate, for denying him his son. He is a good man. If I were able, I'd figure out a way for Nate to know Logan but it is impossible. Unless Logan discovers our secret on his own, I'm afraid he will never know. I gave my word and it must be kept.
Lois

June 1985
Dearest friend, if I could travel back in time and undo the wrongs I've committed, would I? If I could change the days that led me into Nate's bed, would I? As I sat there today watching my wonderful son graduate from college, these thoughts crossed my mind and the answer would be, no. I wouldn't change one thing if it meant I would miss one minute with Logan. My only regret is Nate. Not that I should have chosen him over Joe, for I couldn't do that, but I regret he doesn't know Logan. He would be so proud to see his son graduating with honors. If only he could. If I could, I would tell Logan of him. He's a man now and would understand, I believe. But always, I must be respectful of Joe and his feelings. Logan is his son and I dare not disrupt that relationship. It is pure and honest and based on love. Lois

May 1993
My friend, today was Logan's wedding day and it was beautiful. Melissa is a lovely woman and I can tell by the looks passing between them they are very much in love. The only flaw in the day was misplacing my dia-

mond earrings. If it were an isolated event, it wouldn't bother me but lately I'm forgetting a lot of things...

"Lois," Joe said as he knocked on the bathroom door. "This room only has one bathroom, honey, and I need to shave. Can you unlock the door so I can come in? We'll be late to the church."

Lois looked in the mirror, panic rising. She'd misplaced her earrings again. She was sure she'd brought them in the bathroom to put on in the mirror, but now they were nowhere to be found.

"Just a minute, Joe," she said as she searched frantically. Lately, she'd had this problem of misplacing things, and when the item was found, it would be in a strange place. Her watch had been in the toaster. Luckily, Joe saw it before he turned it on. A hairbrush had been found in the vegetable crisper, her socks in the record player. They either had a gnome hiding her things, or she was losing her mind.

Joe knocked again. "Lois?"

She flushed the toilet, ran some water, and opened the door. "We should have reserved a suite with two bathrooms, Joe. Go ahead and shave. I'll finish out here." She walked from the bathroom in her robe, hoping Joe wouldn't notice her concern.

"Oh, Lois, I found these under the bed when I was looking for my shoes." He handed her the diamond earrings with a smile. "Actually, I found them in my shoes. They must have shifted around in the suitcase. You may want to put them in your jewelry case next time. They could have been lost."

"You're right." She turned from Joe as he went into the bathroom and took a relieved breath. Before they could be misplaced again, she went to the mirror and put the earrings in her ears. She studied her image in the mirror. Her honey-blonde hair had turned to gray, her face was now lined and showing her age. At sixty-three, she was trim and healthy, but she was having difficulty with her memory. Joe brushed it off.

Everyone suffered a little memory loss as they aged. He had turned seventy-two that year and sometimes had to think about things longer. He told her not to be concerned. But she was.

They finished dressing and made it to the church on time. The ceremony and reception were perfect. Logan and Melissa departed the reception hall in a shower of birdseed and well wishes, and they hurried to catch a plane to Miami for their honeymoon cruise.

Joe and Lois returned to their hotel, tired from the busy day. As they undressed for bed, Lois experienced a moment of confusion and wasn't sure what she should be doing.

Joe stepped up behind her. "Need help with your zipper, love?"

"Yes." She nodded.

"What a beautiful day," he said. "Logan looked so happy." He wrapped his arms around Lois and sighed. "He isn't just ours anymore."

"What do you mean?"

"We have to share him now, with Melissa. He won't ever be just ours again."

"Does that bother you?"

"In a way. He's always been ours."

They finished dressing for bed. As Lois settled in for the night, the thought occurred to her what Joe had said wasn't completely true. Logan had never been "just theirs." A part of him had always belonged to Nate and always would. They just hadn't given him a chance to make his claim.

...I wonder as I write this entry, what would Nate think of his son's marriage? Lois

Logan rolled to the side of the bed, put the journal in the box, and grabbed the next in sequence. As he flipped open the pages, a cold draft blew across his bare feet. He hadn't heard a weather report but supposed the temperature could have dropped considerably since he'd retired for the night. He wandered to the hall and checked the furnace setting. It was set on seventy and running, but he felt cold air.

To allay his concern the furnace was operating improperly, he walked through the house, checking the temperature. As he neared the front door, he found it standing wide open.

"Mom!" he called as he backtracked to her room. "Mom!" He stopped short and stared at her empty bed. "Oh no."

Logan ran to his room, slipped on his shoes, and grabbed a coat. On his way through the house, he grabbed his mother's coat and shoved a pair of slippers in the pocket. Most likely she'd wandered out barefoot. He debated calling the police but decided to check around the house first. With a flashlight in hand, he ran around the house and up and down the street. When he couldn't find a trace of her, he dialed 9-1-1 and enlisted the local police in the hunt.

After the initial search of the neighborhood, Logan jumped in his car and drove. The temperature had dropped considerably, and he worried she'd suffer hypothermia. He cruised the neighborhood streets, peering into yards, hoping for a glimpse of her, but saw nothing.

"I'm sorry, Dad," he muttered to himself. "I'm sorry I failed you. You left me in charge of her, and I neglected her." To calm his nerves, he called Melissa.

"I've lost her, Mel. I can't find her," he said when she answered.

"What time is it, Logan?" she mumbled.

"Midnight, and my mother is gone. I lost her." He turned a corner and drove through a grocery store parking lot.

"You lost her?" Melissa was suddenly awake. "Have you called the police?"

"Yes. Two hours ago. They can't find her either. I'm scared, Mel. What if she fell in the ocean? He trusted me to take care of her, and I've failed."

"You haven't failed. Calm down. You'll find her. I know

you will."

"I wish I shared your optimism. It's freezing cold, and I don't know if she's wearing shoes. I found the front door wide open, and she'd been gone long enough I felt the cold air down the hall. She'll catch pneumonia." He finished checking the parking lot and drove through an alley. "She won't know how to get home, Mel. She's confused walking around her own yard." As he talked, his phone beeped. "Just a second, I need to catch another call." He switched to the other call. "Logan McKinnon."

"Mr. McKinnon, Sergeant Trimble here. I have good news. One of our patrols spotted your mother down by Burger Town. She's okay, but they're taking her to the hospital as a precaution."

Logan sighed. "I'll head there now. Thanks for letting me know." He disconnected and reconnected with Melissa. "They found her. I need to run over to the hospital and see what's going on. They say she's okay, but they're checking her out anyway." He stopped for a red light and took a deep breath. "I thought I'd lost her, Mel. He trusted me, and I failed."

"Logan, she has Alzheimer's. You can't watch her every second. I've heard this sort of thing happens a lot. People take off walking, looking for something from their childhood or for someone they knew a long time ago. Don't blame yourself."

"I don't have anyone else to blame. Tomorrow morning I need to install more locks." The light changed, and he drove down the quiet beachside street. It was serene; the moonlight glimmered on the incoming waves.

"That's a good idea," she agreed. "I checked with the Alzheimer's care facility that thought they had a space opening up, and they think it might be a few weeks yet."

"If I step up the locks and watch her closer, hopefully I'll make it." He drove into the emergency room parking area and turned off the car. "I need to run in the hospital. I'll call you later."

He entered the ER through large glass doors and stopped at the front counter.

"McKinnon, Lois McKinnon. Is she here?" he asked a calm-looking woman who probably experienced much worse emergencies than this every day. She typed the name into the computer and smiled.

"She's in exam room four. Go ahead and go back." She pointed down a long hall. Logan walked quickly down the corridor until he saw the number four. He peeked in and saw Lois wrapped in a pink blanket, sitting on the examination table, listening as a nurse talked.

"May I come in? I'm her son," he said through the crack in the door.

"Of course. Lois and I were discussing flowers. She likes sunflowers," the nurse said with a smile. She stepped away as Logan rushed in.

"Is she okay?"

"Yes, but the doctor said he wants to keep her overnight to be sure." The nurse pointed to her sock-clad feet. "She was barefoot, so her feet were scratched up and cold. If you'll stay with her, I'll tell the doctor you're here and start the admission process." Logan nodded as the nurse walked to the door. "Mr. McKinnon? The officer who brought her in said she was looking for her daddy." She gave him a sympathetic look before leaving the room. Logan turned his attention to Lois.

"You scared the hell out of me, Mom." He tried to keep the fear from his voice, but judging by Lois' wide-eyed look, she caught it.

"Why?"

"You don't know, do you?"

She shook her head and looked confused. Logan let out a sigh and smiled. "Never mind. You're okay, and that's what matters." He looked at her for a moment and wrapped his arms around her. She snuggled in and hugged him back. "I'm sorry I let you down, Mom. It won't happen again." He kissed her forehead and let go. Lois looked at him with tear-filled eyes and smiled.

"Love you," she said quietly.

Logan smiled and fought back his own tears. "I know. I love you too."

Lois wiped a tear that strayed down his cheek. "My son," she said.

"Yeah, I'm your son. Always will be." He took her hand in his and squeezed.

"Joe and..." She looked at him seriously and struggled to say more. "Another. There was another. Do you know him?"

Logan was stunned. Was she trying to tell him about Nate?

"The other one," she said with emphasis. Logan debated if he should help her with the memory. Sometimes she struggled for a word, and if supplied it, she was able to continue talking.

"Do you mean Nate?"

"Yes, Nate. The other one. Do you know him?" She squeezed his hand.

"I do. Yes, I know the other one. I met Nate a couple of days ago."

Lois smiled. "That's good. Very good. Father."

"I know. He told me all about it. I know he's my father. I understand." He rubbed his hand across her cheek. "But Joe will always be my dad. It's okay to know both." He smiled at Lois as she squeezed his hand.

"It's bedtime," she said with a yawn. Logan helped her lay on the exam table and covered her with a blanket. The moment disappeared as quickly as it came.

The doctor kept her overnight for observation. Not willing to risk losing her again, Logan spent the night in the chair by her bed. She woke occasionally but settled down when Logan spoke to her.

He called Max in the morning and informed him of the night's activities and told him she wouldn't be released until afternoon. When they arrived home, they found a Chevy Silverado in the driveway and Max busy in the house. Max hugged Lois as she entered her home. She was obviously pleased.

"There's coffee and cookies in the kitchen to welcome our weary traveler home," Max said as they removed their coats.

"I didn't expect to see you today, Max."

"I took the opportunity to do a few things around here for you." He pointed to the top of the front door. "You have a new lock where she can't reach it. There's another one on the kitchen door. I figured you wouldn't have time to stop at the hardware store and get it installed before bedtime tonight."

Logan shook his head and smiled. "Thanks. I don't know what I'd do without you."

"I know." He grinned. "Being indispensable is one of my talents. Come on, Lois. Let's have some cookies."

"I'll be there in a minute. I need to make a phone call. There's someone I forgot to call this morning." He removed his cell from his pocket and dialed. "Nate, its Logan. Sorry I didn't call earlier."

"It's okay," Nate said, but Logan was sure he heard something in his voice.

"No, it isn't okay. I should have called, but Mom wandered off last night and ended up spending the night in the hospital."

"Oh. Is she okay?"

"Fine now. She wandered around town for a couple of hours in the cold and cut her feet. Other than that, she's okay. I spent the night at the hospital with her, and we just got home."

"I'm glad to hear that. Maybe you can make it another day."

"I'd like to. How about tomorrow? My schedule is open."

"That would be great," Nate said. "I have some things to show you."

"I look forward to it." He paused. "Nate, something else

happened last night."

"What?"

"Mom tried to tell me about you. She couldn't put it all together, but when I filled in the blanks, she was happy. She was talking about me being her son. She said there was Joe and another. I filled in your name, and she smiled." He paused. "I think she wants me to know about you. It's hard to say in her condition, but I think she'd be happy about this."

"I'm glad, Logan. I'm glad she approves."

"I'll bring lunch if you like," Logan offered. "Do you like burgers?"

"I love them. Lots of onions, please."

"I'll see you around lunchtime tomorrow. What's the address?" Logan scribbled as Nate told him. "See you tomorrow." He disconnected the call and smiled to himself.

Chapter 20

Logan knocked on the door of a moderate, two-story home nestled into a grove of shore pines overlooking the ocean. The green paint had faded to a mellow, peaceful tone. Nate answered Logan's knock with a smile.

"Come in. Come in." He waved Logan in and closed the door. "Those burgers smell great. Let's eat in the kitchen." He led the way through a cozy living room with photo-lined walls. Nate waved his hand to the table, indicating Logan should sit while he grabbed plates from the cupboard. "How's your mom today?"

"Fine. Her feet are healing, and she doesn't show any signs of pneumonia. That was my biggest worry. She was out in the cold air for hours without a jacket or shoes." He opened the sack and pulled out three huge hamburgers, fries, and milkshakes. Nate looked at the mass of food with wide eyes.

"You must be hungry."

"I thought Gracie might be here, so I brought one for her," Logan said

"Oh." Nate smiled and looked a little sad. "I guess I should have said something. I lost Gracie two years ago to cancer."

Logan frowned. "I'm sorry." He looked at the extra burger.

"Don't be. I should have said something." He grabbed a burger and removed the paper. "If we don't eat that third one, I'll have it for lunch tomorrow. Sounds better than what I'd come up with on my own."

Logan nodded and grabbed a burger. They ate in silence for a few moments while Logan debated what to ask Nate next. There were so many things he wanted to know, but he settled on one that had been weighing on his mind. He set his burger down on the plate and plunged in.

"Nate? Do your kids know about me?"

Nate shook his head and half smiled. "We never had children, so I'm sorry to say, you're still an only child. Gracie wanted children terribly, but it wasn't to be. I always wondered if it was a punishment for my sins, but Gracie hadn't done anything to be punished for. She said I was foolish to think that way." He gazed out the window, his eyes sad. "We'd been married a year when she found out she was pregnant. We were so happy and made all sorts of plans. When she was four months along, she had a miscarriage. Her health deteriorated after that, and her doctor decided she required a hysterectomy. She was only twenty-three, and it nearly broke her heart she would never have children of her own." He sighed. "She never was strong physically. Morally and spiritually she was a sturdy woman, but physically she was a wisp of a thing. I worried over her continually, so afraid I'd lose her, and the whole time she was worried sick about me. She said I'd already lost you, and she was afraid of how the miscarriage would affect me. As long as I had Gracie, I was okay."

"It sounds like you were able to get past your feelings for Mom."

"I didn't have any choice in the matter. She would never leave Joe, so what was the point of pining for her?" He sipped his milkshake. "I have to admit, I was a basket case for a while. But after that trip to the hospital, it wasn't about her anymore. It was you I couldn't get over. I let go of Lois the day I held you in my arms, but I never got over you. Gracie knew, and she was okay with it. You became her son too." He ate a fry. "It was Gracie's idea to go to your kindergarten program. I thought she was crazy. If Joe saw me, there was no telling what he'd do to me. But she convinced me to go, and

I'm so glad I did." He laughed. "They had you dressed up as a reindeer, and it was so doggone cute I almost cried."

Logan smiled at the memory. "I remember that suit. It itched all over, and I couldn't wait to take it off."

"That was the day I knew without any doubt who had fathered you. Just a second." He jumped from his chair and left the room, returning a moment later with an old photo album. After flipping through the pages, he laid the book on the table and pointed to a picture. "See what I mean? We could have been twins."

Logan stared at the photo of Nate at five years old and was astonished. It could have been a picture of Logan himself.

"I don't know what to say." Logan continued to stare.

"Nothing to say, I guess. This is my dad." He pointed to another picture of a man bearing a strong resemblance to Logan. "This is my mom." He continued to point. "My brothers and sisters."

"I'd fit right in, wouldn't I?"

"Yeah. You look like a Ford. We have strong genes." Nate smiled proudly. "Finish up your burger, and I'll show you a few other things."

They finished their meal and moved to the living room. Logan recognized the box from Nate's office. Nate handed him a scrapbook as he sat on the sofa. Nate sat at the other end. Logan flipped through the pages and looked more seriously than he had the time before. There were pictures of every Christmas and spring program, basketball games, and his high school plays. Logan stared at the play program.

"You were there that night? You saw my play?"

"Both nights. We stayed for the weekend so we could catch both performances. Gracie loved a good musical. She was quite amazed to hear you sing." He grinned. "A chip off the old block."

"Mom wrote about that in her journal, that you sang Sinatra songs to her."

"Sinatra, Crosby, sometimes the Platters. She liked the slow romantic stuff."

Logan frowned, remembering. "I know you were there that night. I knew at the time you were there."

"How is that? You didn't know I existed then." Nate leaned forward.

"I was backstage during the intermission, and my friend Tom said, 'Hey, Logan, there's some dude out there that looks like you.' I laughed it off and thought Tom was imagining things. He kept insisting I should look, but by the time I got there, you were gone." He looked at Nate. "If I'd been faster, I might have known about you twenty-five years ago."

"But at what cost, Logan? I don't know what you'd have thought at that time. Knowing could have messed up your relationship with your parents, and I never wanted that. As much as I wanted to be part of your life, I didn't want to do anything to mess you up."

Logan frowned. "Maybe I could have handled it."

"Maybe not. We'll never know now. It's all history anyway. Remember that?" He pointed to a picture of Logan's prize pig.

"This looks like the auction after the fair. You were there too?"

"I wanted to see your pig. The local paper had an article about your FFA class growing massive pigs, and I wanted to see it."

"He was a terrific pig," Logan said with pride. "I hated to see him sold, but I needed the money for the next project, and when somebody paid three times what he was worth, I couldn't feel too badly about that."

"He was an expensive pig, that's for sure." Nate leaned back and smiled.

"You bought my pig?" Logan laughed. "Why?"

"Because he was your pig. Problem was, someone else wanted him real bad and kept driving up the bids. I got him though."

"You bought my pig. I can't believe it. I guess I should say thanks. I earned enough from the sale to raise another pig and start my college fund. Thanks." He looked at Nate sincerely. "What did you do with him? He was huge."

"That's the funny part. Gracie wouldn't let me butcher him. Every time she looked at him, she thought of you. Not that there was a resemblance or anything." He laughed. "It was just that you'd raised him. He was like family. So, we kept him out back in a pen until the neighbors complained about the smell. Gracie still refused to eat him, so I donated him to the local mission. I hear he was quite a hit down there."

"I'm glad he went to a good purpose." Logan continued through the pages and noticed the pictures ended with his college graduation. "You were there too?"

"In the back row," Nate said.

"Mom wrote in her journal that she thought about you that day. She wondered what you would think of your son graduating with honors."

"Damned proud, Logan. They did a terrific job raising you." He blinked, a tear threatening to spill from his eye. "I lost track of you after that. I saw in the paper where your parents sold their property, but I had no way of knowing where they went, and I didn't know where you'd moved after graduation. Can you fill me in on the last twenty years? I've got a few holes of my own I need filled."

Logan looked at Nate and felt something surprising. He was starting to care about the old guy. He cleared his throat. "I was offered a job after graduation as a computer programmer for a company in Seattle. It was a good experience, but I didn't like the big city. Too much farm boy in me, I guess. I stayed for five years until I couldn't stand it anymore. Then a friend talked me into moving to Vancouver. He had an idea to start a software company, so we did. The next few years we worked our tails off and didn't do much else. Finally, we hit it big with a business program and were able to expand and hire some employees." He smiled. "Melissa was one of them. Not only was she a sharp programmer, but gorgeous too. We dated for several years and finally got married twelve years ago. My friend decided he wanted to do something else, so we bought out his share of the company and renamed it McKinnon Software. Not very creative, but Melissa wanted it that way."

"How old are your children?"

"Joey is seven, Derek is five, and Hannah is six months. And poor Melissa has been dealing with them alone for the past month. She's an amazing woman, but I think she's getting worn down."

"How soon will you be leaving?" There was a hint of sadness in Nate's voice.

"As soon as Mom's spot opens at Eagle Crest. Melissa placed her name on a list, and they say she may be able to move in soon."

Nate nodded. "It's the best for her, I'm sure." He was quiet for a moment. "Can you tell me something? You've read Lois' journals, and I'm wondering…did Lois ever mention how she really felt about me? When we were together, I would prod her to say, but she never did. I've always wondered if I was a crutch to get her through a bad time, or did she have real feelings for me?"

Logan thought for a moment, debating if he should repeat what he'd read in his mother's private journal. He looked at Nate and decided he had the right to know. "She wondered how it was possible to love two men as deeply as she loved you and Dad. She said she'd found room in her heart for both of you. If Dad had rejected her, I'm positive she would have gone back to you."

"But she loved him more," he said, his tone matter of fact.

"Yeah."

"Thanks, Logan. It wouldn't have changed anything if I'd

known. Thankfully, I met my Gracie. I loved your mother, but Gracie was the love of my life. If two people were ever meant to be together, it was Gracie and I."

"Mom hoped you found someone to love. She wanted you to marry and have a family. She hoped for your happiness. But she also lived with massive guilt. Her entries had a common theme. She wondered a lot about what you would think of things, how you would feel about me, and the things I did. She spent a great deal of time wondering if she'd been unfair to you."

"Water under the bridge. It couldn't have been any other way, and I'm sorry to hear she was tormented by it. I know you now, and it has to be enough."

Logan thought for a moment. "One thing I'm having a problem with about all this."

"What's that?"

"You promised Dad you'd stay away from me. Didn't you break that promise by being there?"

Nate didn't appear disturbed by the question. "You're trying real hard to get a handle on me, aren't you? Trying to decide if I'm a dishonest man in every respect. Maybe you're carrying bad genes?" He smiled. "I've spent a lot of time contemplating it myself over the years. My behavior with your mother was immoral, and I'd be the first to admit it. But in my own defense, prior to being involved with Lois, I hadn't done anything illegal, immoral, or reprehensible. Other than lacking direction in my life and being a bit impulsive, I wasn't any worse than the next guy. I saw a pretty woman and fell in love. It should have ended when her marital status became known, but I was weak." He looked at Logan seriously. "And I was equally weak where you were concerned, maybe worse. In a way, I did break my word to your dad, but I couldn't stay away completely. You are my son, Logan. I don't care what it says on your birth certificate, you are a Ford. You are my flesh and blood. And no matter how wrong it was, I needed you. I needed to know you were okay and they were raising you right."

"If they hadn't?"

"Then you might have known about me a whole lot earlier. I wouldn't have stood by and watched if they weren't doing it right. But they did, and you're a fine man because of it."

Logan was quiet, soaking in all Nate said. He was trying to get a handle on Nate Ford, trying to decide the old nature versus nurture question. Was he who he was because Joe McKinnon raised him or because he was biologically Nate Ford's son? Maybe both? Maybe he'd never know.

The only things he knew for certain, he couldn't dislike this man who'd given him life and had fought to be in his life if only on the edges. He liked Nate. He had an easy manner, a sense of humor, and though he didn't think it of himself, he appeared to be a highly moral man. He'd made promises and despite the pain, he'd held true to those promises. How all of this would fit into Logan's life, he wasn't sure. It would take some time to figure it out. Could he come to love Nate as a father? He didn't know.

They talked through the afternoon, answering questions, telling stories. Laughing together. Nate showed picture after picture of the Ford family and Gracie. He smiled tenderly as he spoke of her, occasionally touching her picture with his finger as if he could feel her.

"Want to see our family photo?" Nate asked with an amused expression.

"Isn't that what we've been doing?" Logan said, confused.

"*Our* family photo." He wagged his finger between them. "Just a second." Nate again bounded from the room and returned with a framed photo.

"Whoa. How did you do that? Photoshop?" Logan said with awe as he looked at a picture of Nate and Gracie smiling at the camera. Just behind them stood Logan in his cap and gown, smiling.

"Wild, isn't it? And purely accidental too. Gracie decided she wanted a picture of us in front of that mural, so she asked a man if he'd snap it. For some reason, you stepped right into the picture and stood there as he snapped the shot. This has always been one of my favorite photos."

"Unbelievable. I wonder why I did that."

"I don't know. You even looked at the camera. We thought maybe you were looking for someone who was standing behind our photographer. Whoever it was made you smile."

Logan shrugged, not sure what would have caused him to do it. His cell phone rang, and he excused himself while he checked the caller ID. He smiled as he answered the phone. "Hi, honey."

"I have good news and couldn't wait to tell you," Melissa said with excitement.

"What's that?"

"Mom's spot is available at Eagle Crest. They moved the other resident to the hospital and say Mom can move in as soon as they clear the room. Maybe as early as three days."

"That's terrific," he said enthusiastically until he looked at Nate. His time with Nate was over. "Let me know what she needs to take, and I'll start packing her stuff."

"I know she needs a bed and dresser, but I'll have to call you with more details. I'm so glad you can come home. We've missed you so much."

"I miss you too." He tried to avoid looking at Nate, at the sadness in his eyes. "We'll have to talk later. I'm in the middle of something right now."

"What?"

"I'm visiting with Nate."

"How's it going?"

"Great. But I need to be getting back to Mom's soon, so I had better get going. I'll call you this evening. Love you. Bye." He disconnected the call and looked at Nate, trying to read his expression.

"That was Melissa. Mom's spot opened up at Eagle Crest."
Nate nodded. "So you'll be going sooner than you thought."

"I need to get home. Melissa handling things at home and at the office by herself. I've been away too long already."

Nate nodded. "I understand. I wish we could have more time, but it isn't to be."

"I need to get back to Mom's." He and Nate stood, and an uncomfortable silence fell between them. "I'll try to get back over before we leave, if that's okay with you."

"It's always okay with me. You're welcome anytime."

"I know." Logan smiled. "I'd better be going." He walked to the door.

"Logan?"

"Yeah?"

"Would it be possible for me to see Lois before you leave? Just for a few minutes? Or would that be too upsetting for her?"

Logan thought for a moment. "I don't see why not. If it upsets her, she'll probably forget about it in five minutes anyway. But it may be upsetting for you. I can't say for sure she'll remember you."

"If it's all right, I'll take my chances."

"Sure. How about tomorrow? It's Saturday, and Max has the day off. I'll be hanging out at the house with her all day. How about one o'clock?"

Nate smiled. "I'll be there."

Though he tried to sound confident with Nate, Logan worried throughout the morning about his mother's reaction to Nate's visit. Max was off for the weekend, and if Lois became agitated, he'd have a heck of a time dealing with her. He kept to her routine as much as possible, and when the doorbell rang after lunch, she was in a fairly calm state.

Logan answered the door to find a nervous Nate.

"You found us all right?" Logan asked as he invited Nate in.

"Easy enough, but I have to admit I'm having a case of nerves." He removed his coat and handed it to Logan. "I haven't seen her in over forty-three years. Maybe this is a mistake."

"She doesn't know you're here. If you don't want to see her, she'll never know the difference." He held Nate's coat out to him. Nate waved him away.

"No, I'm here." He took a deep breath.

"Come in then." Logan smiled. Nate reminded him of a nervous teen on his first date. He walked into the living room as Lois entered from the kitchen. She stood still and unsure. Nate swallowed hard several times.

"Hello, Lois," he said softly. She stared for some time, looking confused. "It's me..."

"Yes," she said as she walked across the room. "Yes."

She stopped before him, frowning as she looked into his face. She reached her hand to his face, stroked softly. "You." She pulled her hand away, and a look of concern entered her eyes. She glanced around as if looking for someone. "You need to go. Joe..."

"It's okay, Lois. Joe's gone." Nate smiled at her concern for him.

"He'll hurt you."

"No, honey. Joe can't hurt me now. That was a long time ago."

"It was?" She looked frantically around the room, spotting Logan near the door. She rushed to him, frantic and pointing at Nate. "Joe will be mad."

Logan took her agitated hands and held them gently. "No, Mom. Dad's gone. He died last month. He won't hurt Nate."

"Nate? Do you know Nate?"

Logan smiled. "Yeah, I know Nate. Let's sit down and talk to him, okay?" He led her across the room. Halfway, she released Logan's hand and walked to Nate.

"Nate." Tears filled her eyes, her lip quivering. "Nate."

"Yes, honey. It's me, Nate."

She again placed her shaking hand on his cheek, sniffling. "I'm so glad you're here." She looked up into his face, and it seemed the years melted away. "I need you."

Tears sprang to his eyes as she repeated those words to him, the words that started everything so long ago. "I know."

"I need you." She repeated as she stepped into his arms and laid her head on his chest. He laid his cheek against her hair. "Be my friend, Nate."

"I always have been, Lois. I always have."

Chapter 21

Moving day arrived, and Logan found himself bogged down in the details. Max kept Lois occupied as Logan attempted to pack her belongings. If he packed one item, Lois packed six more. When she wasn't looking, he dumped it back in the closet. Her room at Eagle Crest wouldn't hold everything.

Uncle Larry arrived as promised and kept Lois out of trouble while Max and Logan hauled her furniture to the rental truck. When the task was completed, Logan gave a sigh of relief as they leaned on the truck box for a short break.

"Max, I have to say it again. I couldn't have done all this without you. You were truly a godsend, my friend. I'll miss you."

"I'm glad I could help, Logan."

"So you'll go on to another home tomorrow?" Logan asked.

"No. I have a board meeting to prepare for, actually." He smiled at Logan's knit brow.

"Nursing staff attends board meetings?"

"No, but CEOs do." He laughed at the look on Logan's face.

"CEO? Of what?"

"Home Health Care Services Inc. is a network of twelve offices. It's my company." He continued to smile.

"Then what are you doing here with us?"

Max smiled. "We were terribly understaffed the day you called. Several of my nurses had called in sick, and I didn't have anyone available. When my office manager took your call, she almost told you we couldn't help, but she said something in your voice got to her. So she asked me what to do."

"What was in my voice?"

"Desperation, my friend. She thought you were on your last leg and needed help real bad."

"I did. She's very perceptive." He nodded.

"She is. So I volunteered, figured I'd come out for a day or so until I had someone available."

"And three weeks later, you're still here. What gives?"

"I don't know. There's something about you McKinnons that gets to a guy. Maybe it was the huge circles under your eyes the day I got here, or maybe it's that sweet mother of yours. I'm not sure, but once I got here, I wanted to play it out."

"I sure appreciate it. I'm not kidding when I say I couldn't have done it without you."

"I know." Max nodded. "You're doing the right thing for her. I've checked into Eagle Crest, and it is well respected. She'll be well cared for there."

"Thanks. I was concerned since I haven't seen it. Melissa was impressed, and I trust her judgment. I'm feeling guilty though." Logan frowned.

"Why?"

"Because I'm placing her with strangers. I should take her home with me, but it wouldn't work out with my kids."

"Home care works for some, but it's a tough way to go. A specialized care facility is a safe place for her to be. They'll take care of her. There will probably be people who try to make you feel guilty for not keeping her at home, but ignore it. I did when I was faced with it."

"What do you mean, when you were faced with it?"

"My dad had Alzheimer's. Mom tried to care for him herself for years, and even with my help and my nursing services pitching in, she eventually couldn't handle it either. He spent his last two years in a care facility. We lost him last year."

"I'm sorry, Max. You should have said something."

Max shrugged. "He's at peace now. Mom has adjusted and is doing quite well. We were faced with all the guilt you're feeling now, but you're doing what's best for her. Trust me on that."

"Thanks." Logan smiled. "I'd better get on the road before Mom gets tired." He pushed away from the truck and returned to the house with Max on his heels.

While Max and Larry kept Lois occupied, Logan grabbed his cell phone and plopped down in his dad's den chair.

"Nate. It's Logan. I called to tell you we're heading out in a few minutes."

"I appreciate the call." He was silent a moment. "I don't mean to pressure you, but will I hear from you again?" Logan could hear the hope in his voice.

"I can't make any promises right now. I need to get Mom settled, spend some time with my family, and get back to work."

"If you're ever in the area, stop in, okay?"

Logan felt guilty for appearing to brush Nate off so easily. It wasn't easy at all. "Thanks, I'll do that." He nearly hung up, when he felt the need to explain further. "Just a second, Nate. I don't know how to handle this."

"I understand. You've got a lot on your plate right now. I don't want to add to it."

Logan blew out a breath. "I need some time, okay? My dad died a month ago, and I haven't had time to think about that at all. I haven't had a chance to deal with those feelings, and I'm not sure what to do with you yet. I'm afraid..." He paused. "I'm afraid I'm using you to avoid dealing with losing Dad. It would so easy to slide into a relationship with you, but I think I owe Dad more. I need to give him the respect he deserves and consider how he would have felt about this."

"You need to grieve for Joe. I understand that, Logan. Like I said before, if you choose to not see me again, I have to accept your decision. The choices are all yours. Take care of yourself and your mother. I'll cherish these hours we've had for the rest of my life."

Logan listened as his father hung up, and he wondered if he was doing the right thing.

Chapter 22

Joe

Logan's return to Lois' house by the sea proved tougher than expected. It was dark and eerily quiet. As much as Lois had driven him crazy, being in her house alone was awful. He kept expecting to hear her footsteps or her voice.

He'd called a King's Bay realtor the week prior to list the house and now had the difficult task of packing his parents' life into cardboard boxes for the movers. Rather than wallow, he jumped in, wrapping and packing each item carefully. Each dish, pencil holder, and candlestick reminded him of some facet of their lives together, and he found himself damp eyed more than once.

In his father's den he confronted the biggest emotions of all. This had been his father's haven, his special place, and for Logan to dismantle it now was like a knife in his heart. He looked around the cozy room at all the photos and mementos and felt so much grief, he broke down. After a few moments, he regained his composure, dropped into his father's chair, and turned on the computer. This was Logan's domain, and he felt comfortable listening to the whirring and clicking sounds of the computer as it booted up. When the desktop loaded, he clicked on his father's document files to see if there was anything needing his attention and was surprised to see a file labeled For Logan. He opened the document and realized it had to have been written just prior to his father's death. Curious, he began to read.

My dear son,
The hour is late, and your mother has finally gone to bed, giving me a much-needed break. I haven't been feeling well, and the doc believes I'm overstressed. I'm not so sure, although I won't discount his opinion. He scheduled a complete physical, so I'll know soon if there is something more. Mom's condition is worsening, and I know it's affecting me, but we plod along as always, taking each day as it comes. Doc thinks I should put Mom in one of those care places, but I've always taken care of her and would be lost without her here.

You're wondering why I'm sitting here late at night writing to you when I should be sleeping, but I have things on my mind. I considered phoning, but the subjects I need to address deserve more respect than a telephone call. I plan to discuss this with you at Thanksgiving, but just in case something happens and we are unable to talk, I have this letter as a backup. I'm sure you, my brilliant computer wizard, will find this letter without difficulty.

You see, my son, there are things you need to know, things your mother and I have been carrying around like overweight baggage for many, many years. I hope you have a few minutes, because I'm starting at the beginning, and it is a lengthy story. Maybe you'd like to get a cup of coffee and make yourself comfortable? I'll wait...

I know a lot of this is familiar history, but if I don't begin here, what I have to say won't make any sense.

It begins with the first moment I saw her. I finished my dinner at the Apple Blossom Diner in Henley when this lovely blonde walked past the window followed closely by four tough-looking boys. I paid my bill and followed the group down the street. When I caught up, they had her trapped. She was obviously scared, so I did what anyone would do and threatened the boys. They ran away, as I thought they would, leaving her shaking. If there is such a thing as love at first sight, I have to say I was bitten with big teeth. Your mother was the most beautiful woman I'd ever seen. That soft blonde hair and her big blue eyes hit me like a brick between the eyes.

Over the years she frequently referred to me as her hero because of that incident, but if the truth were told, I was cowardly where she was concerned. I lived with a constant fear this glorious woman would leave me. Foolish, I suppose, but I felt it strongly. She was young and vivacious, and I couldn't figure out what she wanted with a bland man like me, a farmer. Miracle of miracles, she fell in love with me and we were married. I've never been as happy as I was that day.

We planned to have a houseful of children, but by our first anniversary we hadn't accomplished the task. Neither of us worried much at that point. Sometimes it takes a while. By our fifth wedding anniversary, it weighed heavily that we'd been unable to conceive. I tried to hide my disappointment from Lois, but she knew. It didn't help when the neighborhood women whispered about us. When they offered blatant advice on the subject, it was more than your mother could bear.

She withdrew from me. I tried to be sympathetic, but only irritated her more. By our tenth anniversary she was in a sad state over her lack of children. I have to admit feeling despair as well, but I tried to hide it from her. Consequently, we stopped talking to each other and became strangers.

She needed more to do than the everyday running of our home, the farm accounts, and the harvests, so she took a job at Sloan's Grocery three or four days a week. I thought it was great she had found something that made her so happy. She loved the store and the interaction with the customers. It also helped our

*relationship. She stopped dwelling on our lack of chil-
dren, and we got along like in the old days.*

*She announced she was pregnant in December. I
was thrilled and danced her around the living room.
Our dream came true. But my joy was short lived when
she told me she didn't know if the baby was mine. At
first I didn't understand what she was saying to me.
Why wouldn't the child be mine? Then she made a confession that ripped my heart out of my chest.*

*She'd been having an affair with another man since
August. Twice a week she would go to him while I igno-
rantly worked in my orchard. I became enraged at the
news. How dare she do that to us? I loved her more
than anything, and she betrayed my love with another
man. Unable to control my anger, I kicked furniture
around the room and scared your mother so bad that
she begged me not to hurt her, and at that moment, I
feared I might do it. I forced her to tell me who she'd
been with. At first she refused, but finally, out of fear,
she told me his name.*

*I was devastated for the second time that night. Her
lover was a friend of mine. Unable to look at her any
longer, I jumped in my truck and drove. I didn't have a
destination in mind, but soon I found myself in her lover's driveway. I was so hurt and angry to know he had
touched my wife, I wanted to kill him. The bastard
stepped out of his house as calm as can be. I asked him
if he could deny he'd been with my wife, and he said no,
he couldn't. He loved her. I lost control and beat him
until he was sobbing on the porch. He told me I should
just kill him because he couldn't go on without her. I
decided if that were the case, letting him live would be
the better punishment. Let him think about what he
couldn't have for the rest of his pitiful life. I left him
there and returned home. I was so sure your mother
hated me, I wouldn't have been surprised if she locked
me out of the house. She didn't. I walked through the
house, unable to look at her. I spent the next month hiding from her. Some hero. I was positive she'd tell me*

she was leaving, so I avoided her as much as possible, not giving her the chance to tell me. I feared the rage crawling through me too. What if I couldn't control my anger and I hurt the woman I loved? And even though she'd betrayed me with another man, I stilled loved her.

I continued to take the coward's route until New Year's Eve. Your mother finally forced a confrontation and asked if I wanted her to leave. I was stunned. I thought she wanted to leave me for the other man, and I found out she didn't want to go. She said she loved him but she loved me more.

I realized then I couldn't fault her for her behavior, as I had caused it. She was pregnant, proving without a doubt she didn't have the problem. I did. It dawned on me then what I had considered a minor injury during the war may have kept us from having a child. She had suffered years of unnecessary guilt because of it, and her self-blame tore us apart. My fear she would look at me as less than a man kept me from telling her the extent of my war injuries, and to be perfectly honest, I hadn't considered it a problem until then.

We'd been in France. My buddies and I were pinned down by enemy fire, when a nearby truck burst into flames. Men were trapped inside screaming for help. Without thinking of the consequences, I ran to the truck and pulled as many out as I could. When the fire reached the gas tank, the truck exploded, sending debris everywhere. I was injured in the explosion and wasn't able to help the remaining men. Medics rushed me into surgery to remove the shrapnel from my abdomen and groin, and the doctor said I would recover fully. Due to the nature of the injury, there was a small chance I would have problems, but I didn't worry about it much, as I functioned perfectly well.

When your mother and I married, I should have told her. She'd questioned me about the scars, but I brushed it off as a minor injury. I thought it was.

Her years of depression and anxiety were unnecessary and would have been avoided if I'd been honest *and told her I could be the problem. So I decided to do my darnedest to make it up to her. If she would stay with me, I'd spend the rest of my life trying to make her happy. I put aside my anger over the affair and pledged to raise her child as my own, even though I was positive the child wasn't mine.*

We talked it over. She said she'd never considered leaving me for the other man. She'd needed him for a short time and now that was over. Fear of scandal worried her greatly. Fear that people would know she'd been unfaithful and call her child names drove her to the decision that the child's father would have no further contact with her or the baby. She asked me to speak with him, and I agreed.

When I drove in, he threatened to call the sheriff, sure I was there to pound him again. All of my anger had dissipated, and the thought hadn't crossed my mind. I assured him I was only there to speak for Lois.

After I explained Lois' fears, he reluctantly agreed to stay silent and at a distance. It was difficult for him, I could tell. What decent man would walk away from his child? But we forced him to do just that.

A few months later, he sold his orchard and left Henley, and I'm not sure where he went. I would think of him from time to time, but soon we were busy outfitting a nursery and thoughts of him faded away. If I tried hard enough, I could pretend the child Lois carried was mine, and that pleased her.

The child arrived in June 1962, and I'm sure you've already surmised it was you, Logan.

If it's possible to be struck by love at first sight more than once, I have to say I was. Oh, I was. The first time I held you and saw your face, I was absolutely in love for the second time. It no longer mattered who had fathered you. I knew I would love you for the rest of my life, and I have. Every day I've been allowed to be your father has been a gift, and no one could have loved you more.

I know you're wondering why we kept this a secret from you, and I hope you can find it in your heart to forgive us. The secret was kept for your own good. People can be cruel, and we were afraid of the consequences for you if the story ever got out. I would do anything to protect you and give you a normal life.

As you grew older, I considered confiding with you on many occasions, but each time, my cowardice won. When you were thirteen, you asked if you'd been an accident. Your mother had become distant, and you were beginning to fight with her frequently. You were sure she didn't love you because as an only child, you must have been an accident. I remember being terrified that you were starting to question us. Rather than be honest, I remember hugging you and assuring you there had never been a more wanted child. That satisfied you at the time.

During your high school years, your mother began having difficulties dealing with you, and that strained your relationship more. You asked me frequently what you had done to make Mom act as she did. I knew the reason but couldn't tell you. How could I tell you your mother was having difficulty looking at your face? At fifteen, you were the spitting image of your biological father, and she was constantly reminded of how she had fallen into disgrace. You carried the face of her shame.

I was fairly confident she no longer loved him, but I still lived with the fear she would leave me, and maybe that's what caused her problems. She was afraid to show love for you because of your resemblance to your biological father. Maybe she believed I would think she was still in love with the other man.

We made a pact before you were born to never speak of him again, and we honored the pact. Unfortunately, by not speaking of him, we made him an even bigger presence in our life, a specter forever looming on the fringes. Sometimes I think a lot of her anguish could have been avoided if I had just asked her if that was the problem. But again, my cowardice reared its ugly head. I didn't ask because I was afraid I was wrong. I was afraid she did still love him. Despite her behavior toward you, I know she loves you deeply, Logan. We both do.

There was also someone else I've always suspected of loving you deeply. Even though we forbade your biological father from having contact with you, he was still a part of your life.

For two years after your birth, we saw or heard nothing of him. A few days after your second birthday, a box arrived, addressed to you. No return address or card included, the handwriting unfamiliar. Inside the box were a teddy bear in a baseball uniform, and a train. We knew immediately where it had come from, and my first urge was to toss it in the trash, but when I saw the look in your mother's eyes, I couldn't. She was touched your father had thought to send a gift. You know the bear and train I'm referring to, don't you Logan? I remember Joey playing with them a few years ago.

Each Christmas and birthday another box would arrive. Lois and I never spoke of the origin of the gifts that continued to arrive until your college graduation. There never was an old uncle in Seattle sending gifts. It was him.

When you were five, he began coming to your school Christmas programs. He looked different, but I recognized him immediately. He would come in after the program began and leave just before it ended. I doubt he knew I had seen him. At first I thought I should confront him and remind him of his promise, but when I saw the look on his face at seeing you, I couldn't deny the man that small pleasure. If the situation were reversed, I know I would have done anything to be near you.

He continued to come each year for each program, and when you began to participate in sports, band, and school plays, he was there as well. Always standing in the back of the auditorium at your plays and concerts

*or hovering near the door at your basketball games. At
your high school graduation, he was at the top of the
bleachers; at your college graduation, he sat in the
back row. I always saw him but never said a word.*

*He was at the FFA auction. The bidding was fierce
between him and another man, but he bought your prize
pig for a phenomenal amount of money, giving you
enough for another project and an addition to your college fund. And it wasn't the first contribution he made
to your fund. Several months before your high school
graduation, a letter arrived from an out-of-town banker
saying there was an account in your name that would
become yours on your eighteenth birthday. We signed
all the papers, and on your birthday, we were notified
your account held over ten thousand dollars for your
college education. He did that for you, starting when
you were two years old.*

*We should have told you when you became an adult,
but I always worried you would hate us for deceiving
you. And as his love for you became more apparent
with each event and each passing year, a new fear began. If I told you I wasn't your father, would you love
me as you had? Would you leave to be with him?
Would I lose my son? You had every right to know, and
I kept you from him. For that, I am ashamed.*

*Now the time has come for you to know the truth, no
matter the cost to me or your mother.*

*Your biological father's name is Nate Ford. I'll tell
you everything I can of him, although it isn't much. He
said he was from the coast but never mentioned the ex-
act location, and I didn't think to ask. When he sold his
orchard, I assumed he went back to his old home. His
father had a commercial fishing operation, and he had
grown up working his dad's boats.*

*He and I were friends for a short time. He was a
good guy, and we clicked immediately. He had a great
sense of humor and was friendly to everyone. The waitresses at the café thought him attractive with his light-*

brown hair and brown eyes. Just look in the mirror and you'll know what he looked like.

Knowing you and your inquisitive nature, you'll want to know more about him, and I don't blame you. I wish I had more to tell you, but I only knew him for six months over forty-three years ago.

If you are reading this, then chances are good I'm not there to talk with you. I want you to know I think it's okay for you to find him if you choose to do so. I've always felt incredible guilt over shoving Nate from your life, and if you want to know him, do so with my blessing.

His relationship with your mother was wrong, but over the years I've had difficulty hating him for it, since it produced you. He proved over and over again he had stronger character than I gave him credit for. He promised to stay away from you, and he did. I know he loved you from the number of times I saw him at your school functions, but still, he didn't break his promise.

We should have told you earlier and allowed you to make the decision to have him in your life or not. I apologize for that.

If you find him, give him a message for me. Tell him I'm sorry for what we did. We thought it was right at the time, but in retrospect, I'm not so sure. When I think of the pain we must have caused him, I feel terrible guilt. He may have stolen a few hours with Lois from me, but I took forty-three years with you from him. I find it difficult to forgive myself. I leave that choice to you.

Always know, dear Logan, that although you aren't my biological son, you are the child of my heart, and you've filled my heart to the brim many times over.

Love, Dad

Logan wiped tears from his eyes with shaking hands. It was so typical of Joe to shoulder the burden, and Logan loved him even more because of it. Everyone involved shared in the guilt, but it was Joe who took it in the gut, and Logan found he didn't care who was to blame for any of it. All he wanted was to see his dad one more time so he could tell him it didn't matter. He loved him no matter what had transpired between him, Lois, and Nate. None of it mattered.

He sat in his father's darkening den with the glow from the computer monitor lighting the room, and as he reread his dad's letter, a thought occurred to him. If Joe had confessed earlier, would he be so understanding? He wasn't sure. If he hadn't read Lois' journal, would he have understood her motivation in having an affair with another man? If he hadn't heard Nate's side of the story, filled with anguish and emotion, would he have felt the kinship so strongly? And now he had Joe's side of things to factor in. Without all three sides, would he have felt this way? He had serious doubts. Without the puzzle pieces laid out in order, he wouldn't have understood. Joe's fear was justified, for Logan was sure he wouldn't have accepted any of it easily. The story had played out as it should, and now he could accept it and go on with his life.

He wasn't sure what he should do about Nate though. He had Joe's blessing if he chose to pursue a relationship with his biological father. Okay, that hurdle was crossed. But Logan wasn't sure if he wanted Nate in his life. He liked the guy and was sorry he'd missed so much of his son's life, but did it mean he wanted him in his life on a permanent basis? He'd need to think for a while yet.

Three days later, Logan filled the last of the packing boxes and called the movers. He considered calling Nate and having dinner with him before he left, but didn't. More time was needed before he could make a decision. He drove back to Vancouver and settled into his normal life.

Chapter 23

Logan parked his car in the Eagle Crest parking lot, his nerves jumping. It was a lovely building in a colonial style, meticulously landscaped and maintained to give the appearance of a fine home, not a care facility. Lois had moved in ten days prior, and following the director's advice, he'd stayed away to give her a chance to settle in. He'd checked in by phone on several occasions and was reassured she was doing well. She was making friends, eating well, and appeared quite happy. Logan wasn't sure why that made him nervous.

He was buzzed in through the entry door and greeted by a cheerful caregiver whose name tag read Daisy.

"I'm Lois McKinnon's son," he said when she looked at him curiously.

"Oh, yes. I remember you now. She and her friend are sitting in the TV room." She pointed the direction.

"Her friend? You mean one of the other residents?"

"No. She's had a friend visiting her every afternoon this week," Daisy said as she led him to the TV room.

"But she doesn't know anyone here."

"She knows him pretty well and is quite pleased when he arrives."

Logan frowned, trying to figure out who her friend could be. He stepped into the doorway and was stunned to find Nate sitting on the sofa with Lois, laughing and singing.

"They are so cute together," Daisy whispered. "When he walks in the door, she runs up and hugs him. Then they come in here and he sings to her. She loves Sinatra songs." She listened for a moment. "But I think that one is Louis Armstrong.

Go on in." She indicated with a shooing motion when Logan seemed reluctant. With their backs turned to him, he wasn't noticed at first, giving him a chance to observe the situation. Lois grinned and occasionally clapped her hands.

Any trepidation he'd had toward Nate melted. Nate apparently cared deeply for Lois even after all these years and had made a special trip to spend time with her. He couldn't fault the guy for that. He walked up behind them and joined Nate in singing "It's a Wonderful World." Their voices shared a similar tone and blended beautifully. Nate turned to him with a smile, continuing his song as other residents wandered into the TV room for the impromptu concert. Lois beamed at both men. When they finished, Nate looked at Logan with uncertainty.

"What a surprise," Logan said.

"I should have called and asked you if this was okay, but I didn't." Nate frowned.

Logan shook his head and smiled. "Not necessary. Mom can have friends visit without me being involved. It's good to see you."

Nate smiled. "Thanks. I had the urge to see her again, so here I am."

"I need him," Lois said with conviction.

"I believe you do, Mom. You know, Nate, she likes 'White Christmas.'"

"She does? Start it up. I'll jump in."

They spent the next hour singing Christmas carols and various tunes from the '40s through the '60s Lois might recognize. Nate surprised Logan with "Yellow Submarine," and Logan followed with some Rolling Stones. Lois laughed and clapped, no matter the tune. When the staff announced dinner would be served soon, Nate hugged Lois and kissed her cheek.

"I have to go, honey. I'll come back tomorrow if you want me to," Nate said sincerely. Lois smiled and nodded and turned to Logan.

"I'll see you later, Mom." He hugged her and kissed her forehead. She seemed confused when the two men walked to the door.

"Where are we going? Wait for me."

Nate turned to her, his eyes sad. "You live here now, honey. You need to stay."

She looked as if she would cry. "No. I need to go with you. I want to go home."

Logan put his arm around her and squeezed. "We'll come back tomorrow, Mom. This is your place now." Her lip quivered, and he knew tears would soon follow. He looked over her head as Daisy walked by, and he silently asked for help.

"Lois, dear," Daisy said. "We need to get washed for dinner. The cook made some lovely pork chops and squash." She looped her arm with Lois' and walked her to the dining room. "And we also have cherry pie for dessert." With her back turned, Nate and Logan were immediately forgotten, allowing them to sneak out the door unnoticed.

"I go through this every day," Nate said as they walked to their cars. "It breaks my heart, but I know it's what's best for her."

"It'll take a while to get used to it," Logan said with a frown. They reached Nate's car and both men stood anxiously, not sure what to do. "Are you in town for a while?"

"Yeah. I thought I'd stay a few more days and help her get settled in. She enjoys it."

"You should have called. Daisy said you've been here every day this week."

"That ball is in your court, Logan. I said it was entirely up to you if we got together again. Calling would put pressure on you."

Logan nodded. "What are your plans tonight?"

"Grab a bite to eat and watch some TV in my motel room," Nate said with a shrug. "Would you like to get some dinner with me?"

Logan shook his head. "No, I have other plans." He noticed Nate's face fell with disappointment. "I was wondering if you might like to come home with me and meet your grandchildren." A lump formed in Logan's throat at the look on Nate's face. He'd stunned him.

"Are you serious?" he whispered.

"Yes. I'll call Melissa and tell her to put on another plate." He waited for Nate to respond.

Nate stared at Logan. It was a massive step for them. "If it isn't too much trouble, I'd love to." He smiled at Logan as tears filled his eyes.

"Get in. We'll come back for your car later."

Logan parked his car in the garage and looked at Nate. He appeared shell shocked. "If you'd rather not do this, I understand."

"I'm just nervous." To prove he was okay, he opened the car door and jumped out. Logan closed the garage door and led Nate into the house. They could hear the boys playing and making spaceship noises in the living room. Logan motioned with his head for Nate to follow. They stood in the living room doorway as Derek and Joey ran around the room pretending to blast each other with their toys. Joey was the first to notice Logan, running up to him with a yell.

"Daddy!" He wrapped his arms around Logan. Derek ran up as well but stopped short when he saw Nate.

"Who's that?" Derek asked with a frown.

"Someone I want you to meet," Logan said. He led Nate into the room as the two boys stared at him.

"How come he looks like you, Daddy?" Derek asked with five-year-old bluntness.

"I'll explain in a minute, after we get our coats off." He removed his own and held out his hand for Nate's. After tossing them on a chair, he turned to the boys.

"Joey and Derek, I'd like you meet Nate Ford. Your grandpa." He waited for a response. Both boys frowned, confused.

"We already have a grandpa. Why do we need another one?" Derek looked serious as a thought crossed his mind. "Is it because Grandpa Joe went to heaven? Do we get a new grandpa now?"

"No. It doesn't have anything to do with Grandpa Joe going to heaven. Nate is your grandpa because he is my father. That's why he looks like me." Neither boy was old enough for a more lengthy explanation, so he limited it to the basics.

"A new grandpa," Joey said with a smile. "Will you take us out for ice cream like Grandpa Joe did?"

Nate laughed. "Sure, I can take you out for ice cream sometime. It would be my pleasure, Joey." He looked at Derek, who continued to look apprehensive. "And you too, Derek. I like chocolate ice cream. How about you?"

Derek looked at him for a moment. "I like chocolate."

"Then we'll get along fine, won't we?" Nate smiled at Derek.

"Oh, Logan. I didn't hear you come in," Melissa said as she entered the living room from the opposite hallway, Hannah tucked neatly on her hip. She held out her hand to Nate. "I am so pleased to meet you, Nate. Logan has told me so much about you."

Nate took her hand and squeezed it gently. "I'm pleased to meet you, Melissa. Everything Logan said about you is true. You are lovely. Although, I think the word he used was gorgeous."

Melissa laughed. "You are a charmer, aren't you? He warned me about that."

Nate continued to smile, but it faded as his gaze drifted to the baby she held. He swallowed with difficulty as the little girl gazed up at him.

"Would you like to hold Hannah?" Melissa asked.

"Could I?" he said, unable to take his eyes from her.

"Of course." Melissa handed the baby to the older man. He was tentative at first, smiling at the little girl as she touched his face with her hand. Tears filled his eyes as she smiled and poked his ear. He took her hand in his and kissed it. Nate closed his eyes and held the little girl close, breathing deeply. His shoulders shook and tears ran down his face.

Logan understood. So many years had passed since he'd been allowed to hold his own son for those precious few minutes, and every second of it must have flooded back to him.

"What did Hannah do to make Grandpop Nate sad?" Derek asked Melissa in a loud whisper. "Did she hurt his ear?"

"I don't think Grandpa is sad, honey," Melissa said. "I think he's happy."

Logan looked at her with tear-filled eyes and motioned for her to take the boys from the room.

She nodded and took the boys' hands. "Come on, guys. Let's let Daddy and Grandpa talk for a while. You can help me in the kitchen."

"Nate," Logan said softly, not sure what to do. He stepped closer and put his hand on his father's shoulder.

Nate attempted to compose himself. "I'm sorry, Logan." He wiped tears from his eyes with his free hand, the other holding Hannah tight. "It's all coming back. I thought I had it all pushed down far enough it wouldn't get to me anymore, but I guess I didn't do such a good job of it. I'm sorry."

"Don't be," Logan said, still trying to hold in his own emotions.

"It's the baby scent." He sniffed Hannah's hair. "That's what I remember most about the day I held you. That wonderful baby scent." He looked at Logan with stricken eyes. "I missed so much with you. I tried not to think about it, but seeing this beautiful baby brought it all back. I missed everything." His shoulders shook again. He tried to hold in tears but failed.

A tremendous wave of emotion crashed through Logan as he stood near his father, and he couldn't stand it any longer. This man needed him to feel complete, and Logan decided he couldn't withhold that from him any longer. The societal pressure that had demanded Nate's banishment from Logan's life was gone. The world had changed, and now the McKinnons needed to change as well. He wrapped his arms around the sobbing man and his baby daughter and held him until Hannah broke the mood by grabbing handfuls of hair on both men's heads.

"Ow!" they yelled in unison and then had to laugh as Hannah squealed in delight.

"I forgot to warn you your granddaughter has a heck of a grip." Logan laughed and took a small step back out of Hannah's range.

"My granddaughter," Nate said as he looked at Hannah with awe. "That hadn't soaked in until you asked if I wanted to meet my grandchildren. I've been so busy thinking about my son it hadn't occurred to me I have three grandchildren." He grinned. "And they're beautiful, Logan. Just beautiful. Thank you for letting me meet them. This means a lot to me."

"I know it does, and I hope you can stay and get to know them better."

"I'd like that."

"Maybe you'd like to stay with us for a few days? We have a guest room upstairs, or if you would prefer more privacy, we have a mother-in-law cottage out back. We'd just need to straighten it up a bit."

"You want me to stay with you?"

"If you'd like to. It's your choice. Maybe you're more comfortable at the motel."

"Does this mean you've come to terms with things? I know you were worried about what Joe would think of this."

"Come with me. I have something to show you." Logan

led the way to his office and indicated for Nate to sit in the chair opposite the desk. Still holding the baby, he sat. Logan shuffled a pile of papers, found what he needed, and handed it to Nate. Nate looked at him uncertainly as he took the paper. Hannah tried to grab it, so Logan lifted her gently from him.

"What is this?" Nate asked.

Logan sat in his desk chair and leaned back. "When I was going through Dad's computer files, I ran across something he wrote shortly before he died. He said he'd intended to tell me about you at Thanksgiving, but he wasn't feeling well and worried he wouldn't get the chance. So he wrote a letter explaining everything. I think you might be interested in reading the last page. It's a message for you."

Nate pulled his reading glasses from his pocket and began to read. When he finished, he looked up at Logan, stunned. "Well, I'll be damned. Joe felt guilty?" He swallowed hard. "You know, that last time I saw Joe, he told me he had to forgive Lois but he'd never forgive me. I guess this means he did after all." A small smile worked across his face. "I always thought he was a heck of a guy, and this proves it, doesn't it?" He thought for a moment. "I wonder how things would have played out if he'd told you earlier." He frowned. "It couldn't have been much different than it was though. Like I said before, the times wouldn't have allowed it to happen any differently. And I doubt you would have taken it so well if you'd known earlier."

Logan nodded. "I've given that a lot of thought, and I think things turned out the way they were supposed to turn out. I don't think I could have accepted this if I hadn't had all the pieces in the order I had them."

A knock on the door interrupted them. "Grandpop?" Derek said as he poked his head in the door.

"He's kind of shy," Logan whispered to Nate. "Come in, buddy. I think we're done." Logan waved his youngest son in. Derek's steps were tentative as he entered the room. He stopped beside Nate's chair.

"Um, I was wondering…" He hesitated, looking at his dad for reassurance. Logan smiled. "I was wondering if Grandpop would like to see my boats in my room."

"I would love to see your boats." Nate removed his reading glasses and stuffed them back in his pocket as he stood. "Is there time before dinner?" Logan nodded. "Let's go then."

Logan smiled as Derek took Nate's hand and led him from the room. He heard their conversation as they walked down the hallway.

"What kind of boats do you have?" Nate asked.

"Big ones and small ones," Derek answered seriously.

"Well, isn't that something. I like big boats and small boats too."

Epilogue

Three years later

They stood together, father and son, as they read the inscription on the marble headstone standing beneath the shade of a maple tree. On the left it read Joseph McKinnon, beloved husband, father, and grandfather. On the right, in fresh engraving, it read Lois Delaney McKinnon, beloved wife, mother, grandmother, and friend. The last had been Nate's contribution. He'd always been her friend, right up to the end.

At first, he visited a few days at a time, staying in Logan's guest room, but as time went by, he stayed longer and longer. It wasn't long before he sold his charter company to his nephews, who'd worked for him, and moved permanently into Logan's mother-in-law cottage. His grandchildren renamed it Grandpop's house.

Lois' condition remained level for a while, but slowly her mental condition deteriorated until she no longer recognized the people she loved the most. For a time, they were familiar, but she was unable to recall their names and began asking Logan and Nate if they were related to her. Undaunted, Nate continued to visit her daily, always holding her hand and singing old songs. Eventually, even his songs failed to reach her as she sat staring into space.

The plaques and tangles won—her brain stopped telling her body what to do, pneumonia settled into her frail body, and she drifted away into blessed peace to suffer no more.

"It's a nice stone," Nate said as he pulled a weed. While bent down, he removed the vase from the center of the stone and placed a handful of yellow carnations in it. In the summer, he'd return with sunflowers.

"It is," Logan said flatly. "For a stone."

"It's funny," Nate said. "You live your life as best you can, and in the end all that's left is a hunk of marble with your name on it."

"There's more than that," Logan said quietly. "There are memories. We'll keep them alive with our memories of them. It's been three months since she died, and I can still hear her voice. Sometimes I'll hear footsteps, and I look up expecting to see Dad coming in the room. They're still here with us."

"I know what you mean. Many times I've woke at night over the past five years and thought I heard Gracie's voice. They never truly leave us."

"I guess we'd better be going. Melissa was frosting Natalie's cake when I left. She threatened me with bodily harm if we were late for Nat's birthday party." He draped his hand across Nate's shoulder. "Let's go home, Pop."

"I wouldn't want to miss my newest granddaughter's second birthday party. I missed one of those once. I won't do it again." Nate fell into step with Logan.

"And don't forget," Logan said. "Tomorrow is Derek's spring program at school. We need to get there early so you can sit in the front row."

Authors note

I wrote Tangles *while my family was in the grip of the disease. With my mother-in-law's diagnosis, my husband and I joined a community of people isolated by the task of caring for a loved one and needing more information. We found ourselves in impromptu mini-support-group meetings in grocery stores, movie theater lobbies, and restaurant parking lots. Everywhere we went, we found people whose families were caught in a similar struggle.*

I noticed a similar theme in these conversations—no one knew what to expect with this disease. No one anticipated the emotional and physical toll of caring for a stricken loved one. The idea for Tangles *was born, and with it, I hoped to show the realities of living with the disease within a fictional framework. I don't believe information dissemination needs to be boring.*

The Tangles *story and its characters are fictional. The Alzheimer's behavior displayed by Lois McKinnon is not. Not every victim of the disease will exhibit the same behavior, but every family will experience similar pain and heartache as their loved one slips away.*

—Sharleen Scott

WWW.ALZ.ORG

An estimated 5.2 million Americans have Alzheimer's disease.

Two-thirds are women.

More than 500,000 seniors die each year because they have Alzheimer's.

It is the sixth leading cause of death.

In 2013, 15.5 million family and friends provided 17.7 billion hours of unpaid care to those with Alzheimer's and other dementias. All caregivers face a devastating toll.

Alzheimer's disease is the most expensive condition in the nation.

HOW YOU CAN HELP

TEAM TANGLES

Join my Alzheimer's Association walk team, Team Tangles, either by becoming a team member and fundraising or by donating to a walk-team member. I'll be walking in Yakima, Washington, and I'd love to see you there. Together, we can make a difference.

WWW.ALZ.ORG

ABOUT THE AUTHOR

Sharleen Scott lives in the foothills of the Cascade Mountains in the beautiful Pacific Northwest with her husband, Brett, two college kids, and two spoiled cats.

You can visit her at
www.sharleenscott.com

If you enjoyed this book, please leave a review at
www. amazon.com/author/sharleenscott
&
www.goodreads.com

Also from Sharleen Scott

and

OUT WEST PRESS

Caught in Cross Seas—Released May 2014
Book one in the CAUGHT series

When country music superstar Clay Masterson finds his supposedly dead father, he wants to do two things: buy dear ol' dad a beer to thank him for being a great father for the ten minutes he spent at it, and kick his dad's sorry butt to Montana to face an eighteen-year-old murder charge. Harlie Cates will try to stop him. Happily ever after could be a problem for them.

Caught in the Spin—Released November 2014
Book two in the CAUGHT series

When Tallie Peters lands the job of assistant to Nashville's premier music manager, she's sure things are looking up for her and her son. Meeting gorgeous former bull rider Tom Black confirms it. But Tallie's new life dives into a chaotic spiral with the premature release of her brutal ex-husband from prison. He wants his son and will stop at nothing to take him from Tallie. Tom offers Tallie and her son refuge behind the gates of the Masterson-Black Ranch, but he soon finds that the best security measures are no match for a determined ex-con with nothing to lose.

Made in the USA
San Bernardino, CA
21 September 2015